PLAYING BY HEART

ENDGAME
BOOK 2

CLEARY JAMES

PLAYING BY HEART
CLEARY JAMES

© Cleary James 2017

The right of Cleary James to be identified as the Author of the Work
has been asserted by her in accordance with the Copyright, Designs and
Patents Act 1988.

ISBN: 9781915369116

This novel is entirely a work of fiction. All characters portrayed in this
publication are the work of the author's imagination and any
resemblance to real persons, living or dead, is purely coincidental.

Published by Balally Books

Cover design by Angela Haddon

1

A SOFT BREEZE from the sea ruffled Lisa's hair as she locked the green door of her flat behind her. It was a clear September morning, the sun bright in a crisp blue sky, and the village was still sleeping as she walked through the narrow, winding streets that sloped down to the harbour. The shops and cafes were shuttered, the curtains still closed in the windows of the old colour-washed cottages, and she felt like she had the world to herself as she made her way to the waterfront.

She loved the quiet of early Sunday morning, and was pleased to find the quay still deserted save for a solitary fisherman sitting far off at the end of the pier, lazily dangling a line in the water. She sat on a bench by the harbour wall and took the travel mug she had brought from home out of her satchel. As she lifted the lid, the rich, aromatic fragrance of the steaming coffee mingled deliciously with the salty tang of sea air. Clutching the cup in her gloved hands, she sipped the hot liquid carefully, grateful for its warmth in the chill of early morning.

Sighing contentedly, she looked out over the bay,

shielding her eyes against the sun. Gulls shrieked and wheeled in the air, and little boats bobbed on the sparkling water, their masts knocking softly against each other. Later there would be stalls set up all around the harbour, and the place would be crowded and buzzing with life. But for now all was quiet and tranquil, and she enjoyed having some time to herself before the hustle and bustle began. It had become a little ritual for her to bring her coffee down here first thing on market days.

It still surprised her sometimes how quickly she had settled here and established a new life. It was only six months since she had first arrived in the little Cornish village, but it hadn't taken long for it to feel like home.

It probably helped that she had been here before with her grandparents. They had come to Porth Heron once for a summer holiday when she was a child. She had only been six years old at the time, and she didn't remember much about it, just a scatter of vague memories – playing ball with her grandfather on the beach; her grandmother holding her hand as they paddled at the water's edge – but she knew it was somewhere they had all been happy together, and she was glad that in leaving London, she hadn't severed all ties with her past.

There was a photograph of the three of them sitting on one of these benches at the harbour eating ice-cream – perhaps even the very one she was sitting on now, she thought with a smile. The sense of connection to her beloved grandparents was comforting, and had made her feel less alone when she first arrived. She couldn't help feeling that they had led her here, still watching over her from beyond the grave, making sure she was all right.

Coming here had been a pilgrimage of sorts, and she hadn't necessarily intended to stay. She had just wanted somewhere peaceful to rest and recuperate for a while after the turmoil of her final weeks in London and her last-minute panicked escape. She was stressed out and exhausted, and she had decided she could afford to take a little time out to recover before she started looking for work.

But she had fallen in love with the place straight away, and within a couple of days she knew it was where she wanted to be. She had felt a sense of calm and wellbeing from the moment she arrived. The peace and tranquillity soothed her ragged nerves. She liked the clean air and the quiet streets, and being by the sea gave her a wonderful sense of freedom. Much as she loved London, she welcomed the slower pace of life in Porth Heron and was happy to trade the anonymity of the big city for the sense of community she found here.

The quaint village was one of the prettiest in Cornwall, and the surrounding area was famed for the beauty of its rugged coastline dotted with craggy coves and wide, sandy beaches. It was a popular holiday destination, and the transient population of visitors had made Lisa feel less conspicuously an outsider while she was finding her feet. But the local people had been friendly and welcoming, and she had quickly started putting down roots and making friends.

The thriving tourist trade meant there was always work to be found in the busy pubs, cafes and guesthouses, and she had quickly got a waitressing job at a little coffee shop in the village. She had been delighted to discover that there was a lively and active group of artists working in the village. She had been shy about approaching them at first, but once she had, they had quickly welcomed her into their community. It felt good to be part of something again after years of isolation.

London and Mark seemed worlds away now, like another lifetime. She still missed the city sometimes. But whenever she felt a twinge of longing for what she had left behind, she reminded herself what she had escaped from and how much she had to be thankful for.

She was safe and happy. She had friends, a job, and a place to live that was all hers. She had found her tribe among the local artists, and she was painting again. Best of all, she had freedom. She tried not to focus on the things she didn't have – family, a career in the art world, love …

Her thoughts drifted to Grayson sometimes – too often for her comfort. She thought with a pang of the week they'd spent together – the things he'd said to her, the way he'd touched and kissed her. She'd felt so happy and alive when she was with him. She had only known him for a few weeks, yet sometimes she missed him so much it was like a physical pain. Leaving him behind was her one real regret. She wondered did he ever think about her. She hated that she didn't get to say goodbye, and she hoped he didn't think badly of her for disappearing with his money before she'd earned all of it. She still intended to find a way to pay it back.

As she finished her coffee, she was aware of the car park filling up behind her as stall holders started to arrive to set up for the day. The air filled with the sounds of van doors sliding open, the chirp of car locks, and the familiar voices of her friends carrying on the air as they called out greetings to each other. She put her cup back in her bag and strolled over to join them.

'Morning, Lisa!' Annie, a middle-aged lady who made beautiful jewellery from sea glass, called to her as she unloaded boxes from the back of her car. 'You're up and about early.'

'It's such a lovely day,' Lisa said to her with a smile. 'I thought I'd make the most of it.'

'Gorgeous weather, isn't it?' Annie said, looking up at the sky. 'Should be good for business.'

'Fingers crossed.'

Lisa saw her friend Katya pulling into the car park in her colourful Volkswagen van. She waved and rushed over to meet her.

'Morning!' Katya said with a sunny smile as she hopped out. She pulled off her pink beanie hat, tossing it onto the driver's seat, and shook out her straight, pale blond hair. 'Great day for it, huh?' she said as Lisa followed her around to the back of the van.

'Yes, perfect.' Katya opened the doors and they both scrambled inside and began unloading canvases and equipment. Lisa had met Katya at a yoga class, and they had hit it off straight away. Originally from Sweden, she had come to Porth Heron on a painting holiday three years ago and met her boyfriend Connor, a musician from Ireland. Six months later, they had both returned to set up home together in the village. It was Katya who had told Lisa about the local artists' co-operative and invited her to join. They pooled their resources to run exhibitions and workshops, and they took it in turns to sell their work at the stall they paid for in the regular Sunday arts and crafts market. Lisa and Katya ran it together once every six weeks.

Lisa enjoyed the atmosphere of cheerful industriousness and camaraderie on market mornings as everyone set up for the day, catching up with people they hadn't seen in a while, and checking out each other's stalls. She loved being part of their little community.

'Connor's playing in the pub tonight,' Katya said as she arranged paintings on the canvas walls of their pop-up gazebo. 'Do you want to go and see him? We could get something to eat first.'

'Thanks, but I'm going to Martha's for dinner – you and Connor are invited too.'

'Oh, great!' Katya grinned. 'Connor will be eating with the band, but I wouldn't miss it!'

Martha was Lisa's employer, friend and all-round guardian angel, and her cooking was legendary.

'Ellie's home, so we could all go down to the pub later?'

'Great! I haven't seen Ellie in ages.' Ellie was Martha's daughter, a student in Manchester.

'Oh, I love that,' Katya said as Lisa propped up one of her canvases against the side of the stall. A large abstract, it was her oldest surviving painting, one of only two that Mark hadn't thrown away. She had sent the other one to Grayson when she left London so hurriedly. It was all she had to offer by way of a goodbye. It meant she couldn't look at this one now without being reminded of him, and she was loathe to part with it.

'Are you sure that's all you're asking for?' Katya pointed to the four hundred pounds price sticker. She knew as well as Lisa that it could fetch ten times that in a London gallery. But they weren't in a London gallery now, and Lisa had to be realistic. There wasn't much chance of finding a casual buyer ready to splurge thousands of pounds on a painting from a market stall.

'It probably won't sell anyway,' she said with a shrug. Part of her almost hoped it wouldn't, even though she could use the money.

Lisa had found running the stall daunting at first. She had been shy, and found talking to strangers difficult. She'd relied heavily on Katya to deal with people. But everyone was so friendly and easygoing, she'd soon started to relax and enjoy it. Now she looked forward to it. It was fun to spend the day with Katya, chatting and laughing together when they weren't busy, and taking turns to do runs for coffee and snacks from the adjacent food stalls. She actually liked talking to customers now, glad to discuss her work with anyone who showed an interest. She was still surprised sometimes when she caught herself chattering away happily to a complete stranger, and felt quite proud of how far she'd come. It was such a small, everyday thing that most people would take for granted, but for her it felt like a real achievement. She was a long way from the tense, timid creature she'd been when she first arrived here.

As predicted, the warm weather brought out lots of visitors, and the market was busy, with a steady stream of day-trippers and locals out for a Sunday stroll. The sunshine put everyone in a good mood, and friends and neighbours stopped to chat to Katya and Lisa as they wandered through. The time whizzed by in a blur of good-natured banter, and they both made enough sales to declare the day a success.

Returning from the final coffee run of the day, Lisa stopped to chat to a couple of stallholders as she wended her way back to Katya.

'Sorry I took so long,' she said, handing Katya her favourite chai latte. 'I got us a couple of brownies too.' She produced a paper bag from the pocket of her jacket and held it out to her.

'Mmm, thank you.' Katya took a sip of her coffee. 'It's a pity you weren't here. You missed a customer who was very interested in your paintings.'

'Oh?' Lisa ran her eyes over the canvases. 'Not interested enough to buy one,' she said wryly, confirming that there were no more missing since she'd gone for coffee.

'No, afraid not,' Katya smiled. 'It was that one he was particularly interested in.' She nodded to The River of

Dreams, the large canvas Lisa had brought with her from London. 'He said it looked very familiar.'

'Oh?' Lisa felt a sense of dread creep through her veins. She had only started painting again recently, and her early work hadn't been seen by many people. Mark had made sure of that. Apart from a handful of fellow students from art college, she could think of only two people who might recognise her work – and one of them was Mark.

Katya nodded. 'He thought he'd seen it before, or something very similar. He said he must have seen other stuff of yours.'

Lisa knew that was unlikely. Her current paintings were in quite a different style to this one. She felt a tightening in her chest. 'Did he ask you anything about me?'

'He just asked if you were local. I told him you'd be back in a few minutes if he wanted to wait.'

Lisa allowed herself to relax a little. Surely if it had been Mark, he'd have waited and confronted her, or at least pumped Katya for more information. Still, she felt exposed and vulnerable, and she wanted to run home and hide. She swallowed hard and forced herself to ask the next question. She dreaded the answer, but she had to make sure. 'What did he look like?' she asked.

'Tall, very attractive,' Katya said, unaware of the increasing pounding of Lisa's heart. 'Grey hair, mid-sixties, I'd say,' she added, and Lisa sagged in relief.

'Do you think you know him?' Katya asked.

Lisa shook her head. 'I thought it might be someone from London. But it doesn't sound like anyone I know.'

'He said he lives here,' Katya said. 'In Cornwall, I mean – near Polperro.'

'Oh.' The man was obviously just mistaken about having seen her work before, whoever he was. Perhaps he had noticed that painting subconsciously at the market before and had simply forgotten where he'd seen it.

But despite the reassurance, she felt unsettled and on edge for the remainder of the day, and she was glad when it was time to count their takings and go home. It had been quite a successful day, and Lisa had sold quite a few prints, and a couple of small, lower-priced paintings. They were both in high spirits as they dismantled their stall and packed up the van, tired and hungry after a satisfying day's work and looking forward to a well-earned glass of wine.

They were crossing the car park, making their final trip to the van with the last of the paintings, when there was a loud burst of laughter from down the street. Lisa looked in the direction it had come from – and froze. A few feet away, a tall, dark-haired man was walking away from them, and there was something about the ramrod straightness of his back, and the way his dark, wavy hair ruffled in the breeze, that hit her like an electric shock. Her stomach lurched, and her heart seemed to jump into her throat. *Mark*.

'Lisa, are you okay?' She turned to find Katya frowning at her concernedly.

'Yes,' she said faintly. She felt dizzy. *Was* it Mark? She turned back to make sure, struggling to hold it together. As she peered at him, the man turned to say something to the woman beside him, and Lisa saw his profile. Relief washed over her like a wave as she realised it wasn't Mark after all.

'Are you sure?' Katya asked.

'Yes,' Lisa answered dazedly. For a moment she thought Katya was asking if she was sure it wasn't Mark. 'I just—I thought I saw someone I knew.'

'You look like you saw a ghost,' Katya said with a light laugh.

Lisa shook her head as if to bring herself back to reality. She'd been spooked by the idea of Mark coming across her painting in the market earlier and had allowed her imagination to run away with her, that was all. 'I was mistaken. It wasn't him,' she said, smiling, as much to reassure herself as her friend.

As they drove towards the village, they passed the couple again, and Lisa turned to get another look at the man, just to reinforce the fact that it definitely wasn't Mark.

LISA WAS ready for a drink to soothe her nerves when she arrived at Martha's that evening for dinner. She had gone home briefly to shower and change, swapping the somewhat tattered jeans she wore to the market for a newer pair, and teaming them with a colourful hand-painted silk shirt she had picked up in a local craft shop. Her newly-washed hair fell loosely around her shoulders, and she had put on a little make-up. She was glad that casual dressing was the order of the day in the village, and a night out at the pub didn't call for anything more glamorous than a good pair of jeans and a bit of jewellery.

When she arrived at Martha's, Katya and Ellie were already sitting at the table in the big kitchen/diner drinking wine.

'Lisa!' Ellie beamed, leaping up as she entered the room. She rushed over to her and pulled her into a hug. 'It's so nice to see you again.'

'You too,' Lisa grinned, squeezing her tight.

'Oh wow, you look amazing!' Ellie said, pulling back

and holding her at arm's length. 'I'd hardly have recognised you.'

'Um … thanks. I think,' Lisa said with a wry smile.

Lisa had only met Ellie once before, when she had been home for a visit, just after Lisa had started working for Martha.

'You've put on weight, haven't you?' Ellie blushed and clamped a hand over her mouth as soon as the words were out. 'God, I mean that in a good way. You've put it on in all the right places,' she added with a cheeky smile. 'No offence.'

'None taken.'

'I suppose Mum has been feeding you up?'

'She needed it,' Martha said, carrying dishes in from the kitchen area. 'She was nothing but skin and bone when she first came here.'

'Not much chance of staying that way with Mum around,' Ellie said conspiratorially to Lisa. Small and curvy, Ellie had her mother's black hair, merry brown eyes and round, rosy cheeks. They even had identical dimples when they smiled.

'No,' Lisa said, smiling fondly. 'Your mother is an amazing cook.'

She had been so lucky to meet Martha in the first week she had come here. In her mid-forties, she was twenty years older than Lisa, but they had become great friends. Martha owned The Kettle, the cafe where Lisa worked as a waitress, but right from the start she'd been more like a mother to her than an employer. It had taken all of Lisa's courage to go in and ask about the job when she saw the 'Help Wanted' sign in the window of the quaint little coffee shop. She had only done it after pacing the street for hours, walking past the cafe several times before she finally got up the nerve to go inside.

Martha had seemed to pick up on her nervousness instantly, and had quickly put her at ease. She'd been so kind and friendly that Lisa had soon forgotten to feel shy. After a few cursory questions, Martha had offered her the job almost on the spot, and then made a pot of tea and sat down with her for a chat. She didn't seem bothered that Lisa's waitressing experience had been a long time ago or that she hadn't worked in years. Lisa suspected that Martha could tell she was in trouble and had decided to give her a hand. She had since discovered that Ellie's father had been an abusive man and Martha had been the victim of domestic violence during their marriage. She wondered now if Martha had recognised something of herself in Lisa when she had turned up that day.

Whatever the reason, she had taken her under her wing, and she didn't know what she'd have done without Martha to guide her in her first few weeks living in Porth Heron. She owed her so much. She had not only given her a job and helped her find a place to live, she had also introduced her to a circle of friends that had become like family to Lisa. Martha seemed to know everyone, and she was the soul of hospitality. She loved entertaining and bringing people together, and Lisa had met most of her friends and neighbours at Martha's kitchen table.

'Potatoes, Lisa?'

'Yes, please.' Lisa couldn't help thinking of Mark as Martha ladled a big spoonful of golden, crunchy roast potatoes onto her plate, already laden with roast beef, Yorkshire pudding and cauliflower cheese. He'd have a fit if he could see her digging into this lot. She smiled secretly to herself at the thought.

'Are you guys coming to the pub later?' Ellie asked as they ate.

'Yes, definitely,' Katya said. 'Connor's playing.'

'Brilliant. I love his band – and they always bring in lots of boys, so hopefully we'll get lucky.'

'What about that guy you were with?' Katya asked her. 'William, was it?'

'We broke up,' Ellie said. 'So I'm on the prowl.'

Katya laughed.

'You should come, Mum,' Ellie said. 'You must be well overdue a shag by now. I'm sure we could find you someone. Never too late, you know.'

'No, thanks,' Martha said, laughing. 'It's probably safer for everyone if I stay home. You know my taste in men is shocking.'

'What about you, Lisa?' Ellie asked. 'Any man in your life?'

'No.' Lisa shook her head.

'Well, we'll have to do something about that,' Ellie said, with a mischievous glint in her eye. 'We can't let all this hotness go to waste.' She circled her knife in the air, indicating Lisa's figure.

Lisa shifted uncomfortably, not sure what to say. She tried to think of a way to tell Ellie to back off without hurting her feelings. She knew she meant well and was just being friendly, but Lisa's luck with men had been every bit as bad as Martha's and she had no interest in meeting someone new. She just wished she could laugh it off like Martha and deflect Ellie good-naturedly.

'I know loads of cute guys I can introduce you to,' Ellie continued.

Out of the corner of her eye, Lisa noticed Martha give her daughter an almost imperceptible shake of her head.

'I don't think Lisa's looking for a boyfriend,' she said.

Ellie shrugged. 'Oh, that's cool. I'm not looking for a boyfriend myself. Just a bit of fun, a one-night stand or whatever.'

Martha rolled her eyes. 'I don't think Lisa's looking for a man at all,' she said.

'Oh!' Ellie's eyebrows shot up. 'Well, that's fine,' she said to Lisa, a slow smile spreading across her face. 'I know lots of great women I can introduce you to, if that's your thing.'

'Thanks,' Lisa smiled, 'but I'm not gay. Just not interested.'

'Really?'

'Not right now,' Lisa said, shaking her head. 'I'm not in the market for a relationship at the moment – or a one-night stand,' she added quickly before Ellie could pursue it.

Martha gave her daughter a meaningful look, and Ellie obviously took the hint.

'Okay, then – girls' night!' she announced, slapping the table decisively. Then she changed the topic, launching into a story about one of her course tutors.

Lisa was relieved as the focus moved away from her, grateful to Martha for her support. She had always respected Lisa's privacy, and while she was happy to listen whenever she wanted to talk, she didn't pry or ask questions. Lisa had told her that she had walked away from a bad relationship, but she had never gone into details about her life with Mark, and she never felt pressured to divulge more than she was comfortable with.

'But don't let me cramp your style,' she said to Ellie with a smile. 'Just because I'm not on the prowl, doesn't mean you can't be.'

'No, we stick together,' Ellie said decisively. 'Besides, I could do with a proper girls' night out. I haven't had one in ages. It could be just what I need.'

. . .

It turned out to be just what Lisa needed to put the stress and strain of the day behind her and finally lay the ghost of Mark to rest. Connor's band were good, and the atmosphere in the packed pub was friendly and high-spirited. As she, Katya and Ellie danced, drank and laughed, she felt all her earlier tension melt away, and she started to have fun. It was good to let her hair down and get a little bit drunk with her friends. By the time she flopped into bed that night, she had forgotten her worries about Mark and she fell asleep as soon as her head hit the pillow.

3

SHE SLEPT FITFULLY. In her dreams Mark was following her, shadowing her every move, and she was constantly on alert, waiting for him to confront her. But he never did. She saw the back of his dark head in the distance walking away from her, a shadow in the trees across from her house that she couldn't quite make out. The tension was unbearable, escalating until she longed for him to make a move just so that it would be over. She ran after him down narrow laneways, hunted for him in crowds, but he always eluded her. The spectre of him was a constant presence in her days, a threat hanging over her entire life and paralysing her. Every time she half woke from one of these dreams, she felt a momentary relief, but it was only a brief respite before she sank back into another, and it started all over again.

She was finally startled awake by a loud, persistent pounding on her door. It didn't stop as she stumbled out of bed and pulled on a robe. She raced blearily into the hall, anxious that the racket would wake up her neighbours. Still immersed in her dream, her heart hammered as she fumbled with the lock, half expecting to find Mark standing there. She threw open the door and gasped, relief flooding through her. Because there on the step was someone she had thought she would never see again – Grayson Fielding.

'Grayson! What—what are you doing here?'

Her relief was short-lived, seeping away as she took in his stony face and the hardness in his eyes. She'd never seen him like this before. It was unmistakeably Grayson, as beautiful as ever, and yet he felt like a stranger. There was something menacing in his demeanour that sent chills through her.

'Thought you'd escaped me, did you?' he said, with a contemptuous curl to his lips as he barged past her into the flat. 'I've come to collect what you owe me.'

Lisa trembled in fear, her mouth dry. She blinked hard, thinking she must still be dreaming. This couldn't be Grayson, so hostile and aggressive. She closed the door in a daze, her legs shaky as she followed him down the hall.

He was standing in the middle of the living room, hands on his hips, his eyes flinty as he glanced around, taking it all in. Finally he focused on her, standing uncertainly in the doorway.

'You know what I'm here for, don't you, Lisa?' he asked taking off his jacket and tossing it on the sofa. 'You owe me.'

'I know,' she nodded, trying to remain calm. Maybe she could reason with him. 'I know I still owe you a thousand pounds, but I didn't mean—'

'A thousand pounds?' He tilted his head to the side and regarded her almost pityingly. 'I think you owe me a little more than that. You've had the use of that money for half a year.'

'I'll pay it back,' she said quickly, 'with interest. I've been saving—'

Grayson snorted contemptuously. 'I don't want your money. I want what I purchased. I paid for the use of your body. I hired you to be my whore, and you still owe me for services I never received. I expect you to make good on that.' He threw himself onto the sofa and sprawled there, his eyes glittering dangerously as he looked at her. 'So, take that thing off.' He nodded to her robe.

'Grayson,' she hesitated, biting her lip.

'I said take it off,' he said, his voice deadly cold. 'Now.'

Lisa's fingers shook as she untied her robe and tossed it aside.

Grayson's eyes raked over her body, a crooked sneer curling his beautiful lips as he took in her thin cotton pyjamas. There was nothing remotely sexy about them.

'Strip and get on your knees.' He snapped his fingers and pointed to the floor in front of him. 'I want your hot mouth on my cock.'

Lisa did as he said, her heart hammering. He leered as she pulled her pyjama top over her head, his eyes raking over her breasts.

'All that money I gave you and you still didn't get your tits done,' he said.

Lisa felt her face burn with humiliation. It's Mark, she thought irrationally. It didn't make any sense, but somehow she knew this was Mark in Grayson's body.

'And the rest,' he said, nodding to her pyjama bottoms. 'Come on, Lisa. You've held out on me long enough.'

She pulled off her pyjama bottoms and tossed them aside. She stood naked before him, and his eyes darkened as they roved over her body with tortuous slowness. There was no warmth in their glittering depths. His gaze was hard, detached as he appraised every inch of her.

'Come here,' he nodded to the space in front of him, and Lisa did as she was bid, standing between his spread legs.

He sat forward and reached for her, his hands sliding over the curve of her hips, stroking the gentle swell of her stomach. 'You've let yourself go, Lisa,' he said softly as his hand moved lower, stroking the light sprinkling of pubic hair and pinching the flesh at her hip. 'This isn't the body I paid for.' He sighed, looking up at her.

Lisa held her breath. Maybe if he found her wanting, he wouldn't make her do this.

'Lucky you're so talented with your mouth to make up for it,' he said. He leaned back against the cushions, undid the button of his jeans and pulled down the zipper. 'So get on your knees and start earning that money I paid you.'

Lisa did as she was told, sinking to the floor in front of him. He lifted his hips as she helped him pull off his trousers and boxers. He was already rock hard. She bent her head to him, taking his thick cock in her hand as she swirled her tongue around the tip. He groaned deep in his throat as she licked along his shaft, then wrapped her hand around him and pumped as she sucked the head, bobbing rhythmically up and down on the tip. She took him a little deeper each time, but Grayson grabbed her head and thrust upwards, ramming his full length into her mouth until she gagged and her eyes watered. She instinctively jerked away, but he held her head firmly in both hands, pinning her to him as he controlled her movements and thrust harder.

'That's it, baby,' he groaned as he pumped her head up and down on his shaft, his hands rough in her hair. 'Deeper. You can go deeper than that.' He shoved himself further down her throat until she gagged again and tears streamed from her eyes. 'Don't hold out on me. I know you can go all the way,' he said as he thrust into her mouth. He groaned deeply as his cock bounced off the back of her throat, and Lisa panicked, flailing as she struggled not to gag.

She was out of practice at this, and she felt like she was going to choke. She flailed and whimpered, but it only seemed to excite him more.

'Oh yeah, baby. That's so good,' he said as she cried out in fright. She massaged his balls, praying he would orgasm soon and this would be over. Finally, he came with a deep groan, squirting hot liquid into her mouth. He held her head clamped to him while he pumped down her throat, so that she was forced to swallow every drop. After what seemed like an age, he softened and pulled out.

'Good girl,' he said, smiling at her almost tenderly as he rubbed his thumb along her swollen lips.

Lisa swiped at the tears still streaming down her face. Before she could catch her breath, Grayson wound her hair around his hand, pulling it painfully as he jerked her head back. Then he swooped in and kissed her, sucking her bottom lip between his teeth and biting down hard, while his hands groped her breasts, pinching her hardened nipples until she squealed in pain. He chuckled deep in his throat at the sound.

'Come on,' he said, surging to his feet and taking her hand. 'I want to fuck you now.'

In the bedroom he removed the rest of his clothes and ordered her to lie down on the bed. He was already hard again as he crawled over her. She tried to stifle her panic as he took both her hands in one of his and stretched them over her head, holding them immobile.

Why was he doing this? He knew she didn't like being held down. But there was a cruel glint in his eyes as he pushed her legs apart and rammed himself into her, and she knew it excited him to intimidate and scare her in this way. She tried to concentrate on breathing deeply as he held her still, her hands trapped above her head, his big powerful body pinning her to the bed as he pounded roughly into her again and again. When he came, he bit down on her shoulder so hard, she thought he would draw blood.

She shuddered as he drew back and his hand slid between her legs, stroking her soft flesh, pumping two fingers inside her.

'You're so wet,' he murmured in her ear. 'You love sucking me off, don't you? It turns you on to suck my cock. My little whore,' he said, his tone almost tender. He bit her earlobe, his breath hot on her neck, and Lisa shuddered as he stroked her clit, trying to resist the shocks of pleasure that were spreading through her. She didn't want this, and she hated that he could make her enjoy it, but she was powerless to stop her body's traitorous response as he roughly massaged her breasts. Her core tightened, every nerve end tingling as he kissed and licked his way down to her stomach. His fingers dug into the flesh of her hips as he buried his face between her legs. She felt his teeth sinking into the soft flesh of her inner thighs, and she squealed as he tugged the sensitive skin between his teeth. He alternated biting her with soft, wet kisses.

'That feels good, doesn't it?' he murmured, his hand stroking soothingly over her stomach, the gentle touch in stark contrast to the sharp pull of his teeth. 'I love that it makes you wet when I hurt you.' He put his mouth to her clit, sucking and nibbling relentlessly while he pumped his fingers inside her, until her orgasm took over and her body bowed off the bed, rigid with tension, and she let out an involuntary moan. The release was exquisite, and she sank back into the mattress, limp and satiated.

Grayson rolled off her and sat up. 'Stay there,' he said, and bent to press a kiss to her lips. 'I'm not finished with you yet.' He trailed a finger down her body, following it with his eyes. 'Not by a long shot.' He got up and left the room, and Lisa lay still on the bed, wondering how long her ordeal would continue. Her heart was pounding and she was trembling in fear as she waited for him to return, but she was afraid to move.

'There's someone I want you to meet.' Lisa turned. Grayson was standing in the doorway, a crooked smile on his face. Then he stepped aside, and her heart leapt into her mouth as she saw the man standing behind him.

'Hello, Lisa,' Mark said, his eyes glinting cruelly as he looked down at her. He loosened his tie and shrugged off his jacket as he stepped into the room. 'My turn.'

She turned to Grayson, silently pleading with him not to do this. But he just gave her a pitiless smile as he came to stand at the head of the bed, spreading her arms wide and holding them there. Bile rose in her throat as she watched Mark removing his clothes and she waited for her torment to begin all over again. She opened her mouth to scream, but no sound came out.

'No!' She woke with a shout, clawing at the sheets like a drowning person trying to fight her way to the surface of the water. She jolted upright, her heart pounding. It was just a dream, she told herself over and over. But she couldn't stop shaking as she looked around the room nervously, half expecting to find Mark lurking in the shadows. She took deep breaths, trying to calm herself. It wasn't real. She flopped back against the headboard, relief flooding through her. Grayson had been in her thoughts today – and then for a split second she'd thought she'd seen

Mark. Obviously the two things had somehow fused in her subconscious to produce that nightmare.

She glanced at the window. It was still dark. But the digital numbers on her bedside clock said six-ten. There was no point in trying to go back to sleep now – and besides, she didn't want to risk another nightmare like that one. She threw back the covers wearily and got out of bed. She might as well get up and get on with some work.

4

Lisa made sure she was too preoccupied in the days that followed to allow her nightmares to prey on her mind. It helped that the cafe was busy all week and she had no time to dwell on dark thoughts when she was rushed off her feet with a constant stream of customers. After long, tiring days at The Kettle, she went home and immersed herself in frenzied painting sessions in the evening, working to the point of exhaustion and only going to bed when she felt sure of falling asleep as soon as her head hit the pillow.

By Friday, she was in need of an early night, and she reckoned she'd worn herself out sufficiently to risk one. She was looking forward to a quiet, relaxing evening as the last customers left, and she and Martha started to clear up.

The Kettle was a quaint little tea shop on a square just off the high street, nestled between a bookshop and a florist. It was popular with tourists and locals alike, and famed for Martha's home-baked cakes and pies. There was a scattering of tables outside on the pavement, sectioned off by planters, where even in winter dedicated smokers would sit huddled over steaming mugs of tea or coffee.

'Are you coming to the pub tonight?' Martha asked her. She was behind the counter, emptying the till while Lisa cleared and wiped the tables.

'No, I'm planning a bath and an early night. Not very rock and roll, I know,' she said with a wry smile, 'but I'm wiped out.'

'You do look tired,' Martha said, eyeing her with concern.

'I haven't been sleeping very well lately,' Lisa said.

'Well, why don't you go on. I'll finish up here.'

Lisa smiled at her gratefully. 'I'll just clear off the tables outside,' she said, nodding towards the door.

As she looked through the window, she saw him, and froze. He was sitting outside, his chair pushed back from the little wrought iron table, his long legs stretched out in front of him. Lisa's stomach lurched as her nightmare came slamming to the front of her brain. Her first instinct was to duck and hide, but it was too late. He looked up and their eyes met through the glass of the window. He nodded to her, his lips curled in a tentative smile that suggested he was unsure of his welcome.

His eyes were soft and kind, the way she remembered them. This was the real Grayson, not the cold, brutal sadist of her nightmare, and she knew she had nothing to fear from him, but she still had to take a deep breath and steel herself before she walked outside on legs that felt like jelly.

'Hello, Lisa,' he said, looking up at her with a gentle smile as she stood in front of his table.

She'd forgotten just how breathtakingly beautiful he was. In her dream his features had been hardened by cruelty, his mouth twisted in scorn, his eyes cold and empty. Now it was as if he was lit from within and all his warmth and kindness shone through in his face. He was dressed casually in black jeans and a grey sweatshirt, the sleeves pushed up to reveal the dark sprinkling of hair on his tanned arms.

'Hello.' Her voice came out as a croak, and she cleared her throat. 'We're just closing up,' she said stupidly. He wasn't here for coffee. She knew why he had come.

'That's okay,' he said. 'I didn't want anything. I came to see you.' He looked up at her, his thick brows drawn together almost questioningly.

She nodded. 'I know.' There was only one reason he would have come looking for her. She decided to confront it head-on and get this over with as quickly and painlessly as possible for both of them. She knew she was in the wrong – she had effectively stolen from him. That part of her nightmare was real, even if the rest wasn't. She had taken his money and left without giving him all the time he'd paid for, and he was perfectly entitled to come after her for it. But he wasn't the heartless monster who had terrorised and humiliated her in her dreams. He was a rational, decent man. She could reason with him, and she felt confident that he would be understanding.

'I'm sorry about the way I left,' she said, pulling out a chair quickly and sitting beside him. 'I haven't forgotten about the money, and I do intend—'

'Money?' Grayson frowned. 'What do you mean?'

'I didn't plan to run off like that, so suddenly,' she said in a rush. 'I honestly intended to … to give you all the time you'd paid for.' She blushed, looking down, her fingers fidgeting nervously in her lap. 'But then something happened and it was my only chance to—' She broke off. She didn't want to bring Mark into this; she didn't even want to mention his name. She resented having to think about him at all. 'Well, I had to leave. You'd paid me a thousand pounds to be with you that night, but there was no time—'

'That's fine,' Grayson interrupted, looking almost as uncomfortable as she felt to be discussing this. 'Please don't worry about it.'

'I've been saving up,' she rushed on. 'I do intend to pay you back. But it will take a while.'

Grayson frowned at her in bemusement as if he couldn't comprehend what she was saying.

Lisa took a deep breath, steeling herself to say what she had to. 'But if you don't want to wait, or if you'd rather have what you paid for,' she said, her words tumbling over each other in her haste to get them out, 'I'm prepared to honour our agreement.' She swallowed hard. 'I'll go to a hotel with you if that's what you want.'

Grayson's eyes widened in shock. 'You think I've come here to … collect?' he asked, aghast.

She shrugged. 'You'd be entitled.'

'Well, I haven't.'

He looked wounded, and Lisa felt bad. Though she'd behaved like a whore with him, he'd never treated her like one.

'Honestly,' he continued, 'I've never given the money a thought. Forget about it.'

'I'd rather not. I *will* pay you back – whatever way you prefer.'

'I wish you'd consider it a gift,' he said, leaning towards her earnestly. 'I'm ashamed to say it, but it's not a lot of money to me.'

'That's not the point. If you're not getting what you paid for, then I want to return the money.'

'Why?' He frowned.

'Because I don't want to owe you anything. I don't want to be under an obligation to you.'

Grayson sighed. 'I would never hold that over you,' he said, his expression pained. 'I didn't come here to harass you, Lisa.' He ran a hand through his already messy hair.

'Nevertheless,' she said implacably. 'If you don't want to—to sleep with me—'

'I don't,' he said firmly. 'Not for money.'

Lisa's breath caught as their eyes met and held. She watched his long fingers as they toyed restlessly with packets of sugar in a bowl on the table, and experienced a sudden, intense pang of longing to feel them on her skin, to have them pushing inside her. She was almost sorry he didn't want to take her to a hotel and have sex with her. He'd always been able to make her feel so good. His turning up here was a complication she hadn't anticipated, but now that he had, she would be more than happy to go to bed with him one last time to fulfil her end of their bargain. It would be no hardship to work off her debt that way, and she could hold onto the hard-earned cash she'd been putting aside to repay him.

But deep down she didn't want it to be a mercenary transaction between them any more than he did. Grayson was a good person, and he'd always been kind and decent to her. She knew he felt diminished by their arrangement. He found it degrading on her part and exploitative on his, and he felt guilty enough already for taking her up on it. He'd only agreed to it reluctantly because she'd refused to let him give her the money any other way.

'Okay,' he sighed, leaning back in his chair. 'If you're dead set on paying me back one way or another, maybe there is something you could do for me.' His mouth twitched a little in amusement and he seemed to relax.

'What?' Lisa asked suspiciously, her heart starting to race.

'Don't look so worried.' Grayson's beautiful mouth widened in a smile. 'All I want is a game of chess.'

'A game of chess?' Lisa's eyebrows shot up. 'For a thousand pounds?'

'I like chess,' he said with a shrug. 'And I don't often find people who can challenge me like you do.'

'Still … that's an awful lot of money for a game of chess.'

Grayson drummed his fingers on the table. 'Okay – throw in dinner as well. How about that?'

'And then we're quits?'

'Yes.'

'Okay,' she said, smiling. 'Deal.'

Grayson held out his hand and they shook.

Lisa stood. 'Well, I have to finish closing up,' she said, glancing back at the cafe.

'So what about dinner? Are you free tonight?'

'Um … sure.' She thought quickly. She couldn't afford to take him out – certainly not to the kind of fancy restaurant he was used to. 'It would have to be a home-cooked meal,' she said.

'Even better,' Grayson said. 'Sounds perfect.'

'Okay. Well, wait here and you can walk home with me, if you like? I live very near.'

'Great.' Grayson nodded, smiling.

'I'll just be a few minutes.'

Lisa felt dazed as she went back inside, took off her apron and said goodbye to Martha. She was nervous, but also excited at this unexpected turn of events. For better or worse, her weekend wasn't going to be as quiet and dull as she'd thought.

5

IT WAS a short walk from the cafe to Lisa's apartment above a bakery on the high street. She felt suddenly shy and awkward with Grayson, unsure what his being here meant and how to behave with him in this new context. Why had he come all this way to see her if he didn't want his money?

'Have you been working at the cafe long?' he asked.

'Pretty much the whole time I've been here, so about six months. Martha, the owner, is great. She really helped me find my feet when I first moved here.'

'It must have been a big adjustment for you. What made you decide to come to this place?'

'I wanted somewhere quiet and secluded, far away from London. I was ready for a change, I guess.' She didn't add that she'd wanted a place where she could hide – somewhere no one would think of looking for her.

'Well, you certainly got that.'

'How did you find me?' she asked.

Grayson shot her a wary look. 'It was the painting you sent me,' he said, watching her carefully. 'My father said he'd seen one very like it for sale in the market here. He couldn't figure out at the time why it looked so familiar. Then he saw that painting again when he was at my house recently, and it clicked.'

So the grey-haired man who had asked about her painting was Grayson's father! How strange. She remembered him mentioning that his parents had retired to Cornwall. 'Do your parents live here?' she asked.

He shook his head. 'No, they live near Polperro. They were just visiting for the day.'

'Well, this is where I live,' Lisa said as they reached the green door beside the bakery. The shop was closed now, its windows shuttered, but the sweet smells of sugar and vanilla still hung in the air.

Lisa was very aware of Grayson behind her as she opened the door and led him through the long, narrow hall and up the creaky stairs, suddenly conscious of the threadbare carpet and peeling paint.

'This is me,' she said, opening a door off the landing. She waved him inside and dropped her keys on the table by the door.

Her little flat seemed to shrink as soon as Grayson stepped inside. He could take it all in at a glance, she thought as he looked around. This was her refuge, and her heart still gave a little excited skip when she came home in the evening, relishing the feeling of freedom and security when she closed the door behind her. Here she was free to be herself and do as she chose, with no one else to please or placate, nobody making demands or trying to control her. It was her home, and it couldn't have been more precious to her if it had been the most luxurious mansion money could buy.

But as Grayson stood in the centre of the room looking around, she saw it through his eyes and realised how small and shabby it must appear to him. She kept the flat scrupulously clean and tidy, and she had added little homely touches with colourful accessories and cheerful cushions – cheap things she had bought at the market to brighten the place up. But it didn't mask the fact that the furniture was old and dilapidated, and the carpet worn and faded.

'This is lovely,' he said, crossing to the large casement window where late evening sunshine streamed in. 'You get great light.'

Lisa smiled, touched that he had zeroed in on the most positive aspect of the room. She had forgotten how kind he was. She should have known he would never try to make her feel small or shame her for being poor.

'Well, have a seat.' She waved him to the two-seater couch beside the window, warmed by a patch of sunlight. 'I'll just get changed and then I'll start on dinner. It won't be anything fancy, I'm afraid.'

'Nothing fancy – my favourite!' He grinned.

'You're in luck, then,' Lisa laughed. 'Is spaghetti with meatballs okay?'

'It's great.'

She went to her bedroom, and quickly changed out of the sneakers and jeans she wore for work and into a pair of loose wide-legged linen trousers, a soft cotton T-shirt and flip-flops. Then she went to the kitchen and started to prepare dinner. Luckily she had planned to make a batch of pasta sauce to last her two days, if not three, so she had enough ingredients for her impromptu guest. She sometimes cooked in bulk for the freezer in order to free up her time for painting.

'Can I do anything to help?' Grayson asked, appearing in the doorway as she added onions to the pan. They sizzled as they hit the hot oil, the delicious aroma rising into the air in a cloud of steam.

'You could prepare the salad?' She nodded to the ingredients she had laid out on the worktop.

'Sure.' He moved into the kitchen, rolling up his sleeves, and she handed him a knife and chopping board.

'Would you like a glass of wine?' she asked, picking up a bottle of red she had left open on the counter to breathe. She liked to have a glass in the evening as she prepared dinner. It helped her relax and switch into leisure mode.

'Yes please.'

She poured two glasses and handed him one. 'Cheers,' she said, raising her glass to his.

'Cheers!'

'Oh, sorry,' she gasped as Grayson took a sip, suddenly remembering that he was quite a connoisseur, used to drinking the finest wine. 'It's probably not very good.' She recalled Mark telling her that the wine Grayson had served when they went to dinner at his house would have cost upwards of five hundred pounds a bottle. This hadn't even cost ten. 'It was on special offer at the supermarket.' She blushed, feeling like an idiot.

'It's very nice.' He smiled at her, and Lisa relaxed.

'Nice!' she mocked, remembering how Mark had scoffed at her use of that word to describe Grayson's expensive wine. 'Is that all you can say? I'll have you know this is the finest the bargain bin had to offer.'

Grayson laughed and took another sip of wine, seeming perfectly happy with it. He put down his glass and started chopping vegetables for salad.

Lisa relaxed as they worked companionably together. She was surprised to realise that he didn't make her nervous, and she didn't resent his intrusion into her home. In fact, she felt very comfortable with him, and it was nice to have some company for a change. Grayson should have seemed so out of place, drinking cheap wine in her poky flat while they cooked together. Everything about him exuded wealth and privilege, from his manicured hands to the designer watch that gleamed at his wrist. That alone probably cost about five times her monthly rent. But somehow it felt oddly natural having him here in her kitchen. He seemed so relaxed that it put her at ease in turn, and she quickly forgot that he was more used to vintage wine and Michelin starred restaurants than super-market plonk and spaghetti around a rickety table.

'So, no hot date tonight?' he asked as he chopped peppers. 'Did I just get lucky that you were free on a Friday night?' The question seemed loaded. His tone was light, but it felt forced and there was a stillness in him as he waited for her answer as if he was bracing himself for her reply. But he kept his head down so she couldn't see his expression.

'No. I was just planning a quiet night in.'

'Well, I hope I'm not intruding.' He looked up at her then.

'No, not at all. It's really nice to see you, Grayson.'

He smiled, relaxing.

'And I'm looking forward to a game of chess too. So far I haven't found anyone here who's really into it.'

She set the table while Grayson dressed the salad, and when the food was ready, he helped her bring it through. They sat across from each other at the little dining table, their knees almost touching.

'Well, here's to … new beginnings,' Grayson said, raising his glass.

'To new beginnings.' Lisa touched her glass to his. 'I'll definitely drink to that.'

'You look really well, Lisa,' Grayson said as they began to eat. 'There's something about you.' His eyes scanned her face. 'You look … different.'

'Fatter,' she said with a little laugh.

He shook his head. 'Happier.' He smiled.

She blushed. 'I *am* happy.'

'You like living here?'

'I do,' she nodded. 'It's … peaceful.'

He frowned slightly, something flickering across his face that looked like sadness, and he fell quiet. 'Do you mind that I found you?' he asked then.

Lisa hesitated, taking a sip of her wine. 'No,' she said finally. 'It's really good to see you again. But—' She broke off, biting her lip. She was reluctant to bring the spectre of Mark into the room. She liked Grayson so much, and she was having a nice time. She didn't want to spoil it.

'You're worried that if I could find you, someone else could too?' he guessed.

'Yes,' she admitted.

'It was just dumb luck, Lisa,' he said. 'I wasn't searching for you – it just happened. Serendipity, a coincidence – whatever you want to call it, it was a chance in a million. Fate, perhaps,' he said, his lips twisting in a smile.

'I guess you're right. Besides, I don't even know if Mark is trying to find me. He might not give a damn where I am.' She was trying to reassure herself more than anything, but deep down she didn't believe it for a minute. Men like Mark didn't let go. She didn't flatter herself that it was because she was special – it was just his nature. It was all about possession for him. One of his belongings had been taken away from him, and he would want it back.

'Maybe I should have stayed away,' Grayson said. 'I didn't come here to harass you or make you anxious. But once I knew where you were, I couldn't pass up the opportunity to see you again. Like I said, it seemed like fate.'

'It's okay,' she said, smiling at him reassuringly. 'I'm glad you're here.'

'My motives weren't entirely selfish. There was another reason I wanted to see you. That painting you sent me – it was extraordinary. I know I'm no expert, but Isabel thought so too.'

'Really?' Lisa felt a burst of pride. 'Isabel said that?'

He nodded. 'And I wanted to tell you because I wasn't sure if you knew how talented you are. I couldn't bear to think you'd given up, that you'd go on letting Mark make you believe you weren't good enough.'

'I discovered he'd lied to me about my work,' she said, looking down at the table. She felt ashamed of how naive and trusting she'd been, depending on Mark for validation instead of believing in herself. 'He told me I'd never make it as an artist, that I didn't have the talent, and he destroyed most of my paintings. The one I sent you and the one your father saw in the market are the only ones that survived.'

'Christ!' Grayson looked stricken.

'He'd taken those two for the gallery – so he said. But I discovered later – the day I left actually – that he'd buried them and hadn't offered them for sale at all. He completely sabotaged my career.' She swallowed hard. 'I was such an idiot,' she said, looking up at him.

'It wasn't your fault, Lisa. Mark was a manipulative asshole. You mustn't blame yourself for what he did to you.'

She nodded. 'I'm trying not to.'

'Well, I'm really glad that you're happy here,' he said, folding his napkin and leaning back in his seat.

'I am.' The mood had become gloomy and she was grateful to him for changing the subject.

'And you're painting again.'

'Yes. How did you know?' She frowned. He hadn't framed it as a question.

He smiled, nodding to her hand.

She examined her fingers and gave a rueful smile as she saw the flakes of paint around her nail beds that she could never quite shift, flecks of vermilion and cobalt blue embedded in her cuticles. 'Busted,' she said with a soft chuckle.

'I'm glad. You're far too talented to give up.'

'I'm doing a lot, actually. There's a very active artistic community here, and I'm part of an artists' cooperative. There are some really talented people. We run little exhibitions and workshops, and we sell our stuff in the Sunday market.'

'This place obviously agrees with you.'

'Yeah, I love it. The people are great – I've made some lovely friends. And I really enjoy being by the sea – being able to swim or surf whenever I want.'

'You surf?' Grayson raised his eyebrows, his mouth spreading in a grin.

'I'm learning.'

'Wow, I'm impressed.'

'I'm not very good yet, but it's fun.' Lisa had initially decided to take a lesson just to challenge herself. She was trying to become braver and build up her confidence, so she had pushed herself to do it, even though it scared her a little. She hadn't expected to enjoy it. But to her surprise she had loved it, and she'd never forget the exhilaration she'd felt the first time she had managed to stand up on the board and ride a wave, even if it was only seconds before she was tossed off into the sea. She'd never felt so alive and invigorated, even when she wiped out and was gasping for breath as waves crashed over her and the salt water rushed up her nose. It was a rush, and it made her feel strong and brave – like if she could do that, she could face anything.

'Yeah, it is fun,' Grayson said.

'You surf?'

He shrugged. 'Occasionally, when I'm staying down here with my parents. It's been a while.'

'Are you staying with your parents tonight?' she asked.

Grayson shook his head. 'I thought I might visit them tomorrow. But I stopped off here first to see if I could find you. I checked into a hotel in the village for tonight. I left my car there.'

'You drove down?' she asked, surprised. It was a very long journey from London.

Grayson shook his head. 'I flew. I picked up a car at the airport.'

'How long are you in Cornwall for?'

'Just the weekend. I have to go back to London on Sunday evening.'

They had finished the wine as they chatted, and Lisa was surprised when she looked at her watch and discovered it was already nine. The time had flown by.

'Well, I'll make coffee,' she said, pushing away from the table. 'And then I'll dig out the chessboard.'

6

Grayson watched Lisa studying the board, a little frown of concentration creasing the space between her brows as she considered her next move. He couldn't take his eyes off her. She was even more beautiful than he remembered. She looked healthier, of course; she was no longer painfully thin. But it went much deeper than that. It was almost as if she was a different person. Before she'd always been so tense and stiff, as if everything inside her was coiled tight, and every line of her features was taut, every muscle in her body rigid with the effort of keeping it all in. Now the tension in her shoulders was gone, and she no longer had that strained look in her face. He'd never seen her so relaxed and natural. There was a softness about her that hadn't been there before, an easy grace in her limbs, a warmth in her smile and a light and vivacity in her eyes that dazzled him. She almost seemed to glow.

When he first saw her at the cafe, he'd been taken aback by how young she looked. Casually dressed in jeans and trainers, with her dark hair loose and tumbling around her shoulders, she was so different to the chic, sophisticated woman he remembered that he hardly recognised her. It had knocked him off balance, and for a moment he wondered if he'd misremembered her. Had he been pining all those months for a woman who only existed in his mind?

But this was the real Lisa, he realised – the person she'd been before Mark had crushed all the life out of her; the woman he'd caught a glimpse of in their last few days together. She was warm, artless and full of life, and he wanted her more than ever.

He couldn't believe he was here with her now. He still wasn't sure he'd done the right thing by coming; if she wished him gone. Even though he'd thought of her constantly, he'd never looked for her. It almost drove him mad wondering where she was and what had happened to her. He could hardly sleep at night, torn between longing for her and worrying if she was all right. Nevertheless, he didn't want to disturb her peace, and he had tried to come to terms with the fact that he would probably never see her again. So he hadn't tried to find out where she was. But when the information just landed in his lap, it had seemed like it was meant to be, and he couldn't stay away any longer.

He'd told himself he just needed to see her once, to satisfy himself that she was safe and well, and he had certainly put his mind at rest on that score. She seemed really happy here, and he was glad of that. But he couldn't help feeling sad when she'd said how peaceful her life was. It broke his heart that she'd settle for so little at her age. She was too young, too bright and far too talented to be content with such a small, sheltered life in this sleepy backwater, happy just to be left alone. He knew why she felt that way, but he still found it troubling. She had so much potential, and he hated to think of Mark cheating her out of more of her life than he already had.

He watched her fingers curl around the rook as she picked it up, longing to feel them on his skin. He wished he could shove the chessboard aside as they'd done in the past, pull her to the floor and make love to her. He remembered all too vividly how soft and warm she was, the magic touch of her hands on his body, stroking, caressing, how it felt when she took him in her mouth …

His breath caught as she smiled up at him.

'Your move,' she said.

She blushed, and he wondered if she was remembering when he'd said that to her once in his library – and she'd made her move, leaning in to kiss him. The heady triumph he'd felt as she touched her lips to his surpassed any victory in his life before or since. He'd left it up to her, and she'd shown him that she wanted him. He'd swept the board aside and pulled her into his arms, caressing her breasts through the sheer material of her blouse …

Get a grip, he thought, feeling himself getting hard. He cleared his throat and bent his head to the board, frowning as he tried to focus on the game. Lisa was playing recklessly, making audacious sacrifices all over the place. Did she have a strategy, he wondered, or did she simply want to get the game over with as soon as possible. She was paying off a debt here, after all. Maybe she just wanted rid of him. He might have some idea if he wasn't finding it so hard to concentrate.

Maybe he should have held out for more than a game of chess. He didn't regret not taking her up on her offer to go to a hotel with him – even though he wanted her so badly it hurt. If she ever slept with him again, it had to be because she wanted him as badly as he wanted her. But he could have at least bargained for another match, he thought wryly, or one more dinner. He might never see her again once this game was over. He wished it could go on forever …

Lisa watched Grayson's face as he studied the board.

Your move. She wondered if he remembered when he'd said that to her in his study. As soon as the words were out of her mouth, they brought vivid images flashing across her brain. *Your move,* he'd said, and she'd made her move. Feeling uncharacteristically bold, she'd shown him that she wanted him, kissing his beautiful mouth. She felt warm all over as she remembered how urgently he'd pulled her onto his lap. She could still see the hunger in his eyes. She could almost feel his arms around her, the soft warmth of his hungry mouth at her breasts, sucking her nipples through the sheer chiffon of that blouse Mark had made her wear. She remembered how good the hardness of his erection felt as she straddled him, grinding her hips against his. Grayson had wanted her so much, and she'd wanted him just as badly. She still did. It was hard to concentrate on the game when she was just itching to push the chessboard aside and climb onto his lap. She longed to feel his arms wrap around her, pulling her close so she could feel the stiffness of his cock pressed into her stomach.

Did he still want her like that, she wondered. It was strange being with him like this now, and she was unsure how to behave. In the past, they'd always had sex. It was agreed between them, so they both knew what to expect. But it had been a financial transaction, a means to an end on her part. With that removed, she felt off balance, uncertain as to where they stood. There were no rules anymore. Anything could happen – or nothing.

'Thank you for the painting you sent to me,' Grayson said, breaking into her thoughts and pulling her back to the present.

She smiled shyly. 'I wanted you to have it.' It suddenly occurred to her that he might think she had sent it as some sort of recompense for running out on him that night. 'Something to remember me by,' she added. She needed him to understand that it was a gift and had nothing to do with the money she owed him.

'It meant a lot to me,' he said quietly. 'I love it.'

'I'm glad. I'm sorry for disappearing on you like that.'

'I was devastated when you didn't turn up that night,' he said deeply. His hands were steepled in front of his face, and he was looking down at the board so she couldn't see his expression.

'Sorry. Mark was coming back, and I needed to go. It was my one chance to get away.'

Grayson looked up at her, nodding understandingly. 'You were leaving him.'

'Yes.'

'That's what I figured – what I hoped.'

'But I'm really sorry for ditching you the way I did.'

'Don't be,' he said, shaking his head. 'I'm glad. Even if it meant I'd never see you again, I wanted you to be free and safe.' He sighed. 'I wish you'd let me help you back then,' he said with a troubled expression.

'You *did* help me, Grayson. You have no idea how much.' She shuddered as she remembered how desperate she'd been when she first met him, how trapped and hope- less she'd felt. She would always be grateful for the lifeline he'd thrown her.

'But I wish you'd let me be a friend to you. I'd have

given you the money you needed to get away if you'd let me – no strings attached.'

She shook her head. 'You helped me in the only way you could – the only way I'd allow you to. I'd never have taken a present of the money. I had to earn it, so I wouldn't be beholden to anyone.' She looked at him earnestly, pleading for his understanding. 'I don't know what I'd have done if I hadn't met you when I did, Grayson. It wasn't just the money. You *were* a friend to me. You played chess with me, and talked to me, and when I had an accident, you looked after me. When we were together, I was happier than I'd been in a very long time. I felt secure and happy and cared for, and I remembered who I was.' Tears clogged her throat as she spoke, and she blinked them away. 'I hadn't been that person in a very long time. You made me feel like myself again – someone my grandparents might recognise if they saw me.' A tear escaped and rolled down her cheek, and she swiped it away.

'Lisa.' Grayson started forward as if to get out of his chair, but he checked himself. She was glad, even though part of her wanted him to take her in his arms and comfort her. 'Sorry,' he sighed, sinking back into his seat. 'I didn't mean to upset you.'

'It's fine,' she said with a reassuring smile.

'I shouldn't have brought it up. I'm sure you don't want to be reminded of that time. It must bring back painful memories.'

'They're not all bad memories,' she said. 'There are some happy ones too.'

He raised a sceptical eyebrow at her.

'You're a happy memory,' she said softly, and was rewarded with a gentle smile. Then Grayson returned his attention to the board. She tried not to grin as he moved his knight into the position she'd anticipated, walking into the trap she'd set.

She'd been playing with apparent recklessness and abandon, but she'd had a strategy, and even though she'd found it hard to concentrate, she'd managed to carry it out. In a few more moves, she had Grayson's king in check.

7

———

'So,' Lisa said as she put away the chess board, 'we're even now?'

'Yes, we're even.' He smiled. 'You don't owe me anything.'

'Good.'

'Well, I guess I should go.' He stood hesitantly, hoping she'd offer him a drink or something – anything to extend the evening a little longer. But she said nothing. 'I'd really like to see you again, Lisa,' he said. 'I'm here until Sunday, if you're free?' He looked at her hopefully. She was biting her lip, regarding him uncertainly.

'Not because you owe me. Just because we … like each other,' he finished with a shrug.

Lisa sighed. 'I do like you, Grayson,' she said with an apologetic smile. 'But I'm sorry, I can't.'

'Not even for a game of chess?'

'I think you want more from me than a game of chess.'

'Maybe,' he said with a rueful smile. 'But I'll settle for whatever I can get.'

She looked down at her hands. 'I'm sorry. I just—I need to be on my own now.'

He nodded, trying to swallow his disappointment. 'I understand.' Still he felt glued to the spot, loath to leave her. With an effort, he turned to go.

'If you ever change your mind, you know how to reach me,' he said as Lisa followed him to the door. 'You still have my number?'

'Oh! Actually, I don't. I … threw away my old phone when I left London.'

'Right,' he nodded. 'Clean break.' He had suspected as much. When he'd tried texting or calling her after her last message to him, her phone always seemed to be out of service.

'But hang on.' She went back into the room and picked up her phone from the coffee table. 'Give it to me now.'

She handed him the phone and he keyed in his number. He noted she wasn't volunteering to give him hers, so he didn't ask. He would just have to hope that some day she would choose to call him.

'Well, thanks for a great game,' he said as she took the phone back from him. 'I really enjoyed it.' He lingered still, reluctant to leave. He couldn't bear the thought that he wasn't going to see her again and he just wanted to stretch out this last moment for as long as he could. 'And thank you for a lovely dinner.'

'Sorry it wasn't anything more exciting.'

'It was perfect.' He hovered uncertainly in the doorway. Every fibre of his being strained towards her, and his feet remained firmly planted on the threshold, unwilling to move away from her.

'Goodbye, Lisa,' he said finally. He leaned in and placed a soft kiss on her forehead. 'It was really good to see you again.'

She tilted her face to his so their lips were almost touching and he felt her soft breath on his skin. For a moment her lips hovered so close to his he could almost taste their sweetness. *Kiss me*, he begged silently, willing her to close the infinitesimal distance between them. He was almost shaking with the effort it took not to reach out and touch her.

'Goodbye, Grayson,' she said softly, breaking the spell. She blinked rapidly as she pulled away.

'Take care of yourself,' he said. Then he left and he heard the soft click as she closed the door behind him.

Lisa willed herself not to run after Grayson as soon as the door closed behind him. She put her phone on the coffee table, determined not to call his number straight away, and returned to the kitchen, busying herself with clearing up after dinner. The time seemed endless as she stacked the dishwasher and wiped down the worktops, half expecting Grayson to come back at any moment and beg her to change her mind about seeing him again. She knew he wanted her. She'd seen it in his eyes. She'd felt it in the way he'd hovered hopefully in the doorway. He hadn't wanted to leave. If she'd kissed him, he'd have pulled her into his arms and kissed her back. If she'd made the smallest move towards him, he wouldn't have hesitated. It had taken all her willpower to resist touching her lips to his, taking that last tiny step that would bring her into the warmth of his body and would inevitably lead to the two of them wrapped around each other in her bed. But she had left it up to him to make the first move, and he hadn't kissed her or touched her; he hadn't tried to seduce her or pleaded with her to go to bed with him. He had simply walked away. Still, she was on alert, listening for the sound of the door buzzer as she worked. But it never came.

When she had finished clearing up, she went back to the living room and sat on the sofa, staring at her mobile on the coffee table in front of her. She listened to the seconds ticking away on the wall clock, forcing herself to wait it out a little longer. When fifteen minutes had passed and he still hadn't returned, she relaxed a little. There had been something final about the way he'd said goodbye to her. He'd seemed so sad, but resigned. He wasn't going to come back, she thought, smiling. If she didn't call him, she would never see him again. She waited another five minutes before she picked up the phone and texted him.

Could you please come back? Now?

She put the phone back on the table and stared at it, her heart sinking as no answering text appeared. It didn't seem possible that she'd been mistaken about how much he wanted her. The heat between them was palpable. Then it occurred to her that he wouldn't recognise her number. She was just picking up the phone to text him again when the doorbell rang. Her heart raced as she ran downstairs. She opened the door to find Grayson on the step, looking flushed and a little concerned. He was breathing heavily and had obviously rushed back.

'Is everything okay?' he asked urgently, concern etched in his features.

'Yes.' She smiled at him as she took his hand and pulled him inside. She was so happy to see him. 'Everything's fine. More than fine. Come in.' She stood aside and he stepped into the little hallway. He looked at her questioningly as she closed the door behind him.

She took a deep breath. 'I wanted to ask you if you'd

like to stay,' she said, touching his arm. 'Here. With me,' she added, just to be clear. She blushed shyly as she looked up at him from under her lashes.

He frowned. 'You mean, you want—'

'You.' She leaned in and kissed his lips softly, tentatively. 'I want you.'

He smiled. 'You've changed your mind?'

'No. I never really wanted you to leave,' she admitted.

'But you said—'

She shook her head. 'Forget what I said. I've wanted you from the first moment I saw you today at the cafe. It's pretty much all I've thought about all evening.' She laughed softly. 'I couldn't even play chess properly.'

'You still won,' he said with a wry smile. 'But then I couldn't concentrate either. All I could think about was how much I wanted you.'

She kissed him again and his arms came around her as their lips clung together.

'But why did you tell me to go?' he asked, frowning down at her in bemusement as he pulled back.

She sighed and bit her lip. It was so hard to explain. 'I wanted to know that you'd walk away,' she said. 'That you'd take no for an answer.'

'Of course I would.'

'I'm sorry. I don't mean to play games. I just—I needed to be sure.' With a sudden flash of insight, she realised she had been testing herself as much as him. She not only needed to know that he would leave, but that she would let him, despite wanting him with every fibre of her being. She couldn't risk letting her heart rule her head.

'I get it,' he said, stroking her arm. 'If you want me to leave, just say the word. I promise I'll walk away right now if that's what you want, Lisa.'

'It's not.' She took his hand, curling her fingers around

his and looking into his eyes. 'I want you to stay.' She tugged on his hand. 'I want *you*,' she finished simply.

She heard Grayson's sharp intake of breath, his eyes searching her face. Whatever he saw there, he needed no further urging.

'God, I want you too,' he said, wrapping his arms around her. 'So much.' Then he was pushing her against the wall, his mouth descending on hers. Their lips met in a soft, lingering kiss, tentative and exploring. 'I've missed you so much,' Grayson breathed against her mouth between kisses.

'Come upstairs,' Lisa said, taking his hand.

8

THEY STUMBLED across the threshold of her bedroom as they kissed frantically, all the pent-up desire of the last hours finally unleashed. They nibbled and bit at each other's lips while their hands roamed restlessly. All Lisa's senses leapt to life at the touch of Grayson's warm, firm lips on hers, the rasp of his stubble against her skin and the feel of his strong arms wrapped around her. She breathed in his warm male scent as he turned his head this way and that, seeking the perfect angle, while her hands roved frenziedly over his body, impatient for more. His darting tongue sent delicious shivers down her spine and she pressed herself closer, loving the feel of his erection against her stomach, thrilled by the evidence that he was as excited as she was.

He broke the kiss briefly to remove her shirt, then he pulled her back into his arms and kissed her again as he unfastened her pants, his hands urgent as he pushed them off and they slid to her feet. She shivered as his lips moved to her neck and up to her ear, sucking on the lobe as he slid her bra straps off her shoulders. But when his hands slid around to the fastening at her back, she froze.

'What's the matter?' he asked, lifting his head to look at her, his brow furrowed with concern. She'd forgotten how perceptive he was. He had always been able to pick up on how she was feeling, and he had obviously sensed her hesitance.

'Nothing.' She shook her head, stifling the momentary panic she had felt, and tilted her face up for his kiss.

As his mouth slanted over hers, hot and demanding, his hands went again to the fastening of her bra. Instinctively, before she could stop herself, she pulled away slightly.

'Lisa?' he asked hoarsely. 'What's wrong? It's something.'

She blushed as his eyes searched her face, acutely aware that she was framed by the moonlight pouring in the window. She suddenly felt shy to be standing before him in her underwear, feeling his heated gaze on her body. She felt a sudden stab of anxiety at the thought of Grayson seeing her naked and finding her lacking. He had seen her naked before, of course – plenty of times – and he had always wanted her. But she had changed since then; her body had altered. She no longer spent hours working out every day, and though she was by no means fat, neither was she as toned and taut as she used to be. Her stomach was soft and rounded, her breasts fuller, her thighs and hips fleshed out and curvy. She didn't spend her days getting pampered and polished at the beauty salon, and she no longer waxed herself bare. She wasn't Mark's perfect sex doll anymore – he would be disgusted if he saw her now. She shuddered as the shadow of her dream flickered across her brain. *This isn't the body I paid for.* What if Grayson didn't want her like this?

He was watching her closely. 'You've changed your mind?' he asked softly, sliding her bra straps back into place.

She felt the tension in his body, his fingers trembling against her skin. His features were taut and strained, his erection plainly visible through his jeans, standing stiff against his stomach. Every muscle in his body was rigid with the effort it took to tamp down his excitement.

Lisa shook her head, unable to meet his eyes.

'It's okay,' he said, taking her chin between his fingers and tilting her face up. 'You don't want this?'

She gasped. How could he think that? She wanted so badly for him to touch her. She had never craved anything so desperately in her life.

'I do,' she whispered. 'I want you so much.'

She saw the answering need in his eyes, dark with hunger.

'It's just that … it's been a long time.'

Grayson nodded understandingly. 'I know. But it's always been good between us, hasn't it?'

Lisa nodded.

'You have nothing to be shy about with me, Lisa.' His thumb stroked along her lips seductively while his heavy-lidded eyes followed the movement. 'You're so beautiful and sexy, and I want you so much it hurts,' he said, leaning in to nuzzle her face. 'I've dreamt of being like this with you again so often. I know it's been a while, but we want each other as much as ever. Nothing's changed.'

'But *I've* changed,' Lisa said, pulling away, panicked. She knew his words were meant to reassure, but they had the opposite effect on her.

Grayson gave her a puzzled frown.

'You haven't seen me in a while, and I'm … different to

how I was then. I've put on a bit of weight, and I'm not as toned as I used to be—'

'Ssh.' Grayson frowned, putting a finger to her lips. 'I want you, Lisa. I want to touch you and kiss you, and make love to you – and I want to look at you. Trust me?' His eyes burned into hers as his fingers went to her bra straps.

She took a deep breath and nodded. This was Grayson, she reminded herself as he slid the straps down her arms and began to kiss her again. She did trust him. His mouth was soft and wet on hers, and their kisses quickly became heated and hungry, their breathing heavy and jagged. Lisa had forgotten herself again by the time Grayson slid his hands around her back and opened the clasp of her bra. Lost in the kiss, her body strained towards him. He lifted his head as he pulled off her bra and tossed it aside, his heavy-lidded eyes darkening as they dropped to her naked breasts.

'So beautiful,' he murmured, cupping their swollen fullness in his hands. Lisa gasped softly as his thumbs stroked over her nipples, excitement spiking deep in her belly.

He bent his head to her again, kissing his way along her throat and down to one breast, his tongue flicking lightly across her nipple before he took it into his mouth. He sucked hard on the tight, swollen nub, while his fingers gently caressed the other one.

Lisa gasped at the sensation of cool air against her wet, heated skin as he lifted his head and kissed his way down her body, sinking slowly to the floor until he was kneeling in front of her. She was grateful for his hands gripping her waist, steadying her as his lips trailed across her stomach from hipbone to hipbone, and then moved down to her abdomen and along the edge of her underwear. She trembled as his head dipped between her legs and she felt the heat of his mouth through the thin fabric of her panties, while his hands stroked along her thighs. Her legs started to shake as heat built inside her. He looked up at her as he hooked his fingers into the sides of her panties and slowly slid them down her legs, the light touch of his hands against her skin sending shivers down her spine. He leaned forward, nudging her legs apart and kissed her soft, heated flesh.

'You're so sweet,' he murmured huskily as he licked gently along her folds. She gasped as he parted her flesh with his fingers. As his tongue slipped inside her, she placed her hands on his shoulders to steady herself.

She cried out as his mouth found her clit, clutching his shoulders tightly. She felt the little spasms building inside her, growing stronger as he sucked and licked, his little groans of pleasure vibrating against her feverish skin. It was almost unbearably intense, and her body instinctively recoiled, but he clasped her thighs firmly, holding her still against his unrelenting mouth until she screamed her release as her orgasm took hold, the delicious waves of pleasure racking her body.

'Lisa,' he whispered her name against her sensitive skin as she trembled, little fluttering pulses of pleasure sending shivers through her. He pressed soft butterfly kisses across her thighs as the spasms subsided, and her body relaxed, spent. He stood, and she collapsed into his arms, feeling boneless.

'You're more gorgeous than ever,' he murmured, watching his hand as it trailed across the slight mound of her stomach and stroked over the soft curve of her hip. 'I like the way you've changed.'

'You like me fatter?' She smiled up at him.

He laughed softly. 'I like you happier.' Their eyes caught and held, and she saw his smile fade to be replaced by an intent, hungry look as he bent his head to hers.

She tasted herself on his lips when he kissed her again, the musky tang of her arousal mingling with the scent of his body wash and his own distinctive taste to became a flavour that was uniquely them. As their kisses deepened, Grayson pulled her closer and her senses leapt as she felt the hardness of his erection pressing into her stomach. She slid her hand between them, stroking him over his jeans, impatient to take his cock in her hand, to feel him moving inside her.

She broke the kiss. 'Come to bed,' she murmured huskily against his lips.

Grayson nodded, and she took his hand and led him to the bed. She sat on the edge and watched as he quickly removed the rest of his clothes, openly gazing at his body, drinking in the beauty of his broad shoulders and wide, muscled chest, the sprinkling of dark hair on his flat stomach leading her gaze downwards. He didn't take his eyes off her as he stripped, and she saw how much he wanted her in the heat of his eyes and the urgency of his movements. When he pulled off his boxers, the sight of his hard cock stiff against his stomach sent a little shiver of excitement though her. She felt a strange burst of pride at the effect she had on him.

He joined her on the bed, pushing her back onto the mattress as he crawled over her. His mouth opened against hers, his tongue slipping inside as he nudged her thighs apart. Lisa spread her legs wide, pumping her hips up to meet his, urging him on. He pushed inside her slowly, and she cried out in ecstasy at the feeling of fullness, the weight of his body on hers, the thickness of his cock, and the power of his thrusts inside her. It felt so right to be joined like this with him again, as if she'd finally found what she hadn't realised she'd been missing all these months. She felt complete. The intensity in Grayson's gaze told her it was the same for him. He looked into her eyes and held her hand as he thrust deeper and harder, driving them both to an earth-shattering climax.

9

Lisa woke to the weight of an arm draped across her waist, a warm hand cupping her breast possessively. *No.* Adrenalin shot through her body, and she wrenched away, jolting upright and throwing off the restraining arm. She whimpered as she scrambled to the edge of the bed, her heart thudding. Still barely conscious, she felt the warm body behind her stir. A hand touched the bare skin of her back and she gave a panicked cry, jerking away from it.

'Lisa?' The husky voice was croaky with sleep, but there was something about it that had an instant calming effect. She blinked hard as her pulse slowed, trying to wake herself up properly.

'What's happening?' She felt the light touch of a hand on her shoulder. 'Are you okay?'

Grayson. She let out a breath, relief flooding through her. It was Grayson. She relaxed as her sleep-fogged brain cleared. Trying to shake off the jittery feeling, she mustered a reassuring smile. It obviously wasn't very convincing, because his eyes widened in alarm as she turned to face him.

'Hey, what's wrong?' He frowned in concern, reaching out with one finger to stroke her face lightly.

Her skin felt clammy, and her breathing was short. 'Nothing.' She shook her head. 'Sorry, I just—I was half asleep and I freaked out when I woke up and there was someone else in the bed.' She gave a wry laugh. 'I guess I'm just not used to having company.' She gave him a shaky smile.

He sat up, still looking worried. 'Do you want me to go?' he asked, studying her face intently.

'No!' It came out so vehemently that she laughed. 'Don't go. I'm glad you're here.'

He hesitated, regarding her uncertainly.

'I want you to stay,' she said and was relieved when he smiled, his features relaxing.

'Okay.' He nodded. If you're sure, I'm more than happy to oblige. There's nowhere I'd rather be.'

Lisa suddenly felt emotional in the aftermath of her adrenalin rush, and she blinked back tears, overwhelmed as relief seeped through her.

Grayson frowned, putting an arm around her. 'What happened just now?' he asked. 'Were you dreaming?'

She shook her head, wiping away a stray tear with the back of her hand. 'No, not exactly. But I wasn't properly awake and I panicked when I felt you in bed with me.'

He frowned broodingly. 'You thought I was him. Mark.' His tone was flat, his expression solemn.

'I wasn't thinking at all. It was just an instinctive reaction. I guess I subconsciously sensed danger and my body automatically went into fight or flight mode.'

Grayson sighed. 'Well, I'm glad your body chose flight and you didn't try to beat me up.'

Lisa laughed softly, grateful to him for lightening the atmosphere.

'Are you sure you're okay?' he asked, squeezing her shoulder. 'I don't want to make you uncomfortable.'

'You don't. I really like that you're here, Grayson. I feel ... safe with you.'

'Good.' He gave her forehead a soft kiss.

She curled into his side, laying her head on his shoulder and he stroked her arm soothingly as her breathing returned to normal.

'I hope you're not paying too much for that hotel room you didn't use,' she murmured. 'Where were you going to stay?'

'Cliff House.'

'Ooh, nice.' It was a boutique five-star hotel just outside the village. 'Seems a shame to miss out on that. I've heard it's lovely.'

He shrugged. 'I think the accommodation here is far superior.'

'I doubt that,' she laughed.

'Well, the bed is much more comfortable, and I can't fault the room service,' he said with a grin, his eyes twinkling.

'And we *do* serve a very good breakfast.'

'You see – no contest. Breakfast wasn't even included at Cliff House. And I, for one, am starving.'

'Me too,' Lisa grinned. 'I seem to have worked up quite the appetite somehow last night. But first I'm going to take a shower.'

Grayson nodded, relaxing back against the pillows as she got out of bed.

'Would you like to join me?' she asked, holding out her hand to him.

Grayson's mouth spread in a wide smile. Without another word, he swung out of bed and took her hand. His cock was already hard as she led him to the bathroom.

. . .

Lisa hummed to herself as she made breakfast, taking special care to make the bacon crispy, and the scrambled eggs soft and creamy. This morning felt special, and she wanted to make it a treat for Grayson – for both of them. She hadn't felt so happy in a long time. She'd been content here, but this pure, giddy joy was on another level. She felt so light, she thought she might be in danger of floating away.

She was still tingling from their lovemaking in the shower. They had kissed as they stood under the warm spray, their hands gliding languorously over each other's naked bodies, massaging and stroking, unhurried as they luxuriated in their closeness. Then it had become urgent and heated as the excitement built between them. Grayson had lifted her, and she'd wrapped her legs around his waist as he thrust forcefully inside her, driving them both to an explosive climax.

She'd pulled on a robe and left Grayson getting dressed while she started on breakfast. She was glad to have a little alone time to gather her thoughts. Last night had been incredible; and this morning, she thought dreamily. She'd never known lovemaking like it before – so passionate, yet so tender it almost brought tears to her eyes thinking about it. She hadn't expected to ever really yearn for sex again after Mark. But she couldn't get enough of Grayson, and her desire for him was a revelation. She craved his touch with a hunger that took her by surprise.

He made her feel more alive than she had in a long time, and she was glad he'd found her. But it was tinged with sadness because she knew nothing could happen between them. They were worlds apart in every way – not just geographically, but socially. Grayson lived in London, and was part of the city's wealthy elite, while she eked out a living as a waitress and part-time artist in this tiny village in Cornwall. She knew last night was just a one-off thing, and her heart ached at the thought. But she didn't regret that it had happened. Grayson had awakened something in her that she had thought was dead, and nothing could take that away. Even when he was gone, she would still have that spark inside her and the memory of one last precious night with him.

'Mmm, something smells good,' Grayson said, coming up behind her and putting his arms around her. He dropped a kiss on her shoulder and she breathed in the delicious male scent of him, fresh from the shower.

'It's just ready,' she said. She loaded up their plates with scrambled eggs, bacon and toasted sourdough, and they took them through to the living room. Lisa felt dazed as they sat opposite each other at her little table, as if she was in a dream. They weren't touching, but she had never felt closer to anyone than she did to Grayson right now. The sun poured in the window, and the sky outside was a perfect cloudless blue. It couldn't have been a more perfect morning.

Grayson kept his eyes on her almost the entire time, as if afraid she might disappear. He grinned at her goofily when their eyes met, his happiness almost palpable.

'I can't believe I found you again,' he said.

'Me either,' Lisa said, smiling back at him.

'So, do you plan on staying here for good? Do you think you'll ever go back to London?'

'I don't know.' She shrugged. 'I miss it sometimes. It's a big change living in a small village, but I've made a life for myself here. I feel like I belong, and I feel … safe.'

Grayson's smile faded and a flicker of concern passed across his face. 'Do you think Mark is looking for you?'

'I don't know. But if I try to find out, it could lead him to me, so I don't risk it.' She didn't dare look Mark up on social media in case it would give him a way to find her.

Grayson gave her a cagey look. 'I could get Isabel to try to find out, if you like? She still sees him sometimes.'

'Oh.' Of course Mark would come across Isabel from time to time. They were both important art dealers with galleries close to each other in Mayfair. But it wasn't the idea of Isabel seeing Mark that caused her heart to plummet. It was the thought of Grayson still being involved with her that was causing that corrosive gnawing in her belly.

'How is Isabel?' she asked, trying to sound casual.

'She's great.' Grayson's fond smile cut through her. She knew it was silly to feel that way. Of course Grayson would speak of Isabel affectionately. They were old friends, she told herself, trying to be reasonable. But she couldn't block out the needling voice in her head reminding her that they were old friends who slept together. It was a sharp reminder that sex didn't mean to Grayson what it did to her. It had been easy to forget that when she was with him last night. He'd been so completely focused on her, so intense and passionate that it felt like more than just the physical act. The heat in his eyes and the tenderness of his touch had beguiled her into believing he felt the same way she did. Caught up in the moment, it had been all too easy to forget that to him it was nothing more significant than sharing a pleasant physical activity with a friend. She didn't doubt that Grayson liked and desired her; but sex didn't mean anything to him beyond that.

She had never understood the kind of casual sexual relationship he had with Isabel. She still didn't. She wished she could be sophisticated about it, but she knew she couldn't be that intimate with someone and not want an emotional connection too. So it was probably a good thing in the long run that this was just a one-off thing. Falling for Grayson wouldn't do her any good. He wasn't mean or uncaring, and she knew he would never deliberately hurt her. But that wouldn't stop him doing it. The jealousy would eat away at her and make her miserable.

'Has Mark ever said anything to her about me, do you know?'

'She bumped into him just after he came back from China. He asked if we'd seen you while he was away.'

'Oh!' Lisa tensed up. The thought of Mark looking for her gave her a horrible hunted feeling. She could imagine how angry he'd have been.

'She didn't tell him anything, of course. She didn't even know that I'd seen you that week. She suggested the two of you come to dinner, and he said you'd gone to stay with an aunt.' Grayson smiled crookedly. 'I knew you didn't have an aunt. I guessed then that you'd gone and he didn't know where you were.'

'He wouldn't want to admit that I'd left him.' It would have been humiliating enough for him that she'd walked out on him. His ego couldn't take anyone else knowing.

'Would you like Isabel to try to find out if he's looking for you? She'd be subtle about it, I promise.'

Lisa thought for a moment. 'No,' she said finally. 'I think I'm better off not knowing.' Maybe it was cowardly, but she didn't want to think about Mark any more than she had to. If she knew he was searching for her, it would make the threat of him a constant looming presence in her life, and she didn't want that. If he found her, she would know all about it soon enough and she would deal with it as and when it happened.

'You don't have to work today?' Grayson asked her when they had finished eating.

'No. I'm really lucky. I only work weekdays. Martha has plenty of part-time staff to cover Saturdays and Sundays.'

'That's great. So, any plans for the weekend?' he asked.

'I was just going to do some painting.'

'Where do you paint?' he asked, looking around the room. 'Do you have a studio?'

'There's an attic conversion at the top of the house,' she said. 'It was just being used as a junk room. My land-lady let me have it for no extra rent if I took care of clearing it out.'

'Can I see?'

'Sure.'

When they'd cleared away the breakfast things, she led him up the steep flight of stairs to her little eyrie on the top floor. The pungent smells of oil paint and turpentine hit her nostrils as she opened the door and waved him in ahead of her. It never failed to give her a little thrill entering her makeshift studio. It wasn't a large room, but devoid of furniture apart from a long workbench, it felt airy and spacious. Fitted shelves were filled with art supplies, jars full of brushes jostling for space with little bottles of varnishes and thinners, and a collection of paint-smeared rags. A skylight and a row of windows along two walls flooded the room with light. An easel stood in the corner opposite the door.

'This is great,' Grayson said, his eyes lighting up as he followed her into the room.

'I know. I was really lucky Kay couldn't be bothered clearing it out. But she said it wasn't really usable space anyway.'

'Really?' Grayson asked sceptically, looking around.

She could tell he was looking at it with an architect's eye, seeing its potential.

'Yeah, I know,' she said drily. 'Kay's a friend of Martha's. It was Martha's suggestion she give me this room.' She smiled crookedly. 'I think there may have been some strong-arming involved.'

Grayson chuckled. 'I'd like to meet this Martha. She sounds like a paragon.'

'She is kind of a force of nature. She's been a really good friend to me.'

'I like her already,' he said. 'May I?' He nodded towards the easel and the canvases stacked against the wall behind it.

'Yes, go ahead.'

He walked over, but to her horror, he stopped on the way and picked up one of the smaller canvases laid out to dry on the workbench. They were typical postcard scenes of the village and surrounding landscape that she sold in local souvenir shops, and they were everything Mark had accused her of being – trite, derivative and completely devoid of originality, with no real artistic merit. But they were quick and easy to produce, and they were very popular with tourists, so they were a useful source of extra income. She smiled to herself as Grayson looked at the beach scene in his hands, a bemused look on his face, and decided to have some fun with him. She went over to stand beside him.

'So, what do you think?' she asked, folding her arms and nodding to the painting he was holding. She looked at him hopefully, as if eagerly awaiting his opinion.

His eyes flicked over the other paintings on the table. 'They're very ... um ... They're quite different to what you did before, aren't they? I mean, maybe the painting you sent me isn't your typical style, but—'

She swallowed a giggle as he struggled to find something positive to say. 'Relax. They're terrible,' she said, relenting. She took the painting from his hands and placed it back on the bench.

'No, I wouldn't say—'

'Okay, maybe they're not terrible,' she smiled. 'They're … fine. I just do them for the tourist trade. They sell really well,' she shrugged. 'It's handy extra money.'

'Oh,' Grayson grinned at her. 'I must admit that's a relief.'

'That's my own stuff,' she said, nodding at the large canvases stacked in the far corner. There were four finished paintings and one on the easel that she was currently working on. She watched as Grayson picked up the first of the paintings to examine it, feeling genuinely anxious about his opinion now.

'Wow!' he said, holding it out at arm's length. 'This is amazing.' He lifted one painting after another from the stack, his expression thoughtful as he studied them carefully in turn. Then he stood in front of the easel. 'This is brilliant, Lisa.'

She went to stand beside him. 'Do you really think so?'

'It's breathtaking.' He turned to her, real excitement in his eyes. 'You're incredibly talented.'

She smiled, blushing with pleasure. 'Thanks.'

'I mean it. You don't need to waste your time doing that stuff.' He nodded to the pictures on the bench.

'They're the ones that bring in the money,' she said with a sigh. 'I mean, I sell a few of my pieces at the market, but not that many.'

'These don't belong in a village market, Lisa. I know I'm no expert, but I'm sure you could get a couple of grand for one of these in a London gallery – probably more, especially once you'd become established. I bet

Isabel could sell them for you like that,' he said with a snap of his fingers.

'Maybe,' she shrugged, smiling. It was really nice to hear. 'But I'm not interested in showing in London galleries anymore.'

'Why not? Didn't you want this to be your career?'

'That ship has sailed. I guess I'm just not as ambitious as I once was. The London art scene is so competitive, and talent is no guarantee of success. People way more gifted than I am never make it.'

'But isn't it worth trying? Your work deserves to be seen.'

She shook her head. 'I'm happy to do it as a sideline now. I can enjoy painting and make a bit of extra pocket money without all the stress of trying to make a career of it.' The truth was she couldn't risk putting her paintings in a London gallery where they might come to Mark's attention and lead him to her. He was such a dominant figure in the London art world, it would be impossible to have a career there without encountering him, and she wasn't ready for that. She didn't know if she ever would be.

'Whatever makes you happy,' Grayson said, frowning. 'As long as it's not because you don't think you're good enough. Because you are.'

'Thank you. That means a lot.'

'Well, I'd better go and check out of my hotel,' he said, glancing at his watch. 'How would you feel about abandoning your painting and spending the day with me?'

She smiled. 'I'd love to. But don't you want to visit your parents while you're down here?'

He thought for a moment. 'Come with me,' he said.

'To your parents'?'

'Yes. Why not?'

'They won't be expecting me. I wouldn't want to impose.'

'You won't be imposing. They love when we bring friends home.' He glanced out the window. 'It's going to be a beautiful day. We could go surfing on the way.'

Lisa grinned, delighted by the suggestion. 'I'd love that! It's a great time of year for it.'

'Do you have all the gear?'

'No, I usually just hire everything. I don't go that often. I've only had a few lessons.' Surfing was expensive, and it was only an occasional treat when she could afford it.

'Well, I'm pretty rusty myself. But I know a great beach on the way that's perfect for beginners and doesn't get too crowded at weekends.'

'Sounds perfect.'

Grayson beamed happily at her. 'Then we could go on to my parents' for dinner and stay the night. What do you say?'

Lisa was almost shaking. She was so happy, it didn't seem real. She decided she wasn't going to over-think this. 'I say yes!'

'Great! Well, throw some things in a bag and I'll go get the car.'

10

It was a mild, sunny day, and Lisa couldn't have been happier as they bowled along the twisting roads with the windows open, the music pouring from the car stereo providing the perfect soundtrack to the stunning scenery of the coastline flashing by. Every bend in the road revealed another wide sandy beach or rocky cove, the sunlight sparkling on the water far out to the horizon while foamy waves crashed against the rocks below. Each vista was more breathtaking than the last, and she was torn between looking out at the scenery and watching Grayson as he drove. She still found herself constantly awed anew by the beauty of this place – she didn't think she'd ever take it for granted, no matter how long she lived here. She and Grayson spoke little as they drove, but it was an easy, comfortable silence. It felt like they were both on the same wavelength, giddily happy to be in each other's company and enjoying this lovely day.

The beach Grayson brought them to was a little off the beaten track, so it wasn't too crowded even on a sunny Saturday, and there was plenty of room on the long stretch of sand for the small crowd of surfers who had gathered there. As she got out of the car, Lisa shielded her eyes from the sun to survey the beach. Its relatively sheltered location and gentle shelving made the waves perfect for beginners honing their skills, evidenced by the abundance of surf schools in the vicinity.

They hired boards and wetsuits at a nearby surf shop, and Lisa felt a familiar shiver of anticipation as she changed and tied her hair back in a ponytail. Adrenalin was already kicking in as she picked up her board and headed for the sand. Grayson was waiting for her, and the sight of him in a wetsuit set her pulses racing even faster.

'Are you ready for this?' He grinned at her, jerking his head towards the sea.

She nodded. As they ran to the shoreline, she enjoyed the familiar rush of excitement mixed with fear she always felt before she got in the water, and there was a little flutter of butterflies in her stomach as they paddled out. But as soon as she caught her first wave, her nerves were swept away in the pure high she felt when she stood up on her board and suddenly she was gliding effortlessly, skimming across the curve of the water. She was so intensely in the moment, unaware of anything but the feeling of weightlessness, the power of the water pushing her board along the top of the wave, the spray on her face and the crashing of water around her. Everything else zoned out until there was nothing but her and the sky and the sea, and for a brief few seconds the world was perfect and she was exactly where she was supposed to be. It was unlike anything else she'd ever experienced. It would only last seconds before she plunged into the water, but it was enough to get her hooked again every time and eagerly chasing the next wave to recapture that moment where she was at one with the ocean, a part of it. The only thing that came close was sex with Grayson.

She looked across at him as he wiped out, crashing into the water, the sun glinting off his board as it flew into the air behind him in a high arc. He turned to her, laughing as he shook water from his hair, and she saw the same exhilaration in his face that she felt, the same pure visceral joy.

'God, it's been too long since I've done this,' he called to her breathlessly. 'I'd forgotten how much I love it.' Droplets of water sparkled on his skin and dripped from his hair. 'Thanks for reminding me.'

'You're welcome.' She grinned back at him. She was so happy they'd come here. Surfing was always a high, but sharing it with Grayson just made it more wonderful than ever.

Several hours later, they walked back up the sand together, happy and exhausted after a morning chasing the waves.

'Are you hungry?' Grayson asked.

'Starving!' Lisa grinned. The taste of salty water on her lips as it dripped down her face sharpened her appetite.

'The beach shack here does really good food. We can have lunch before driving down to my parents' place.'

When they had changed, they went to the restaurant at the edge of the beach. It was a basic wooden shack right on the sand, with simple picnic tables and benches outside. It was obviously a popular spot, full of tanned, sun-kissed surfers refuelling with burgers and freshly caught fish, washed down with bottles of ice-cold beer. They ordered a large seafood platter to share and a couple of beers, and Lisa dug in hungrily to the mouth-watering selection of prawns, crab and razor clams. She caught Grayson watching her with a mixture of awe and amusement as she peeled a prawn and dipped it into the bowl of delicious spicy sauce on the side.

'What?' she asked.

He grinned, shaking his head. 'It's just great to see you cutting loose like this – enjoying yourself and having fun. I've never seen you so relaxed.'

'I *am* having fun,' she said. 'And this food is amazing.' She popped the prawn into her mouth. The physical exertion and the tangy sea air had given her one hell of an appetite.

'It is,' he said, reaching for a crab claw. 'But we'd better save some room for dinner. My mum's expecting us, and she'll be cooking up a storm. She likes to feed people.'

'Will your sisters be there?' Lisa asked, a little nervous about meeting Grayson's family.

'No, just Mum and Dad. Alison and Emma still live in London, and Sarah is in Edinburgh.'

At least she wouldn't have to cope with meeting all of them at once, she thought, feeling a little less intimidated. 'I hope your parents won't mind me turning up.' They saw little enough of Grayson, as she understood it. They would probably rather have him to themselves.

'They'll be delighted to meet you, honestly,' he said with a little laugh, as if enjoying some private joke.

'Why do you say it like that?' she asked, alarmed. 'What did you tell them about me?'

He shrugged. 'Just that you're a friend I was spending some time with down here.'

A friend. She wondered were they used to him bringing friends home to spend the night – women friends who shared his bed. Had Isabel stayed with him at his parents' house?

Damn! She shook her head as she caught her thoughts straying. She had promised herself she wouldn't over-think this, and here she was doing exactly that. She resolved anew to just go with the flow, enjoy her time with Grayson for what it was and not stress about making it last or trying to turn it into something more.

'My mum's always complaining she doesn't see enough of me,' he continued. 'She'll be absolutely thrilled with you if you're luring me down to Cornwall more often.' He smiled at her and lifted his beer bottle, throwing his head back as he took a long slug, so he didn't see her flush of pleasure. She couldn't help feeling pleased by the implication that he wanted to spend more time with her and his assumption that they would be seeing a lot more of each other from now on.

Despite Grayson's assurances, Lisa's nerves returned as they got closer to where his parents lived. They drove through the quaint village of Polperro and out the other side.

'That's it.' Grayson pointed to a large white house perched on the side of a cliff, standing out brightly against the blue sky. A few minutes later, they pulled up outside a set of electric gates. Grayson leant out to enter a code into the panel, and the gates opened onto a paved granite driveway.

'Gosh, what an amazing house!' Lisa gasped as they pulled up in a carport to the rear of the property.

Grayson smiled at her as they got out of the car. He took their overnight bags out of the trunk, grabbing them both with one hand.

'Come on,' he said, taking Lisa's hand and leading her around to the front of the house.

Lisa didn't know which way to look as they rounded onto a slate-covered terrace, planted with mature trees and exotic plants and shrubs. In front of her there were stunning views over the wide expanse of the bay, and steps led down through a series of smaller terrace gardens to a little beach at the bottom of the cliff. Behind her, the house was as stunning as its setting. Its stucco facade standing out stark white against the blue sky, it was a classic example of art deco architecture, with its flat roof and bold geometric shapes, the walls a mixture of lines and curves. A rounded glass-block wall in its centre divided the house in two, and on either side, a wide railed deck at the upper floor faced out to sea.

Grayson smiled at her reaction as she stood there gaping speechlessly. 'We can explore later,' he said. 'Let's go inside.' He led her towards the huge oak door. It opened before they got to it, and a tall, slender woman with ash-blonde hair stood on the step smiling at them welcomingly.

'Hi, Mum.' Grayson dropped the bags as he leant in to kiss her cheek, and they embraced. 'This is Lisa,' he said as he pulled back. His mother turned to Lisa, holding out her hand.

'Hello, Mrs Fielding,' Lisa smiled, shaking her outstretched hand. 'It's lovely to meet you.'

'Call me Janet, please,' she smiled warmly. 'I'm very pleased to meet you, Lisa. Well, come in, both of you.' They followed her into a double height entrance hall with floors of polished oak. 'Grayson, you can bring Lisa to your room and show her where everything is. Dinner's almost ready. Come on down when you've dumped your stuff and sorted yourselves out.'

'Where's Dad?' Grayson asked as they headed for the wide, open-tread staircase.

'He's just gone to get a few things in the village. He'll be back shortly.'

The delicious smell of roasting meat wafted from

somewhere else in the house as Grayson led Lisa upstairs. He opened a door off the landing and waved her ahead of him into a large, airy room with walls painted a soft corn-flower blue and pale wood floorboards. A big bed faced glass-paned double doors leading out onto the deck, and white muslin curtains blew softly in the gentle breeze from the half-open windows.

'What a beautiful room,' she said, automatically drawn to the balcony doors that stood slightly ajar. She pushed them open and stepped out onto the wide deck that looked out over the sea.

She heard Grayson follow her outside. He wrapped his arms around her, resting his chin on her shoulder as she leaned against the rail and took a deep breath of salty sea air.

'Thank you for coming,' he said. He nuzzled into her neck and dropped a soft kiss on her shoulder.

She turned in his arms. 'Thank you for bringing me,' she said, smiling up at him.

There was the sound of a car door banging followed by the crunch of feet on the gravel below. A rangy grey-haired man appeared around the side of the house and gave them a cheery wave, smiling up at them.

'Come on,' Grayson said, disentangling his arms from around her. 'Come and meet Dad.'

Downstairs, Grayson led Lisa into a large open-plan living/dining room, dominated by a wall of floor-to-ceiling windows at one end overlooking the wide expanse of the bay. In front of them, a long table was set for dinner.

'Good timing,' Janet said, looking up as they entered. 'Everything's just ready.' She was laying dishes on the table, while Grayson's father opened wine.

'Dad, this is Lisa,' Grayson said, ushering her forward with a hand at her back.

'Very pleased to meet you, Lisa,' Mr Fielding said with a warm smile as he shook her hand. 'I'm Don.'

He was tall and lean, and had the same blue eyes and strong, square jaw as Grayson. His hair was mostly grey now, but thick and luxuriant, and he was still a handsome man. Lisa could tell he would have been just as devastatingly attractive as his son when he was younger.

'This looks great, Mum,' Grayson said as they took their seats at the table.

'Well, it's nothing special, but there's plenty of it.' Janet began to pass around dishes. 'I hope you're both hungry.'

'Starving!' Grayson grinned, catching Lisa's eye. 'We worked up quite an appetite surfing earlier.'

'Surfing?' Don raised his eyebrows. 'You haven't been surfing for a long time.'

'No. I'd forgotten how much I love it. Lisa reminded me.'

'Well, that's good news,' Don said, smiling approvingly at Lisa. 'Hopefully that means we'll see more of you down here,' he said to Grayson. 'There's not much surfing in London.'

Lisa was relieved to find she still had quite an appetite despite gorging herself on seafood earlier, and she was able to do justice to the delicious food. There was roast chicken with stuffing, cheesy gratin potatoes, buttered leeks, and carrots roasted with cumin and garlic.

'You have a beautiful home,' she said to Janet. 'This house is amazing.'

'Thank you. But Grayson can take most of the credit.' She nodded at her son proudly.

'Oh?' Lisa turned to him. 'You designed it?'

'Partly,' he said with a shrug. 'It was mainly a restoration job, but there was some restyling involved.'

'The house was originally built in the thirties,' Don told her, 'but it had been vacant for about twenty years when we found it.'

'It was practically derelict,' Janet added.

'But we fell in love with it, and we had to have it – even though there were lots of perfectly lovely houses around here ready to move into, that would have been far more suitable for a retired couple. We just kept coming back to this place. We couldn't get it out of our heads.'

It was easy to see why the house would have got such a grip on them. The location and setting alone were outstanding, and even as an empty shell, some of the house's former glory and future potential must have shone through. 'Lucky you have such a talented architect in the family, then.' She smiled at Grayson.

'Yes, Grayson did an amazing job on it,' Janet said. 'It was his retirement gift to us.'

Not only talented, but generous too, Lisa thought. She liked that Grayson was close to his family. It made her admire him even more than she already did.

'Are you from around here, Lisa?' Don asked her.

'No, I grew up in London. I just moved down here about six months ago. I live in Porth Heron now.'

'What brought you to Cornwall?'

'I just … wanted a change,' she said to Don, shifting uncomfortably.

'Do you have connections in Porth Heron? Family?'

She shook her head. 'No, I'd only been there on holidays once when I was a child.' She smiled fondly at the memory.

Grayson raised his eyebrows. 'With your grandparents?'

She nodded, realising she hadn't told him that before. She felt Don and Janet looking between the two of them. She hoped it didn't strike them as odd that Grayson seemed to know so little about his overnight guest.

'So, how did you two meet?' Janet asked, looking at her.

Lisa hesitated, not sure what to say. Grayson's parents were so kind and welcoming, she hated not being completely honest with them. But there was no way she could tell them that they had met when her ex-boyfriend had brought her to Grayson's house for an evening of partner-swapping.

'We met at a dinner party,' Grayson said smoothly. 'Through a … an acquaintance of Isabel's.'

'You knew each other in London, then?' Janet asked.

'Yes,' Lisa said. 'But we'd … lost touch.'

'It's thanks to you that I found Lisa again,' Grayson said, turning to his father. 'She did that painting you admired at my house recently.'

'Ah, so you're an artist?' Don asked her.

'Well, not professionally or anything,' Lisa said, 'but—'

'Yes, she is,' Grayson said firmly, frowning at her slightly.

'Well, you're a very talented young lady,' Don said.

'Thank you,' Lisa blushed.

'She is.' Grayson shot her an admiring look that made Lisa swell with pride. 'Anyway, you said you'd seen a painting just like it for sale in the market in Porth Heron.'

'Of course – and that's where you live now,' he said to Lisa. 'So I was right!' he said delightedly.

'Yes,' Lisa smiled.

'Well, I'm glad I was able to bring the two of you together again,' Don said.

'Me too,' Grayson said, looking at Lisa. 'Very glad.'

Don and Janet were so warm and friendly, Lisa soon felt completely at ease with them. They bombarded her with questions, but it was obvious that their curiosity stemmed from genuine interest and a real desire to get to know her, and it didn't feel intrusive or unwelcome. They encouraged her to talk about herself, gently drawing her out until they knew all about her childhood with her grandparents, her move to Cornwall, and her life in Porth Heron. There were lots of things she left out, of course. She didn't want them to know her whole story – the sad, sorry tale of Mark and what a naive idiot she'd been with him; the truth about how she'd met their son and the sordid nature of their previous relationship; the whole sorry mess she'd made of her life. But despite her omissions, she felt she could be herself with them.

They told her about themselves in turn. Don had been a barrister in London, and Janet had been a psychotherapist with a busy private practice at their home in Hampstead before they had retired to Cornwall. They spoke with great affection and humour about their family, and proudly showed Lisa photographs of their grandchildren. By the time they were having coffee on the terrace, the distant sound of waves crashing on the rocks far below, Lisa felt as if she had known them all her life.

Nevertheless, it had been a tiring day and she felt a little drained from all the exertion and excitement. So much had happened in such a short space of time, and she felt in need of some breathing space. So she was grateful when Grayson caught her stifling a yawn and suggested that she might like to go up to their room while he helped his parents clear up. She took him up on the offer readily and said her goodnights to Janet and Don, thanking them for their hospitality.

11

'THANKS, MUM,' Grayson said as he helped his mother stack the dishwasher while his father cleared up outside. He had sensed that Lisa was feeling a little overwhelmed and would appreciate a bit of time to herself, so he'd suggested she go ahead to their room while he stayed behind to help clear away the dishes.

'Oh, it was nothing special,' his mother said, bending to stack plates in the machine.

He smiled. 'Not just for dinner. For being so kind to Lisa.'

'Well, who wouldn't be?' she said, straightening. 'She's a sweetheart.' She looked at him carefully. 'She's special, isn't she? To you, I mean.'

Grayson nodded. 'Yes, she is. Very special.'

His mother smiled. 'She's lovely, Grayson. But there's something about her.' She gave a worried frown. 'She seems ... I don't know ... fragile. She reminds me a little of some of my old PTSD patients.'

Grayson sighed, leaning back against the sink. He should have known something like that wouldn't slip past

83

his mother. She was trained to see trauma and damage; to spot the tiny, almost imperceptible cracks on an apparently smooth, flawless facade. 'She was in a bad relationship when we … when I knew her before, in London.' He frowned, suppressing a shudder as he thought of the way he and Lisa had met when, without her consent – without even her knowledge – Mark had brought her to his house for him to fuck. As if she were his toy to share with whomever he pleased. He paled, his fist clenching at the thought of what he might have done to her that night if he hadn't found out in time that she wasn't a willing participant in Mark's games. It still haunted him. 'Really bad,' he said.

His mother frowned, concern etched on her face. 'Well, I'm glad she's found you, then,' she said, putting a hand on his cheek, her troubled expression clearing as she smiled fondly at him.

Grayson couldn't help smiling back, her faith in him chasing away some of the shadows. He just hoped he could live up to it – that he could be good for Lisa.

When they had finished tidying up in the kitchen and said goodnight, he went upstairs. When he entered the bedroom, the doors to the deck were open and Lisa was outside, leaning against the railing, her back to him. She had changed into a short silky nightdress, the thin material shivering against her skin in the soft evening breeze.

'Hello,' he said quietly so as not to startle her as he stepped out onto the terrace. He stood behind her, placing his hands over hers on the rail, his body pressed lightly against her back. He dropped a kiss on her bare shoulder. She took a slow, deep breath, then let out a long sigh.

'It's so beautiful here,' she said, gazing out to sea. The sound of the waves crashing below carried on the air.

'It is.' He lifted her hair, pushing it aside to trail soft

kisses across her neck, her ear, her shoulder. He felt his cock stir as she shivered lightly against him, a soft moan escaping her lips as he nibbled her earlobe. His hands drifted slowly to her breasts, cupping their soft weight in his palms, her nipples hardening beneath the thin material as he stroked them gently. Christ, he wanted her so much.

Overtaken by a sudden desperate ache for her, he slid a hand between her legs gratified to find she was already wet. Knowing she wanted him too caused a surge of excitement deep within him, that set his pulses racing. She gasped softly as he slid a finger inside her. Her breathing deepened, her hands tightening on the railing as he stroked her slowly, languorously while he pressed soft, wet kisses on her neck and shoulders. She trembled in his arms, moaning softly as he pumped two fingers inside her. He quickened his pace, her skin hot and feverish as he sucked and nibbled on her neck and ears. She cried out as his fingers found her clit, rubbing the sensitive nub until she was gasping and moaning with pleasure. His heart pounded as he felt her excitement mount to a climax, and he kept up the pressure until her knees buckled and she sagged, shuddering in his arms, crying out her release. Her sticky arousal coated his fingers as she came, and he tightened his arms around her to hold her up as wave after wave racked her body. When she stilled, he withdrew his fingers and turned her to face him.

Her face was flushed, her pupils wide and dark with desire. The need to be inside her, to bury himself in all her warmth and softness, was overwhelming.

'Lisa,' he whispered, reaching down to grab the hem of her nightdress. But he felt her stiffen as he lifted it, pulling it slowly up her legs. He stilled, the material bunched in his hands. Her breathing was shallow, her eyes darting around nervously.

'We're not overlooked here,' he said, his voice husky with desire. He looked at her questioningly, asking for permission. 'Please,' he said when she hesitated. 'I want to see you.'

He held his breath as she bit her lip uncertainly, still hesitating. And then, miraculously, she looked up at him and nodded quickly, her eyes urgent with need.

He pulled the silky material slowly up her body, his fingers playing lightly over her skin. He took it off over her head and dropped it on the deck at their feet, and then he just stood back and gazed at her, letting his eyes drift leisurely over her, drinking in the perfection of her naked body. Moonlight played across her skin so it appeared almost translucent as his gaze lingered on her soft, rounded abdomen and the curve of her hips. Her breasts were swollen with desire, the pink nipples hard and taut. She had always been beautiful, but now she was a goddess. Her body was full and lush where before it was all flat plains and sharp angles, the bones and hollows replaced by soft curves.

'I want you so much,' he said, his voice thick with desire as he reached for her.

'I want you too, Grayson,' she said breathily. Her eyes locked with his and his heart leapt at her open unguarded expression. The frank desire in her eyes combined with those words on her lips affected him deeply. He swallowed a lump in his throat, incredibly moved and humbled that she could trust him enough after all she had been through to stand naked in front of him and tell him she wanted him. He felt privileged that she could allow herself to be so vulnerable with him.

Her hands went to the waistband of his jeans, her fingers fumbling in their haste as she undid the button, while he pulled his T-shirt off over his head. He quickly removed the rest of his clothes, and his skin flushed beneath her heated gaze. Then he pulled her into his arms, a deep shudder racking his body as his naked skin met hers. He bent his head to kiss her, and her mouth opened against his while his hands roamed over her body, exploring every inch, every swell and hollow. She was so soft and hot and wet. Their feverish breath mingled as their kisses deepened, tongues tangling as they devoured each other's mouths hungrily. Then he lifted her and she wrapped her legs and arms around him, crying out as he sank himself inside her with a groan.

'Mmm, I could stay like this forever,' Grayson said sleepily the next morning. They were spooned in his bed, Lisa's back curled into his front.

'Me too,' she sighed. She turned to face him, yawning deeply.

'Tired?' He smiled, brushing a strand of hair off her face.

She nodded. 'I didn't get much sleep last night.'

'Me neither.' Grayson grinned. 'And yet I've never felt so good. That was the best sleepless night I've ever had.'

They had made love endlessly, first outside on the deck under the stars, and later here in his bed, slowly and languorously, savouring each other. Grayson had held her hand as he moved inside her, groaning her name as he came.

'I wish I didn't have to go back to London today.' He sighed, running a hand through his hair. 'But I have a bunch of meetings I have to get back for tomorrow.'

She nodded understandingly, trying not to let it show how much she wanted to cling to him. This weekend had been wonderful, and she couldn't bear the thought that it had to end. But she knew it wasn't real life and it never could be. She and Grayson were worlds apart in every way. The past two days had been like a lovely holiday, a time out for both of them. She would just enjoy it for what it was, and savour it as a precious memory when Grayson was gone.

'I didn't know if I'd even find you,' he murmured, a finger tracing a pattern on her shoulder. 'And if I did, I didn't know if you'd want to see me. I wasn't expecting … this.'

'Neither was I.'

'So what happens now? Can I see you again?'

She tried to ignore the frantic leaping of her heart. She needed to be sensible about this. There were so many reasons why it wouldn't be a good idea for her to get involved with Grayson. If only he was on the same page as her – then she'd say yes in a heartbeat. But she knew that he wasn't, so it was better to stop this now before she got in any deeper. 'I'm not sure that's a good idea,' she said, lowering her eyes, unable to look at him.

'Oh.' She looked up and was shocked by his stricken expression. She hadn't expected him to take it so badly.

'Okay,' he said. His jaw clenched, and she could tell he was struggling to cope with his disappointment. 'I thought —I mean, last night—' He broke off with a frustrated sigh.

'Last night was lovely, Grayson.' She bit her lip, struggling to find the right words. 'This weekend has been … perfect. But it was just a one-off thing, wasn't it?'

'It doesn't have to be. I'd really like to see you again, Lisa. I guess I thought you felt the same way.'

'I do.' She sighed. 'I'd like that too. But … it's complicated.'

'How so?'

She shrugged. 'We have … very different lives. I live here, you live in London.'

'That's hardly insurmountable,' he said, his features relaxing a little. 'Yes, my work is in London. But I could come here at weekends.'

'It's a long way to come for a weekend.'

He shook his head. 'Not for you. I'd go to the ends of the earth, Lisa.'

Her breath hitched as their eyes locked and held, taken aback by the depth of emotion in Grayson's gaze. But it didn't frighten her, like Mark's intensity had. She knew Grayson would walk away and leave her alone if she wanted him to. She also knew she really didn't want him to.

'It's not as if it's another planet,' Grayson continued. 'And if it was, I'd just have to buy a spaceship,' he added with a crooked smile. 'People do the long-distance thing all the time, and over much greater distances.'

She really wanted to say yes, but she had to protect herself too. Could she handle a long-distance relationship with Grayson? What would it even mean to him? She thought of Isabel. Could she risk letting herself fall in love with him knowing what she did about his free-spirited attitude to sex? Would she be driven crazy with jealousy not knowing what he was doing all week in London or who he was with?

She bit her lip, scrabbling around in her brain for words that would make him understand. 'I just think we're very different people,' she said. 'We want different things.'

He frowned, tilting his head to the side. 'Such as?'

Lisa shrugged. Because what could she say? She couldn't very well demand exclusivity on the basis of two days together.

'I think we've got a lot in common,' Grayson continued

when she didn't answer. 'We both like playing chess and surfing. We like being together,' he said tentatively, looking at her questioningly.

She nodded. 'I love being with you, Grayson.'

'I don't want to crowd you,' he said earnestly. 'I know you need your space, and any time you want me to go, just say the word and I'll disappear. But what we have … it's too special to just let it go without even trying.'

She nodded, taking his hand. Who was she kidding? She was already in too deep with Grayson. She wanted to be with him any way she could be, even if it meant he had a whole other life away from her that she would know nothing about. Maybe the less she knew, the better. She could enjoy her time with him for what it was – make the most of having him at weekends and try not to think about what he did when he was away from her. When he was here, he'd be hers alone.

'I don't know about you,' he said, 'but this sort of thing doesn't happen to me every day. I've never been—' He broke off. 'I've never felt this way about anyone before,' he finished.

'I feel the same, Grayson. This has never happened to me before either.'

'So … we're going to do this?' His face lit up hopefully.

She smiled. 'Yes. Let's try the long-distance thing. It might not work, but—'

His face cleared with relief. 'We'll make it work,' he said. He lifted her hand to his lips and kissed it. 'I promise.'

12

———

'WHERE DID you disappear to at the weekend? Katya asked her. It was the following evening and they had met up for a drink after work. The weather was still mild, and they sat outside a pub overlooking the harbour, sharing a bottle of wine. 'We didn't see you at all.'

'Oh, a … an old friend turned up unexpectedly on Friday and we ended up spending the weekend together.' She took a sip of her wine. 'I hadn't seen him in ages, so we had a lot of catching up to do.'

'*Him?*' Katya emphasised the word suggestively, raising her eyebrows.

Lisa knew her answering smile gave her away, but she couldn't help it.

'Interesting,' Katya said. 'Tell me more.'

'He's just someone I used to know in London,' Lisa shrugged. 'We lost touch when I moved here.' She smiled dreamily to herself as she thought of Grayson. 'It was really good to see him again.'

'You say old friend,' Katya said with a sly smile, 'but

I'm getting more of an old flame vibe from you. Were you involved with him before?'

'Not really. We were chess buddies mostly,' she said, skirting around the edges of the truth. There was no way she could tell Katya the details of her twisted relationship with Grayson. 'I guess we liked each other a lot. But we were both with other people at the time, so nothing could happen,' she finished with a shrug.

'But you're not anymore. Is he single now too?'

'Yeah.' Lisa blushed. As far as she knew, Grayson was as single as he'd always been.

'So you're free to be more than chess buddies!' Katya beamed delightedly. 'And he came all the way down here to see you. It sounds like he's smitten.'

'Well, his parents live near Polperro. He stopped off here on his way to visit them.'

'So what did you get up to at the weekend?' Katya asked. 'Apart from the obvious,' she added with a grin.

'You mean apart from playing chess?' Lisa said with a laugh. 'We went surfing. And we stayed over with his parents on Saturday night.'

'It sounds pretty serious if you're already spending time with his parents.'

Lisa shook her head. 'It's not − not yet anyway. It's … I'm not sure what it is, to be honest.'

'New flame maybe?'

'Yeah, maybe,' Lisa said shyly. 'We're going to try the long-distance thing.'

'Great! So when do we get to meet him?'

Lisa faltered, overcome by an inexplicable feeling of dread in the pit of her stomach. 'I don't know. He's coming back next weekend, but I don't think we'll be going out.'

Katya grinned. 'You'd rather spend all your time together in bed?' She wiggled her eyebrows mischievously.

Lisa laughed, relieved that Katya was letting it go. 'Yeah, something like that.'

'That's understandable when you spend so much time apart. Long distance relationships are hard. Connor and I did it for a while, before we moved here.' She took a sip of her wine. 'But they have their compensations. The time you do spend together can be pretty intense.'

There were other benefits to a long-distance relationship, Lisa decided as she settled back into her normal routine for the rest of the week – working at the cafe during the day, painting in the evenings, spending time with her friends – the mundane rhythm of everyday life grounding her. She couldn't wait to see Grayson again, but she didn't want to spend all her time aimlessly awaiting his return, counting off the minutes until they could be together again. She wanted him to be a part of her life, not the whole of it. She had let herself be so consumed by Mark that her entire existence had revolved around him. If that was a tendency she had inside her, maybe this was an ideal situation for her. She would have no choice but to get on with her life during their time apart; to build a life separate from Grayson that had purpose and meaning. She wouldn't be in danger of making him her sole focus and source of happiness.

Nevertheless, she couldn't suppress her mounting impatience as the weekend approached. With their time together so limited, it didn't seem unreasonable to let those two days be entirely given over to him. When Friday rolled around, she couldn't contain her excitement any longer, and she felt agitated and jittery all day as she looked forward to Grayson's arrival.

'Do you want to come to the pub tomorrow night?'

Martha asked her as they closed up the cafe. 'There's a table quiz in aid of the Search and Rescue, and a few of us are making up a team. You're welcome to join us.'

'Thanks, but Grayson's coming for the weekend.' She had told Martha about their fledgling long-distance relationship.

'Well, why don't you bring him along?' Martha said with a smile. 'We'd all love to meet him.'

'Thanks, but … maybe another time,' Lisa said. She felt awkward, but she really didn't think answering trivia questions over pints in the local pub would be Grayson's idea of a good time.

'Yes, another time,' Martha said briskly as she wiped the counter. Lisa thought she detected a false note in her breezy tone and hoped she wasn't offended at her turning down the invitation. The last thing she wanted was to hurt Martha's feelings.

'Well, have a great weekend,' Martha said, and to Lisa's relief there was nothing forced in her cheerful tone now. 'Have fun with your mystery man.'

'Thanks,' Lisa smiled. 'I will.'

She went grocery shopping on her way home and stocked up for Grayson's visit, spending more than she should on luxurious food, splashing out on fillet steak and smoked salmon, luxurious chocolate and cheese, crusty sourdough bread and a couple of bottles of the best wine she could afford.

She bumped into Katya as she made her way home, laden down with bags.

'Hey, are you coming to Connor's gig tonight?' Katya asked her. 'He's playing at the Smuggler's Rest. I could pick you up.'

'Thanks, but Grayson's coming tonight.' She lifted her bags, indicating her shopping.

'Why don't you bring him?' Katya said enthusiastically.

'Thanks, but … I think we'll just have a quiet night in.'

'Oh okay.' Katya's face fell, but she brightened again quickly. 'I guess you're not ready for the outside world yet.'

'Yeah, it's early days.'

'Well, have fun! If you change your mind, you know where we are.'

Lisa felt bad as she walked away, a little of her pleasure at the thought of seeing Grayson ebbing away. Maybe she just wasn't cut out for relationships – even long-distance ones. It was so hard juggling people's demands on your time, trying to give all your relationships the attention they deserved and keep everyone happy. If she was going to do this, she had to make a real effort to spend more time with her friends during the week when Grayson wasn't around.

'What happened to spaghetti and meatballs?' Grayson asked later as they ate dinner.

Lisa had cooked fillet steaks with mushrooms and onions, roasted vine tomatoes, sauté potatoes and pepper sauce.

'Don't you like it?'

'It's delicious. But you shouldn't be spending your money on me.'

She shrugged. 'I wanted to treat you,' she said, blushing as soon as the words were out of her mouth. It was ridiculous to think that she could treat Grayson. He could eat like this every day of the week, and the wine that she considered an extravagance was probably like supermarket plonk compared to the stuff he was accustomed to drinking.

'Well, thank you. I feel very spoiled.'

'You're welcome,' she smiled, pleased that he appreciated the effort she'd made. After all, she reminded herself, it was the thought that counted, and she'd put a lot of effort into making this dinner special.

For dessert she served berries with thick, creamy Greek yoghurt drizzled with honey, and they chatted about what they had been doing during the week. But every so often, when he thought she wasn't looking, Grayson's smile faded and Lisa caught him glancing at her warily. She felt he was on the verge of saying something he knew she wouldn't like. But then he'd catch her eye and smile again, and she'd think she'd imagined it.

'I was talking to Isabel the other day,' he said finally, pushing away his empty bowl.

'Oh?' He had that cagey look again as Lisa glanced at him, and it filled her with foreboding.

'Yes.' Grayson cleared his throat, looking down at the table before continuing. 'She saw Mark last week at some exhibition.'

Lisa heard the apprehension in his tone and swallowed hard. She wasn't sure she wanted to hear more, but she got the feeling Grayson wanted to tell her.

His eyes flicked up to hers. 'He was with someone.'

Lisa frowned. 'You mean …'

'It seems he has a new girlfriend,' Grayson said with a shrug that was meant to appear casual, but didn't come off that way. 'I wasn't sure if you'd want to know.'

Lisa didn't know what to say. She wasn't sure how she felt.

'Isabel thought you might know her,' Grayson continued. 'Her name's Rose, and she's an artist. I think she may have gone to college with you?'

'Rose!' Lisa gasped. Her heart started to pound in her throat, and her skin felt clammy. She didn't know why she suddenly felt so unsettled. 'Yes, I do know her,' she said, her throat tight. Her stomach lurched queasily.

Grayson was watching her carefully. 'Do you mind?'

She hardly knew what she felt, but it must be obvious to Grayson that the news had shocked her and that she wasn't happy about it.

'I'm not jealous, if that's what you mean. I don't want Mark back – not at all. But …'She bit her lip, trying to identify exactly what she was feeling.

'I thought you'd be glad that he's moved on. You wouldn't have to worry about him trying to find you anymore.'

Lisa frowned. She couldn't explain it. Logically she knew Grayson was right – she should be glad that Mark had found someone else. She could be completely free of him at last. She wouldn't have to worry about him bothering her if she should move back to London. But she wasn't happy – not at all. She just couldn't put her finger on why.

It wasn't jealousy – she was sure of that much. She thought of the last time she had seen Rose, when she had bumped into her on Bond Street shortly before Mark left for China. She had been so full of energy and excitement about her upcoming solo show. The world seemed to be opening up before her. She was young and carefree, and seemed on the cusp of something big, her life full of promise and possibility. Lisa had envied her *then* – not now. She hated to think of Mark squashing all that youthful exuberance, turning that vivacious, vibrant girl into a cowering shadow of herself as he'd done to her.

'Was this Rose a friend of yours?' Grayson asked.

She felt dazed and realised she'd been silent for a long time. 'No.' She shook herself back to the present. 'We were at college together, but we weren't particular friends.'

'But you don't like the idea of her being with Mark,' Grayson said.

She shook her head gravely. 'I wouldn't wish Mark on my worst enemy,' she said. 'I hate to think of him treating someone else the way he treated me.'

'Maybe he'll be different with her.'

'Maybe,' she said, unconvinced. She didn't think Mark would ever change, not really. But perhaps Rose would be stronger than she had been. Maybe she'd stand up to him and not let him control and manipulate her. Suddenly she recognised the feeling she hadn't been able to pinpoint. That corrosive gnawing in her gut wasn't jealousy; it was guilt.

'Rose doesn't know what he's like,' she said. 'No one does. He can be so charming. She doesn't know what she's getting into, and I feel like it's my fault.'

'Why?' He frowned. 'You're not responsible for Mark.'

'No, but … I know it doesn't make sense.' She shook her head. 'But maybe if I'd stood up to him, if I'd been braver—'

'None of it is your fault,' Grayson interrupted, covering her hand with his. 'You had nobody. You were vulnerable and alone, and Mark took advantage of that. He abused your love and your trust, and that's all on him. You're not to blame for anything, Lisa.'

'But maybe if I'd spoken up – if I'd let people know what he was really like, maybe Rose wouldn't even be with him now.' She sighed. 'If only I could talk to her, try to warn her somehow …'

'She probably wouldn't want to hear it,' Grayson said. 'She'll find out for herself soon enough.'

Lisa knew he was probably right. Rose wouldn't welcome her interference, and besides, how could she even find a way to talk to her? They weren't friends. She could only hope that Rose would be stronger than she was, and that if Mark was abusive towards her, she would have the strength to walk out.

Lisa tried to put all thoughts of Mark behind her and had another idyllic weekend with Grayson. They surfed, swam, played chess and made love endlessly. On Saturday, Grayson's parents took them to dinner at a wonderful seafood restaurant in Polperro and they spent the night at their house again. Don and Janet were as friendly and welcoming as the first time she'd met them, and the more Lisa got to know them, the fonder she became of them.

After brunch at their house on Sunday, Grayson dropped her home before heading to the airport for his evening flight. Lisa's heart sank a little as he parked outside her flat and cut the engine. A whole week without him stretched out before her – seven long days before she could touch him or kiss him or feel his arms around her – and it seemed like an endless time to wait.

Grayson turned to her, sighing deeply as he took her in his arms.

'I wish you could stay,' she breathed against his mouth as he bent his head to hers.

'Me too.' He gave her a long, lingering kiss and Lisa hugged him closer, breathing him in, as if she could somehow absorb the smell and feel of him and store it up for when she was alone.

He pulled back with a reluctant sigh and rested his forehead on hers. 'I wish you were coming to London with me,' he said, his thumb tracing her jaw line. 'This long-distance thing is harder than I thought.'

'I know. It's the same for me. But my life is here now.'

He nodded. 'I just miss you so much when we're apart.'

He leaned in and nuzzled her face, placing soft kisses on her lips, her eyes, her cheeks.

'Me too,' Lisa sighed as he pulled back. 'But there are advantages to the long-distance thing too.'

'Really?' He gave her a sceptical look. 'How so?'

'Well, at least this way you won't get bored with me so easily.'

He rolled his eyes. 'Like that's a possibility.'

'If we saw each other all the time, you'd get tired of me soon enough.'

He shook his head. 'Never.' He leaned in and kissed her again, his lips clinging to hers as if they never wanted to let go. 'I'll never get enough of you,' he said.

13

'I'm beginning to wonder if this Grayson really exists,' Katya said, topping up her glass from the pitcher of margarita in the centre of the table.

'You think I invented an imaginary boyfriend?' Lisa laughed.

'Well, he allegedly spends all his weekends here, but I've never seen him. Have you, Martha?'

'Nope.' Martha dipped a tortilla chip into guacamole and popped it into her mouth. 'But I think he exists all right,' she said with a sideways smile at Lisa. 'I don't think an imaginary boyfriend would give her that glow.'

It was Friday night, and they were all seated cross-legged on the floor around Lisa's coffee table.

'I have a glow?'

Katya nodded. 'Just a little, yeah.'

'It can probably be seen from outer space,' Martha said dryly.

Lisa knew she was smiling goofily, but she couldn't help it. Just the thought of Grayson made her feel warm and happy, and tingly all over. She wasn't surprised it was visible to other people.

'Besides,' Martha added to Katya, 'where do you think she disappears off to every weekend?'

Lisa had spent the last three weekends in a row with Grayson, and they had all been as perfect as the first. She would cook dinner for him on Friday and they'd stay in and catch up, and then they'd spend the next two precious days wrapped up in each other, whether they were in bed or taking trips along the coast. Their time together was intense and blissful, and every Sunday evening when Grayson had to leave was harder than the last. She missed him so much when they were apart, aching for his touch, the feel of his body next to hers, the warmth of his smile. They spoke on the phone often, but it wasn't the same as having him there with her.

Despite that, she had planned to spend this Friday night with her friends. She was still haunted by how she had let herself become isolated when she was with Mark, and she was determined that she would never again ditch her friends for the sake of a man. So she'd been making a conscious effort to spend more time with Katya and Martha during the week.

But they still complained that she never joined them in the pub on Friday nights anymore, or for Sunday dinner in Martha's. She felt guilty that she was spending less time with them. They'd both been such good friends to her, and she didn't want them to think she took them for granted. So she'd invited them over tonight for drinks and nachos, and put Grayson off coming until tomorrow.

'I need to get on with some work,' she'd told him when they spoke earlier in the week. 'I never paint when you're here, and there are some things I need to finish.' She felt awkward about lying to him, but she didn't want to hurt his feelings by telling him she simply wanted to have a girls' night with her friends.

'Sure,' he'd said readily. 'I wouldn't want to get in the way of your painting.'

She knew he was disappointed, and she hated cutting the little time they had together even shorter. But she forced herself to stay strong and resist the temptation to change her mind.

'I'll see you on Saturday? Maybe you could drive down on Friday anyway and spend the night with your parents. I'm sure they'd love to have you to themselves for once.'

'Nonsense. They love having you around, Lisa. But that's a good idea. That way, I could drive over to you in the morning and we'll still have almost two whole days together.'

'But when are we going to get to meet him?' Katya broke into Lisa's thoughts. 'I thought he might come to see our exhibition last week.'

Katya and Lisa along with several of their friends had donated paintings to a charity auction in the village hall the previous Wednesday, and there had been a small preview exhibition beforehand.

She shook her head. 'He can only come on weekends.'

'It's the weekend now,' Katya persisted. 'I thought he might be here tonight. Doesn't he usually come on Fridays?'

'He's spending tonight with his parents,' Lisa told her. 'He'll be here tomorrow.'

'You should bring him to the pub, then!' Katya said brightly. 'Connor's band are playing.'

Lisa shrugged noncommittally. 'Maybe. I don't think it's really his kind of thing, but we'll see.'

'Oh, back off, Katya,' Martha said good-naturedly. 'It's their first night together all week. I'm sure they've got better things to do than spend it down the pub with us.'

'True,' Katya laughed.

'But if he's still here on Sunday,' Martha said, 'why don't the two of you come to dinner at my place?'

Lisa smiled shakily. 'Thanks, Martha. I'll ask him, but he may already have made plans with his parents.'

'Well, you know you're always welcome. Anyway, we'll meet him next Saturday, won't we?' She looked expectantly at Lisa. It was her birthday and she had already invited Katya, Connor and Martha over for dinner to celebrate. She had planned it ages ago, but for some reason she still hadn't mentioned it to Grayson. 'He'll definitely be there, won't he?'

'Yeah … hopefully,' Lisa said awkwardly.

Martha's smile faded suddenly, and Lisa caught her and Katya exchanging worried looks.

'What?' she asked, looking between the two of them.

'It's just … you said you knew Grayson before when you were in London,' Martha began tentatively.

'Yes?'

'I know you told Katya you were just friends, but … was there more to it than that?'

'Sort of.' Lisa blushed, glancing at Katya. She brushed imaginary crumbs off her jeans, not sure how to answer. 'We had a bit of a fling' she said with a casual shrug. 'It was a very short-lived thing.'

'Sorry,' Martha said. 'I don't mean to pry. It's none of our business, and I know you don't like to talk about it, but we know you were in a bad relationship before you came here …'

'Oh, no!' Lisa gasped, suddenly grasping why they were concerned. 'It wasn't Grayson.'

'It wasn't?'

'No.' Lisa shook her head vehemently. 'In fact, he helped me get out of that relationship.'

'Well, that's a relief,' Katya said.

Martha visibly relaxed. 'Sorry, we don't mean to be nosy. We were just a bit worried.'

Lisa nodded. 'It's fine,' she smiled. 'I get it.' She'd been spending all this time with Grayson, but he'd never met her friends. She realised they were concerned that he was trying to isolate her, just as Mark had done. Far from resenting their interference, she felt incredibly lucky to have people who cared so much looking out for her.

'His name was Mark,' she said, resolving to tell them all about him some time. She felt bad that she'd been so reticent and guarded with them in the past. She'd shut them out, and they deserved for her to be more open with them. But she would tell them about Mark another time. Tonight was about having fun and she didn't want to spoil the light-hearted mood.

'Grayson couldn't be more different,' she said, smiling. 'He was a really good friend to me when I needed someone, and he never expected anything in return.'

'Well, I like him already,' Martha said, raising her glass. 'To the man who put that smile on your face!'

'To Grayson,' Lisa said softly, and they all clinked glasses.

Grayson arrived the following morning and offered to take Lisa out for brunch.

'Where's good to eat around here?' he asked. 'What about the cafe where you work?'

Lisa shrugged. 'It's a beautiful day. Why don't we go somewhere down by the sea? There's a nice place right by the harbour.'

'Sure. Lead the way.'

It was a mild autumn day as they strolled down to the restaurant hand-in-hand. They sat at a table overlooking the harbour and ordered strong black coffee and plates of huevos rancheros.

'How were your parents?' Lisa asked as they ate.

'Great. Though they were sorry not to see you. They're very fond of you, you know.'

Lisa smiled. 'I'm fond of them too. We could go and see them today, if you like?'

'Why don't we just stay here?' Grayson suggested. 'We never really spend any time here. You can show me around.'

'Sure, if you like. Though there isn't a whole lot to see.'

'It's where you live,' Grayson said. 'I'd like to be able to picture your life here – imagine what you do when I'm not around. So far all I've really seen is your bedroom. Not that I'm complaining,' he added with a grin. 'It's an area of outstanding natural beauty.'

Lisa smiled. 'Okay, I'll give you the tour, such as it is.'

'So, how was your week? Did you get much painting done last night?'

'Yeah, a bit,' Lisa hedged. 'Not as much as I'd hoped.'

'Should I have stayed away longer? You can just tell me, you know, if you want to get some work done without me around distracting you and leading you astray.'

'I like you distracting me,' she said, with a crooked smile.

Grayson took her hand across the table. 'I really missed you last night,' he said, his fingers curling around hers.

'Me too,' she said huskily as their eyes locked and held. 'I look forward all week to having you here, leading me astray.'

Grayson lifted her hand and held it between both of

his, playing with her fingers. 'So, that tour … does it take in your bedroom, by any chance?'

Lisa nodded. 'It starts there.' She gasped as his finger dug into her palm, heat building inside her. 'I know you've seen it before,' she said shakily, 'but—'

'It's always worth a repeat visit.'

The way he was looking at her as his finger stroked her palm sensuously was doing crazy things to her. Her insides melted and her blood felt like it was on fire. 'Let's get the bill and get out of here,' she said.

14

THEY WERE WALKING along the high street hand-in-hand, hurrying back to her flat, when Lisa saw Katya coming towards them. She felt unaccountably anxious as Katya spotted her and waved, quickening her steps to catch up with them.

'Hi!' she beamed as she reached them.

'Hi,' Lisa smiled back at her, but her face felt stiff. 'Grayson, this is my friend Katya,' she said to him. 'Katya, Grayson.' She felt her shoulders tense as she introduced them.

'Hi, Grayson!' Katya gave him a friendly smile, shielding her eyes from the sun as she held out her other hand to him. 'It's lovely to finally meet you. I've heard so much about you.'

'Really?' Grayson grinned, raising an eyebrow as he shook her hand firmly. 'I'm afraid I can't say the same.'

'I'm sure I've mentioned Katya,' Lisa mumbled defensively, a knot of tension forming in her stomach.

'Oh, don't worry about it.' Katya waved away her concern. 'Lisa doesn't get to see you that often,' she said to

Grayson. 'I'm sure she has better things to do than talk about me when she does. But we were actually starting to doubt your existence,' she said with a little laugh. 'Well, *I* was. Martha always believed you were real. It's a pity you couldn't make it to our exhibition last week.'

'Oh … yeah.' Grayson shrugged, giving Lisa a curious look.

Lisa willed her friend to stop babbling, too on edge to pay proper attention to what she was saying. She glanced at Grayson. He was chuckling as Katya prattled on, and he didn't appear to be annoyed. But maybe he was just being polite.

'You missed a good night last night' Katya said, unaware of Lisa's mounting tension. 'I think I went overboard on the margaritas, though. How was your head this morning, Lisa?'

'It was fine,' Lisa said quietly. She felt Grayson looking at her, but she couldn't meet his eyes. She just hoped he wasn't finding Katya too irritating.

'So what are you two up to today?' Katya asked breezily.

'Lisa's just showing me around the place. I wanted to see where she hangs out.'

'Well, in that case you should come to the Anchor tonight. I know it's not your kind of thing, but it's where everyone around here meets up.'

Grayson raised his eyebrows. 'Sounds good to me,' he said.

'My boyfriend's band are playing. They're really good.'

'Thanks,' Grayson said. 'Maybe we'll check that out.' He flicked a glance at Lisa.

'Yeah, maybe,' she said faintly.

'Great!' Katya smiled happily. 'Well, I might see you later, then.'

Lisa relaxed a little as she seemed about to go.

'And if not, maybe I'll see you at Martha's tomorrow? She's going to start taking it personally if you keep refusing her invitations to dinner.'

'Um … yeah, maybe.' Lisa gave Grayson a nervous glance

Katya laughed. 'Relax, I'm just kidding. Martha totally understands. And she'll get to meet you next week anyway,' she said to Grayson. 'You'll definitely be here for Lisa's birthday, won't you?'

Lisa's heart plummeted.

'Um … I—' Grayson looked at Lisa questioningly. 'I'm … not sure yet.'

'Oh.' Katya's smile faded and she looked taken aback. 'Well, I hope you can make it.' She cast a worried glance at Lisa.

Grayson frowned slightly. 'I'll … do my best.'

Lisa was grateful he hid his confusion from Katya, but she could tell he was puzzled – and hurt, she realised with a stab of guilt.

'Well, it was nice to meet you,' Katya said blithely to Grayson as she turned to go. 'See you both later maybe.' She gave them a cheery wave and strode away up the road.

'Sorry,' Lisa said as Katya walked away.

'For what?' He frowned.

Lisa shrugged. 'Katya – she chatters a bit.'

'I thought she seemed lovely.'

'She is.' She smiled, relieved that he didn't seem annoyed by Katya's prattling. He was obviously put out about something, though – and it wasn't hard to guess what. The mood had changed, and he fell silent as they started to walk back to the flat. His pace had slowed, all the urgency of earlier gone.

'So … big night last night?' he asked eventually.

'Not really.' Lisa blushed. 'I just had Katya and Martha over for dinner,' she shrugged, trying to play it down.

'Sounds fun. And what's this show that I wasn't able to make?'

'It was just a little exhibition we put on for a charity auction in the village hall.'

'You didn't mention it. I could have come if I'd known.'

'It wasn't a big deal – certainly not worth coming all the way down from London for.'

Grayson nodded, but she could tell he wasn't satisfied. 'Lisa, can I ask you something?' he said, stopping. He looked uncomfortable, and his hesitant tone unnerved her.

'Sure,' she said, her voice a little shaky. She licked her lips nervously, bracing herself for whatever he was about to say.

He looked at her carefully, his expression serious. 'Are you—' He paused for a moment, as if trying to formulate the question in his mind, unsure of what he wanted to ask. 'Are you ... seeing someone else?'

'No!' Lisa gasped, shocked. Where on earth had that come from? 'I promise, I'm not,' she said urgently, putting a hand on his arm and looking pleadingly into his eyes. 'I swear,' she said, panic mounting inside her.

'Hey, calm down,' Grayson said softly, putting a hand over hers. 'I mean, you can tell me if you are. It's fine. We haven't said anything about being exclusive. I suppose I just assumed ...' He sighed. 'I just want you to be honest with me.'

'I'm telling the truth. There's no one else. Why would you even think that?'

'Because you told me you wanted to work last night, and now it turns out you were partying with your friends.' He shrugged. 'I don't know what to think.'

'Look, I would have asked you to come, but it wasn't anything special – just Mexican food and beer.' She looked at him beseechingly.

Grayson huffed out a laugh. 'And what, I live on caviar and champagne? I like Mexican food and beer.'

Lisa's insides were starting to churn. He wasn't shouting at her – not yet. His tone was still reasonable and quiet, his manner calm. But she started to feel a familiar knot forming in her stomach, and she desperately needed to make this stop.

'I'm sorry,' she said, desperate to appease him. 'But Katya and Martha are good friends and I feel I haven't been spending enough time with them lately, so ...' She trailed off helplessly.

Grayson frowned, looking puzzled. 'It's not that.' He shook his head and let out an exasperated sigh. 'You wanted to spend a night with your friends – I get that. I don't expect an invitation. But why lie to me about it?'

'I just ... I didn't want to hurt your feelings, I guess.'

'It still doesn't explain why you were behaving so oddly when Katya was talking to me just now. You visibly tensed up, like you were terrified she was going to say something she shouldn't. What were you so afraid she was going to tell me?'

Lisa shrugged. 'Nothing. I was just worried she'd annoy you by talking too much.'

He frowned, looking unconvinced by her answer. He shoved his hands into his pockets and resumed walking. Lisa fell into step beside him.

'So it's your birthday next weekend?' he asked quietly, glancing at her.

'Um ... yeah. On Saturday.'

'Why didn't you tell me?'

Lisa shrugged. 'It's not the sort of thing you tell people

out of the blue, is it? I didn't want you to think I was angling for a present,' she said with a shaky smile, trying to make light of it.

He didn't smile back at her. 'It's something a boyfriend should know, isn't it? I'd like to give you a present, Lisa. I'd like to be with you on your birthday.'

Lisa squirmed uncomfortably. She took a deep breath. 'Look, I would have told you it was my birthday and suggested we do something to celebrate together, but I arranged ages ago to have people over for dinner, so ...' She shrugged helplessly.

Grayson frowned at her in bemusement. He was quiet for a moment, and she glanced across at him to find him looking at her warily. She felt slightly panicked by his solemn expression.

'Lisa, are you ... ashamed of me?'

'What?' she gasped incredulously. 'No! Of course not.' How could he think such a ridiculous thing?

'Ashamed of us, then – of our relationship?'

'No.'

'I know the way we met was pretty fucked up, but I thought we'd got past that. It doesn't have to define us.'

'It's not that.'

'Then why don't you want me to meet your friends? We never spend any time here, and even when we do you always seem to keep them away when I'm around. We don't go to the pub because apparently it's not 'my kind of thing'. We don't go for dinner with your friend Martha, though Katya seems to think I've been invited. And you clearly don't want me around on your birthday.'

Lisa stopped in her tracks. She was silent for a moment, too stunned to speak. Had she really been doing that – deliberately avoiding having Grayson and her friends meet? But as soon as he said it out loud, she realised that it was true. Without even thinking about it, she had contrived to keep her life neatly compartmentalised, with Grayson in one section and her friends in another – as if she could only have one or the other, but not both at once. And it hit her with sickening clarity why – because that was how it had been with Mark. He had demanded exclusivity. He had never wanted to meet her friends and he resented the time she spent with them, not happy until she had shut out everyone but him. Anything that took her attention away from him had to go – even her painting.

Grayson was looking at her expectantly, waiting for her to speak. He looked so hurt and bewildered, and her hand flew to her mouth as it hit her like a thunderbolt how unfair she'd been to him. He'd been so open and generous in sharing his life with her, and she'd been shutting him out of hers.

'I'm sorry,' she said, her eyes welling up. 'I didn't mean to do that. I just—I didn't think you'd be interested in meeting my friends.'

He frowned, looking unconvinced. 'Why wouldn't I want to meet them?'

'I don't know,' she said with a shrug, too ashamed to admit the truth. How could she tell him that, albeit subconsciously, she'd been treating him as if he was the same as Mark, carefully arranging everything to avoid confrontations and jealous rages. Mark's conditioning was so deeply ingrained in her psyche that it had become automatic, an instinctive survival strategy. But Grayson was nothing like Mark. He didn't grudge her spending an evening with her girlfriends. He would never try to manipulate or control her. It sickened her that Mark's influence still had the power to damage her relationship with Grayson.

'I'm not him,' he said, as if he could read her mind.

'I know,' she said. 'I'm sorry if I've treated you like you are. I just—I got so used to—to keeping things separate.'

Grayson nodded understandingly, his features softening.

'Forgive me?' Lisa sobbed.

Grayson pulled her into his arms and kissed her forehead. 'Hey, I'm sorry,' he said, brushing away her tears. 'I didn't mean to upset you.'

She looked into his kind eyes, and her heart leapt as it hit her that it didn't have to be that way with him. She could introduce him to her friends. She could have all the people she cared about together all at once, and she didn't have to constantly choose between them.

'Come to my birthday party next week,' she said, smiling. 'Dinner at my place on Saturday.'

Grayson smiled. 'I'd love to,' he said. 'But don't feel you have to invite me. I don't expect you to spend all your time with me. I totally understand if you'd rather just have a night with your friends.'

'I wouldn't. I really want you to come. Please?'

'Really?' His face relaxed, and he gave her the most gorgeous smile as he took her hands in his.

'Yes,' she said, surprised and gratified she could make him so happy with such a simple thing. It startled her to realise she had such power over him. 'Please?' She squeezed his hands for emphasis. 'It would make it perfect if you were there.'

He grinned. 'Well, in that case, I'd love to come.' He leaned in and brushed his lips softly against hers. 'I don't want to intrude on your life, Lisa. But I'd very much like to be part of it.'

'I'd like that too,' she murmured against his mouth. 'Very much.'

15

GRAYSON ARRIVED EARLY the following Friday to help Lisa get ready for her dinner party.

'Happy Birthday!' He dropped a kiss on her cheek and handed her a carrier bag with two bottles of champagne as he came through the door.

'Thank you.'

'Have you had a good day?' he asked, loosening his tie as he followed her through to the kitchen. He had gone straight from a client meeting to the airport and was wearing a beautifully cut dark suit and crisp white shirt.

'Yes, it's been lovely so far. Thank you for the flowers.' She nodded to the stunning arrangement of white and purple orchids in a tall vase on a side table. It had been a wonderful surprise when they had been delivered in the afternoon. 'They're beautiful.'

'I'm glad you like them.' He leaned in the doorway of the kitchen as Lisa put the champagne in the fridge. 'Mmm, something smells good,' he smiled.

'It's slow cooked lamb,' Lisa told him.

'I hope you haven't spent your whole birthday cooking,' he said.

Lisa shrugged. 'I liked doing it.' She had had the day off and had enjoyed taking the time to prepare a special meal for the most important people in her life.

'Well, I just have to get the rest of my stuff from the car, and then I'll get changed and join you.'

'Here, I got you these,' Lisa said as he turned to go. She took a set of keys from her pocket and handed them to him.

'Really?' Grayson seemed touched as he looked down at the keys in his hand.

Lisa shrugged. 'It'll save me running up and down the stairs every time you come,' she said gruffly, making light of it. But it was a big deal for her, and she could tell he appreciated that.

'Well, thank you.' Grayson leaned in and kissed her. 'I'll be back in a minute.'

When he returned, dressed more casually in black jeans and a cream sweater, Lisa poured them both a glass of wine and they chatted companionably as they cooked together, effortlessly falling into sync as they moved around each other in the tiny kitchen. Lisa was struck by the mundane domesticity of it: she was cooking with her boyfriend, getting ready to have friends over for dinner on a Friday night. It was the sort of thing most women her age would take for granted, but she couldn't quite believe that this was her life now, and she suddenly felt over-whelmed with happiness. Tears stung the backs of her eyes as she watched Grayson bend to put a tray of gratin pota-toes into the oven.

'Right, what's next?' he asked, brushing his hands as he

straightened. 'Lisa?' His eyes widened in alarm as he saw her face. 'What's wrong?'

She shook her head, brushing away a stray tear. 'Nothing.' She smiled reassuringly at him.

Grayson frowned, stepping closer. 'It's something.' His gaze flicked over her face. 'What is it?'

'I'm just being silly,' she said as he put his arms around her.

'Tell me,' he said softly, brushing her cheek with the back of his hand.

'I'm just so happy, that's all.' She felt her cheeks flush in embarrassment. 'I'm so happy that you're here, doing this with me.'

Grayson smiled gently, his eyes crinkling at the corners. 'Me too.' He swept a strand of hair behind her ear. 'I can't quite believe that I get to be here with you,' he said, echoing her thoughts. He bent to kiss her, his lips warm and firm as they clung to hers in a sweet, tender kiss.

Lisa melted into his body, her eyes fluttering closed. She'd never felt so safe and loved as she did in his arms. They kissed softly, lingeringly, their lips coming together again and again as if drawn by an irresistible force. They only broke apart when the hiss and sizzle of hot liquid hitting the stove brought them back to the moment. They turned to find the water in one of the pans bubbling over.

Grayson sighed. 'We'd better stop or we'll never get this dinner ready,' he said, pulling away reluctantly.

Lisa nodded. 'You keep an eye on things in here, and I'll go set the table.'

She hadn't been so excited about her birthday for a long time – not since her grandparents were alive – and she felt a little fluttering of anticipation as she arranged colourful candles and a tiny posy of flowers in the centre of the table. She was looking forward to Grayson meeting her friends and she felt so lucky that she could celebrate with all the people she cared about most.

It would be a squeeze around her little table, but she knew no one would mind. She smiled to herself as she looked around the room, pleased with how pretty and festive it all looked. She had draped fairy lights around the window frame and placed candles along the shelving, so the room was lit by a soft glow. It felt cosy, intimate and informal, and was a million miles from the elegant dinner parties she had organised for Mark in the past.

Katya and Connor were the first to arrive, followed swiftly after by Martha. When Lisa had introduced everyone and Grayson had got them all drinks, she left them getting to know each other, while she put the finishing touches to dinner.

'Well, I'm not surprised you've been keeping *him* to yourself,' Martha said, joining her in the kitchen. 'He's gorgeous!'

Lisa turned to her, unable to suppress a smug grin. 'He is, isn't he?'

'This is your birthday cake,' Martha said, placing a large round tin on the counter. She was the official baker for all their celebrations. 'No peeking.'

'Promise.' Lisa smiled.

'Can I do anything?' Martha asked.

'No, thanks. Everything's under control.' She glanced at the clock on the wall. 'We can eat in about twenty minutes.'

'Well, come and open your presents, then.'

Lisa wiped her hands on her apron, then took it off and they went to join the others in the living room. She was relieved to find Grayson, Katya and Connor chatting happily together, with no awkwardness between them. Grayson handed her a glass of champagne, and they all toasted her and wished her a happy birthday. Then Katya sat her down on the sofa and she opened her gifts – a smoky grey hand-crocheted cardigan from Martha, as fine and intricate as a spider's web; a sea glass necklace from Katya that Lisa had admired in the market; and a pair of beautiful ceramic wine goblets from Connor, who had recently taken up pottery. She was surprised when Grayson handed her a flat rectangular parcel wrapped in shiny purple foil and tied with a big silver ribbon.

'More?' She looked up at him questioningly as she took it from him. She wasn't expecting a present as well as the flowers and champagne. 'You're spoiling me.'

'I don't think that's possible,' he said, sitting beside her as she undid the ribbon. 'You're the least spoiled person I've ever met.'

'Well, that could change if you keep this up,' she said, aware of everyone watching her as she peeled off the paper carefully. Inside, a framed canvas was covered in a layer of bubble wrap, which she tore off impatiently.

'Oh wow!' she gasped as she held the painting out at arm's length to study it.

'Is that what I think it is?' Katya said, her eyes wide as she leaned in to see.

Lisa nodded. 'It's a Hugo Watling. Thank you so much,' she said, turning to Grayson. 'I love it! I'm such a fan of his work.'

'I know,' Grayson smiled. 'You told me once.'

She frowned, confused for a moment – and then she remembered. It was the night she and Grayson had first met. They'd talked about art, and she had admired a painting by Hugo Watling in Grayson's library. She'd said how much she loved his work. She'd never imagined she could actually own one.

'You remembered,' she said wonderingly.

'Of course,' he smiled. 'I remember everything about you.'

'I love it so much, Grayson,' she said, gazing at it again. 'Thank you.' She leaned in and gave him a quick kiss on the lips. Much as she adored the painting and was thrilled to own it, what made it most precious to her was the fact that Grayson had listened and remembered when she told him what she liked; that he had put so much thought into pleasing her.

'You're welcome,' he murmured.

'Thank you all again for your presents,' she said, looking around at her friends as she gathered up the wrapping paper. 'Okay, let's eat.'

Dinner was fun. Everyone enjoyed the food, and Lisa was delighted to see Grayson getting along well with her friends. He was so friendly and easy-going with them, and there was no stiffness or formality. She felt a flush of pleasure as she watched them chatting and laughing together, and she could tell they all liked each other right away. The conversation flowed effortlessly, and the sound of laughter reverberated around the room as they all drank a little too much.

She looked around the table at her friends' smiling faces warmed by the soft glow of the candlelight, and thought how far she'd come, how much her life had changed in the past year. Her last birthday had been such a sterile occasion compared to this. Mark had taken her to an upmarket restaurant, and they had eaten exquisite food and drunk the finest wine. It had all been elegant and refined, and very expensive, just the way Mark liked it. But there had been no laughter or fun, no getting tipsy and letting their hair down. She'd spent the evening feeling tense and uncomfortable in the tight, sheath dress and vertiginous heels Mark had picked out for her to wear. She couldn't even remember what bit of expensive jewellery or sexy lingerie he'd given her. She did recall with a shudder that it was the first time he'd suggested the boob job – it had been part of his birthday gift to her. She had longed to tell him he should buy himself a blow-up doll and have done with it. But she had swallowed it down and said nothing, instead pretending to be pleased and grateful for his generosity. Later, after he had fallen asleep, she had cried into her pillow, wondering how she had sunk so low, and despairing of ever escaping. She had never felt so alone.

'Lisa?' Grayson's voice murmuring in her ear brought her back to the present.

'Sorry.' She shook her head as if to clear it of such dark thoughts as she turned to smile at him. 'I was miles away.'

'You okay?' He frowned, putting an arm around her shoulders.

'Yes,' she nodded, nuzzling her face against his hand. 'More than okay.' She sighed contentedly.

Martha and Katya had disappeared into the kitchen, where they could be heard whispering and giggling together. Moments later, they reappeared, singing Happy Birthday and bearing a large chocolate cake between them, topped with flaming candles. Lisa blushed as everyone joined in the singing and Martha placed the cake on the table in front of her. It was covered in a thick layer of chocolate ganache with 'Happy Birthday Lisa' piped in swirly pink icing.

'This looks amazing, Martha,' she said as the singing came to an end and everyone clapped.

'Don't forget to make a wish,' Grayson murmured in her ear.

Lisa racked her brain as she drew a deep breath, but she genuinely couldn't think of anything to wish for. What could she possibly want that she didn't already have right now? Today couldn't have been more perfect, and she loved her life. She felt safe and cherished; she had great friends, a job she enjoyed, financial independence and a fulfilling creative life; and she had Grayson. Surely it would be greedy to wish for anything more? She looked around at all the faces smiling at her expectantly, and then her eyes fell on Grayson. She closed her eyes, drew a deep breath and blew out the candles in one go, as everyone clapped and cheered.

'What did you wish for?' Connor asked.

'She can't say or it won't come true,' Katya chided him.

Lisa shook her head. 'It's already come true,' she said, her eyes shining as she turned to Grayson and took his hand. She leaned in and whispered in his ear. 'I wished for you.'

16

'I HAVE NEWS,' Grayson told her the next morning. They'd stayed in bed until midday after a late night, and Lisa was cooking them brunch.

'Oh?' She added herbs to the frittata in the pan and turned to face him. He was leaning against the worktop, arms folded.

A slow smile spread across his face as he nodded. It was obviously good news.

'I've been shortlisted for the Stirling award,' he told her, his eyes lighting up with excitement.

'Stirling award?'

'It's an architecture prize,' he explained. 'For the building of the year. I've been nominated for a children's library I did in the inner city.'

'Oh wow!' Lisa gasped. 'That's wonderful, Grayson! Congratulations!' She threw her arms around him and kissed his cheek. 'Why didn't you tell me this last night?'

He shrugged. 'It was your birthday. I didn't want to steal your thunder.'

She grinned. 'Well, now we have to have another celebration.' She turned back to the stove and transferred the pan to the oven.

'There's something else,' he said, pushing away from the counter and going to his jacket that hung on the back of a chair. 'There's an awards ceremony at the end of the month.' He delved into the inside pocket and pulled out an envelope. 'Come with me?' he asked, handing it to her.

Lisa took the envelope from him and opened it. Inside was an invitation printed on thick white card. Her eyes ran quickly over the elegant silver script, scanning the details: Grayson Fielding and guest, six pm on Friday the twenty-seventh of October, drinks reception followed by dinner at …

Lisa frowned. 'But … it's in London,' she faltered, looking up at Grayson.

'Yes.' Grayson raised his eyebrows questioningly.

'I can't go.' She held the invitation out to him, handing it back.

Grayson's face fell, but he didn't take the card from her. 'I know it's a long way to go, but I'm sure Martha would give you the day off – maybe you could even take a couple of days and—'

'It's not that,' she interrupted. 'It's just – I don't want to go back to London.'

He became very still. 'Ever?' he asked, his eyes wide. 'Not even just to visit?'

She realised with a sinking feeling that they had never discussed the details of their long-distance relationship, and it was obvious Grayson hadn't expected it to continue like this permanently.

'I'm not asking you to move there. It's just one night.'

'I know, but … I just can't. I'm sorry.'

'Why not?' He frowned.

She took a shaky breath. 'I just … I don't feel safe there.' She looked up at him, pleading for understanding.

His frown deepened. 'Because of Mark?' He sounded almost incredulous, and she felt foolish.

'Yes,' she said faintly. She hated disappointing him, but she couldn't help it.

Grayson sighed. 'London's a big place, Lisa,' he said reasonably. 'It's one night. What are the chances of you running into Mark?'

'I know, but …'She bit her lip. She felt awful for letting him down. He'd been so good to her, and she couldn't do this one little thing for him. She knew he was right: it was highly unlikely she would come across Mark, and she was being completely irrational. But she still couldn't bring herself to say she'd go.

'Even if you did see him, what do you think would happen?' Grayson continued. 'I'd be with you the whole time. Anything you need to make you feel safe, Lisa, I'll do it.'

She shook her head, holding out the card to him. 'I'm sorry. I know it's silly, but I can't help it. It's just how I feel.'

He huffed out a deep breath. 'It's fine,' he said, taking the invitation from her with obvious reluctance. He'd been so happy and excited a few minutes ago, and she hated seeing him so deflated. She couldn't bear that she'd spoiled the moment for him. He was obviously trying to hide it, but she could tell from the stiffness of his jaw and the tightening around his mouth that he was frustrated with her and was finding it difficult not to show it.

'I'm really sorry, Grayson,' she said miserably. 'I'd love to be there with you, but—'

He took a deep breath and let out a long sigh. 'It's fine, Lisa,' he said, his tone softer this time. He was clearly making an effort to shrug off his disappointment.

'I wish—'

'Hey,' he said softly, reaching for her as tears pooled in her eyes. 'Really, don't worry about it.' He pulled her into his arms, and gave her forehead a soft kiss. 'It's not a big deal – just a black-tie dinner and a lot of speeches. It'll probably be really boring.' He brushed a stray tear away with his thumb. 'I'll ask Isabel to come with me,' he said.

Lisa flinched. She knew he didn't say it to be cruel, but her heart twisted at the thought of Isabel sharing his special moment with him when it should have been her – and all because she was too much of a coward. Why was she still letting Mark poison her life? What was the point of leaving everything behind and moving halfway across the country if she was still allowing him to control her? Would she ever be really free of him?

'I'm sorry,' Grayson said, frowning as he saw how upset she was. 'I didn't realise you felt this way. I wouldn't have brought it up if I'd known the idea of going to London would scare you so much. But let's not let it spoil our weekend.' He kissed her forehead and released her.

'We can still celebrate, can't we?' she asked meekly. 'I'm so happy for you, Grayson.'

'Of course. We'll have our own celebration.'

That evening they drank champagne in front of the fire, and toasted Grayson's success. He showed Lisa the building he'd been nominated for on his laptop, getting carried away as he talked about how he'd created it and what he'd tried to achieve. The exterior was constructed of timber and mirrored glass. It was beautiful and surprising, standing out in its drab urban setting, and yet at the same time completely harmonious with its surroundings. The plain glass panels reflected the trees and sky, so that the structure blended seamlessly with the landscape. Inside the building was full of colour and quirky, playful features – hidden doors, secret staircases, and even a slide from one floor to another – all aimed at making the library a fun and magical place for the local children, somewhere they they would want to use, and that would feel like it belonged to them.

'It's amazing, Grayson,' she said, scrolling through the images. 'Like something out of a storybook.'

'That was the idea,' he smiled.

'I'd love to see it in the flesh sometime.'

'I'd love to show it to you,' Grayson said.

There was a hint of sadness in his tone, and even as they drank champagne and celebrated, Lisa felt leaden, like a pall had been cast over the whole evening and no matter how hard they tried, they couldn't reclaim it.

She felt awful. Grayson had given her so much, and the first time he had asked her for something, she had let him down. It didn't bode well for the future of their relationship, and it left her feeling shaky and insecure. Grayson had agreed to try the long-distance thing, but he clearly hadn't realised until today how one-sided the arrangement would be. She knew it wasn't fair to expect him to always be the one making the effort to be together. How long before he got tired of it? Was she going to lose him now when they'd barely begun? Did they even have a future if she couldn't share the most important moments of his life with him?

The question niggled at her for the rest of the week. Grayson never mentioned the awards dinner again when they spoke on the phone, but she felt it hanging in the air between them, and it preyed on her mind when she was alone. Was she being unfair to him? If she couldn't be a real part of his life, would it be better for both of them to stop now before they got in any deeper?

But she couldn't bear the thought of losing him. Instead, she began to entertain the idea of going to London. She tried to imagine herself there, testing her feelings as she visualised herself walking the familiar streets. The idea still scared her, but for Grayson maybe she could overcome it.

He had played down how much the awards ceremony meant to him, but she guessed he was just doing that for her sake, because he didn't want her to feel bad. She went over and over it in her mind, agonising over what to do. Eventually, she decided she would try. But there was someone else she had to talk to before she could tell Grayson that she'd changed her mind. She looked up the number of Isabel's Mayfair gallery and called her.

'Who may I say is calling?' the receptionist asked her.

'Lisa … um, Lisa Matthews,' she replied. She didn't know if Isabel would even remember her. They had only met on a couple of occasions, albeit in rather extraordinary circumstances. She drummed her fingers nervously as she waited.

'Lisa! This is a nice surprise,' she said, sounding like she meant it. Lisa relaxed, melting into the warmth of Isabel's welcoming voice. 'It's lovely to hear from you. How are you?'

'I'm good,' she smiled, remembering how much she had liked Isabel from the first time they'd met. She'd always been so open and friendly. 'I don't know if Grayson told you, but we've been … seeing each other a bit.' She felt awkward saying it, even though she knew Isabel and Grayson had never had a monogamous relationship.

'Yes, he told me he'd found you,' she said, and Lisa

couldn't help feeling a little twinge of jealousy at the reminder of how close Grayson and Isabel were. 'I'm so glad,' she continued. 'But don't worry, he hasn't told me any details.'

'Oh, it's fine. I know I can trust you.' Isabel had never been anything but kind to her. She had even stuck up for her against Mark.

'I'm just glad to see him so happy,' Isabel said. 'You know he cares about you very much, Lisa.'

Lisa smiled. 'I care about him too.' She cleared her throat. 'That's why I'm calling really. I wanted to ask you about this award he's been shortlisted for—'

'Oh, isn't it marvellous?' Isabel gasped. 'I'm so thrilled for him.'

'It is important, then? I mean, he said it's not that big a deal, but ...'

'Are you kidding me? Grayson getting this is huge! It's like the architect's equivalent of an Oscar. I mean, even the short-listing is a big deal. If he wins, it'll be a total game-changer.'

'Are you going to the awards dinner with him?' Lisa asked tentatively.

'Yes. It's such a shame you couldn't get away. I'm sure you'd love to be there with him on the night.'

'Well, things have ... changed.' She bit her lip, feeling awkward. Grayson obviously hadn't gone into the reasons why she'd refused to go to the ceremony, and she didn't want to admit to Isabel that it was just because she was a coward.

'You can go after all?' To her relief, Isabel sounded delighted.

'Um ... yes, I can. I was wondering, would you mind awfully if ... I mean, he's already invited you, so—'

'Oh, don't worry about that!' Isabel said breezily. 'I don't mind in the least.'

'Are you sure? I don't want to put you out.'

'Absolutely. I was only going because you couldn't. I know it would mean a lot to him to have you there.'

Lisa smiled, relieved that she sounded so genuinely blasé.

'Have you got something to wear?' Isabel asked.

'Oh! No, I don't.' She hadn't even thought that far ahead. 'I suppose it'll be very dressy.' She tried to remember what the invitation had said, but she hadn't taken in much apart from the location.

'Yes, it's black tie, so you're going to need a cocktail dress.'

Lisa's heart sank. 'I don't have anything remotely suitable. There's not much call for evening wear where I live now.'

'Have you told Grayson yet that you can go after all?'

'Not yet. I wanted to talk to you first, make sure you were okay with it.'

'Right,' Isabel said, a smile in her voice. 'I've got an idea ...'

17

THE LAST TIME Lisa had been on a train, she'd been running away from Mark, and she couldn't help feeling nervous at the thought of returning to London as she boarded the express from Gatwick Airport. She knew she was being silly. Grayson was right – London was a huge, crowded city, and the chances of her running into Mark were close to zero. Still, she couldn't quite quell the jittery feeling in her stomach as they left green fields behind and rattled through the outer suburbs of the city. Along with the nerves, she felt a little tingle of excitement when the train pulled into Paddington Station and she stepped out into the familiar buzz and bustle of London.

She made her way quickly through the crowded platform to the taxi rank outside. When she had given the driver Isabel's address, she sank back against the upholstery and enjoyed the journey, drinking in the sights and sounds of her beloved home town. She felt a familiar little tug as she looked out the window at the distinctive red buses and black taxis, the majestic stone buildings and iconic monuments, and the crowds jostling for space as they poured in and out of Tube stations. She had missed this – she hadn't realised how much. She'd only been away for six months, but already it felt new and exciting, if a little daunting. As the taxi weaved through the streets, she felt like a tourist, her nose pressed to the glass, taking it all in.

Grayson didn't know that she was coming to London. She hadn't told him she'd changed her mind about accompanying him to the awards dinner this evening. It had been Isabel's idea.

'Why don't we surprise him?' she'd said. 'Come to London for the day. We'll go shopping and get you a dress. You can get ready at my place, and then when he comes to pick me up, he'll find you there instead.' Isabel's enthusiasm for the idea was infectious, and Lisa found herself agreeing readily.

'He's going to be so thrilled,' Isabel squealed. 'And this way, if anything happens and it turns out you can't make it after all, he won't be disappointed.'

Lisa couldn't help wondering if Isabel suspected why she'd turned down the invitation in the first place, and was giving her the opportunity to still flake out at the last minute. If so, she was grateful to her for her understanding.

Isabel's home in Belsize Park felt a little too close for comfort to the house Lisa had shared with Mark in nearby Hampstead, and her nerves increased as they drove through the familiar leafy roads. She was very glad to see a friendly, welcoming face when Isabel opened the door.

'Lisa!' She beamed, pulling her into a hug. 'You made it!'

'Yes,' Lisa smiled, realising Isabel hadn't counted on her turning up until she actually saw her on the doorstep.

'It's so good to see you.' Isabel ushered her into the house.

'It's really good to see you too,' Lisa said, realising that she meant it. Even though she only met Isabel on a couple of occasions, and then in very weird circumstances, she felt instantly comfortable with her. She had such an open, warm manner that Lisa felt like they were already old friends.

'Grayson's going to be so happy when he sees you,' Isabel said excitedly. 'I can't wait to see his face!' She took Lisa's coat and overnight bag from her in the hall. 'We've got a big day ahead,' she warned her. 'But I expect you'd like a cup of coffee first?'

'I'd love one,' Lisa said gratefully. She could do with a shot of caffeine to wake her up. Even though the flight had been short, she had been up very early this morning and was a little tired already.

She had never been in Isabel's house before, and she looked around with interest as she followed her through to the kitchen. The decor was as eclectic and flamboyant as she'd have expected, with colourful painted walls and lots of dramatic pieces of art. In the kitchen Isabel waved her to a seat and handed her a steaming mug of coffee. Lisa breathed in the delicious aroma gratefully.

'I have a big girlie day planned for us,' Isabel told her as she sat opposite. 'We're having facials and manicures this morning, and I've booked us a table for lunch. And then we're going to buy an amazing dress for you to wear tonight.'

'Nothing too expensive,' Lisa reminded her nervously. 'I'm on a strict budget.' She had already spent more than she could afford getting here, and she hadn't counted on paying for beauty treatments as well as a dress.

'That's no problem,' Isabel said breezily. 'Don't worry,

I can do style on a budget. I didn't always have money myself.'

'I hope you hadn't already bought something to wear tonight yourself,' Lisa said.

'I had, as it happens – any excuse. But don't worry about that,' Isabel said, shrugging off her concerns. 'I have a big party coming up next week that I can wear it to. Although it might be a bit too much for that particular occasion,' she added with a little laugh.

Lisa looked at her questioningly.

'It's a sex party,' Isabel explained with a cheeky grin, her eyes sparkling. 'An orgy.'

'Oh.' Lisa tried to hide her shock, but Isabel just laughed.

'Anyway,' she said, 'do you like vintage? I know this shop that has fabulous stuff, but it's all too small for me. You're so petite, it'll be easy to find you something – and I'll get to shop there vicariously.'

'It sounds perfect!' Lisa said. 'I love vintage.' She was glad Isabel didn't try to persuade her to spend more than she could afford, or worse, offer to buy a dress for her.

'Great! I've already picked out a few dresses that I think will work, to save us time. The manicure and facial are on me,' she said. 'No argument. It's fun to have someone to do that stuff with, so indulge me, please?'

'Thank you,' Lisa said, deciding to accept graciously. She could see Isabel genuinely wanted to treat her, and it would be churlish to turn her down. After all, she reminded herself, there could be as much pleasure in giving gifts as in receiving them.

'I'll do your hair and make-up myself,' Isabel continued. 'I'm good at that. Ooh, we're going to have so much fun,' she said, her eyes sparkling. She drained her coffee and glanced at her watch. 'We'd better get going. Drink up!'

The salon Isabel took Lisa to was very upmarket. They were served champagne while they were pampered and buffed, and Isabel kept up a constant stream of chatter. Lisa felt quite giddy by the time they left and Isabel led the way to a fashionable restaurant where she had reserved a table. They both ordered chicken and pineapple salad and sparkling water, and the food was deliciously light and tasty.

'How's your work going?' Isabel asked her as they ate.

'It's fine,' Lisa shrugged. 'There's a film crew in town, so it's been very busy the last couple of weeks.'

Isabel smiled, looking at her quizzically. 'I meant your painting.'

'Oh!' Lisa blushed.

'What is it you do?'

'I'm a waitress. I work in a cafe five days a week.'

'But you *are* painting again?'

Lisa nodded. 'Yes, I'm working really hard at it actually, and it's going well. I'm pretty happy with what I'm doing at the moment.'

'Good. Have you got any photos?' Isabel nodded to Lisa's phone on the table beside her. 'Grayson showed me that painting you sent him, but I'd love to see more.'

'Yes, I've got a few.' Lisa picked up the phone and scrolled through to some photos of her recent work. She handed the phone to Isabel.

Isabel put down her knife and fork and gave her full attention to the screen, a little frown of concentration between her brows as she scrolled through the images. She seemed to stop a long time on each one, and Lisa began to feel self-conscious as the silence lengthened. She wished she knew what Isabel was thinking. Maybe she didn't think they were very good and didn't know what to say. Lisa had been confident about them until now, but faced with the judgement of an expert like Isabel, she suddenly felt unsure of herself.

Finally Isabel lifted her head. 'Wow,' she said as she handed the phone back to Lisa. 'They're amazing!' Her expression was deadly serious.

'Really?' Lisa smiled in relief. Even though deep down she'd believed in her work, the external validation meant a lot – especially coming from Isabel, whose opinion was so highly valued.

Isabel nodded. 'They're wonderful, Lisa. I'd love if you'd let me have some for the gallery. You're very talent-ed.' She picked up her knife and fork again, but didn't resume eating. 'You do know that, don't you?' she asked carefully, her eyes narrowed.

Lisa shrugged. 'Well, I guess … I mean, I'm satisfied with my work—'

'No.' Isabel reached out a hand and placed it over Lisa's, commanding her full attention. 'You're *really* talent-ed.' She looked her squarely in the eye. 'You should be having solo shows, and selling internationally. Don't guess. Know it.' She squeezed Lisa's hand for emphasis. 'Own it.'

'Thank you,' Lisa said quietly. 'That means a lot.'

'Seriously, I'd love to represent you,' Isabel said. 'Would you consider giving me some pieces for the gallery? Or if you have enough work and you feel you're ready, I could give you a show. I have a slot available around the end of November.'

Lisa's heart soared and plummeted almost at the same time. It was an amazing offer. Having the backing of a major gallery owner like Isabel was the kind of recognition she'd always dreamed of. It would be the break into the London art world that she'd aspired to for so long. But it was bittersweet to have such a wonderful opportunity held out in front of her when she knew she couldn't take it.

She shook her head, dropping her eyes to the table. 'That would be amazing, Isabel, and I appreciate the offer – more than you could know. Really, I can't thank you enough.'

Isabel gave her a quizzical look. 'I'd be the one thanking *you* if you say yes. I'd have as much to gain as you would – maybe more. Apart from my hefty commission, I'd have the kudos of being the dealer who launched Lisa Matthews on the world.'

Lisa smiled sadly. 'Thanks for the offer – it means the world to me. But—'

'But you're saying no? If you're not ready—'

Lisa shook her head. 'It's not that. I don't really want to show my work in London. I'm not looking for an art career anymore.'

Isabel was looking at her speculatively, her eyes narrowed. 'Is this because of Mark?' she asked.

'Yes,' Lisa admitted. She looked down at the table, drawing patterns on the cloth, steeling herself to ask Isabel the questions that had been buzzing around in her head all day. She was having such a nice time, she hadn't wanted to spoil it by talking about Mark. But now that he'd already been mentioned, she couldn't pass up the opportunity to find out what Isabel knew.

'Do you see him at all?' she asked.

Isabel shrugged. 'I see him around sometimes.'

'Do you know Rose?'

'Not really – at least not personally. I've been aware of her as an artist. I remember she had a show at Gallery Six a while back that was very well received. She seems to have disappeared off the radar a bit since then.'

Lisa's heart clenched. 'But you don't … socialise with them?'

'No.' A shadow flickered across Isabel's face, and Lisa guessed they were both thinking of the dinner party at Grayson's where they'd met.

She flushed. 'I just thought you might have some idea what their relationship is like.'

Isabel shook her head. 'Sorry. They do seem to be a couple, but I don't know how serious they are.'

'Mark seems to have moved on, but …'

'But you can't be sure,' Isabel finished for her. 'Do you think he's still looking for you?'

'I honestly don't know. But I don't want to run the risk if he is.'

Isabel eyed her thoughtfully. 'If that's all that's stopping you, you could always use a pseudonym,' she said, toying with her glass. 'Or you could even be anonymous, and we could keep your identity a secret.' She smiled. 'It might help with publicity – who doesn't love a bit of mystery and intrigue?'

Lisa considered. It was a tempting idea. It would be wonderful to sell in a major gallery, to get recognition for her work, even if no one knew her real name. And it would be a dream come true if she could earn a living doing what she loved. But could it work?

'You wouldn't even need to be in London,' Isabel said persuasively. 'You could stay in Cornwall and Grayson could act as a go-between. Think about it anyway.'

Lisa nodded. 'I will.'

Isabel flicked a glance at her watch. 'Well, we'd better get going,' she said, signalling for the bill. 'We've got some serious dress shopping to do.'

18

GRAYSON TRIED to shake himself out of his gloomy mood as his town car made its way to Isabel's house to pick her up. What was wrong with him? This should be one of the best nights of his life. He was getting recognition for his work from the industry he loved. Whether he won or not, it was an incredible accolade, and an honour he had never even dreamed of. He should be excited and happy, looking forward to an evening with his peers, celebrating the best of their profession. Instead he felt edgy and strangely dissatisfied.

Of course, he knew what the problem was. Lisa wasn't here. It was one of the proudest moments of his life and he wanted to share it with the woman he loved. He understood why she didn't feel able to come, but he still couldn't help wishing she were here.

At least Isabel would be there to share it with him, he thought as they pulled up outside her building. She knew how much tonight meant to him, and she had cancelled a date so that she could be there for him on his big night. She was really excited and happy for him. So he should show his appreciation for her support and stop being such a moody bugger – that wouldn't make the evening fun for either of them.

Determined that he was going to make the best of things and enjoy the night, he hopped out of the car and walked up the steps to her door, mustering a smile as he rang the bell. The door swung open immediately, as if Isabel had been waiting just inside, but his smile faded instantly as he saw her standing there in jeans and a big over-sized sweatshirt.

'Grayson,' she smiled calmly, ushering him into the hall. 'Hi.'

'You're not ready,' he said as he passed her, unable to hide his dismay.

'Change of plan,' she said. 'I'm not coming.'

'*What*?' He frowned, aghast. 'Why not?'

She shrugged. 'I changed my mind.'

'And you didn't think you might have told me?' He glanced at his watch. It was too late to find another plus-one now. He would just have to go solo, he thought miserably, feeling very sorry for himself. But really, was it too much to ask that there should be one person who cared about him there tonight to share his moment of glory?

'It was a last minute thing,' she said, still with that damn calm smile. 'Better offer.'

'Better offer! Christ!' He couldn't believe Isabel was being so blasé about letting him down at the last minute. It was so unlike her to be thoughtless. What the hell had got into her?

'But don't worry,' she said, taking his arm and pulling him in the direction of her living room. 'I'm not leaving you high and dry. I've arranged a substitute.'

'You've got me a date?' he asked disbelievingly. 'For tonight?'

'Yes. Come and meet her.'

She tried to tug him towards her living room, but he dug his heels in and remained immovable. 'Christ, Isabel,' he whispered, 'I don't want a blind date tonight. I'd rather go alone.'

'You'll change your mind when you see her. Anyway, she's all dressed up now. And she's come a long way. You can't just stand her up.'

He didn't resist as she grabbed his arm again, and he allowed her to lead him to the living room, but only so he could tell his 'date' that there had been some terrible mistake and she wouldn't be coming to the ceremony with him. He was still scowling at Isabel as they reached the open door, and was only aware of a flash of dark blue in his peripheral vision.

Then he turned towards it and his breath caught in his throat because there, standing by the window with her back to them, was Lisa. She turned around to face him, and his heart seemed to stop for a beat.

'Lisa!' he breathed, his voice barely above a stunned whisper. 'What—'

'Like I said,' Isabel said quietly by his side, 'you got a better offer.'

He glanced at her with a surprised smile before turning his attention back to Lisa. She was stunning, in a strapless, floor-length dress of midnight blue that made her pale skin almost translucent, her hair falling around her shoulders in soft waves. Everything about her seemed to glow. 'I can't believe you're here,' he said, blinking at her dazedly.

'Good surprise?' Her delighted smile told him she already knew the answer.

He walked across to her and bent to give her a soft kiss on the cheek. 'It's a wonderful surprise, but you didn't have to come,' he said, scanning her face worriedly. Much as he wanted her here with him, he hated the thought of her putting herself through stress and anxiety for his sake. He'd tried to brush off his disappointment when she'd refused the invitation, and he hoped she hadn't felt pressured into coming to make him happy.

'I wanted to come,' she said. 'I know how important tonight is, and I want to share it with you. I'm so proud of you.'

'Thank you.' He bent and kissed her again. 'You look amazing.'

'You two had better get going,' Isabel interrupted. 'The man of the moment shouldn't be late for his own party.'

'You're right.' He took Lisa's hand and Isabel followed them out to the hall.

'Well, good luck!' she said as they stood in the doorway. 'I hope you win.'

'I feel I already have.' He squeezed Lisa's hand, smiling down at her. 'Thank you,' he said to Isabel.

'For standing you up? You're welcome,' she said, exchanging a smug smile with Lisa.

'Thanks for everything, Isabel,' Lisa said softly.

Isabel gave her a final hug and waved them off.

In the back of the car he took Lisa's hand, clasping it tightly. 'I can't believe you're here,' he said, looking at her dazedly, still not quite able to believe she was real. He half expected her to disappear in a puff of smoke. 'Thank you for coming.' He raised her hand to his lips and kissed it.

'You were right – it was silly of me to be afraid. London's a big place.'

He frowned. 'It wasn't silly. It's understandable. I'm sorry if I pushed you.'

She shook her head. 'You didn't. But I realised I can't

hide out in Cornwall forever,' she said. 'If I do that, I'm as much a prisoner of Mark as I ever was, and I'm done with letting him control me. I want to be part of your life, Grayson. And your life is here, in London.'

He leaned in and kissed her, a soft, sweet kiss that quickly became hungry and heated. His tongue slid into her mouth as his hands began to rove restlessly over her body, stroking over her breasts and along the curve of her waist. His cock stiffened as he pulled her closer against him, his breathing becoming deep and ragged. He slid one hand beneath the bodice of her dress and felt her pulse quicken as he caressed her soft, warm flesh. His fingers moved to the zip of her dress as if of their own volition.

The car jolted as it pulled up at a traffic light, snapping him back to reality and he pulled away reluctantly.

'Sorry,' he said with a rueful smile. 'I don't want to mess up your beautiful dress.' In fact, he wanted nothing more, and it was all he could do not to push her back against the plush leather, peel off her dress and bury himself deep inside her right here on the back seat of the car in the middle of the traffic. He took her hand in his, clutching her fingers tightly as if to absorb the pain. 'Not yet anyway,' he said with a crooked grin, and Lisa smiled back at him, her eyes sparkling. 'Will you stay with me tonight? Will you come to my house?'

'Yes,' Lisa nodded.

'Thank you.' He kissed her knuckles.

'Oh,' she gasped, 'I left my case at Isabel's.'

'We can send for it in the morning,' he shrugged. 'I can give you a spare toothbrush for tonight. Anything else you need from it?'

'No,' she shook her head. They both knew she wouldn't be needing any clothes until at least tomorrow.

'When do you have to go back to Cornwall?'

'I can stay the whole week if I want to. I only asked for the day, but Martha insisted.'

'Have I ever told you how much I like Martha?' he grinned.

Lisa laughed. 'I haven't taken any leave since I started working for her, so she arranged a replacement and told me to take the whole week, whether I want to stay in London or not.'

'And do you?' he asked.

'Yes,' she said softly. 'Very much.'

19

———

THE AWARDS CEREMONY was being held in a beautiful old building in the east of the city. Lisa felt a little fluttering of nerves as they were ushered down a long corridor, through a set of double doors and into a vast, high-ceilinged hall where the drinks reception was already in full swing. They were greeted by the celebratory hum of chatter and tinkling glass. Above their heads, ornate crystal chandeliers shone down onto a sea of diaphanous silk and taffeta, catching the light of sparkling jewels and sequinned dresses. It was a long time since she had been to such a glitzy event, and she found it a little intimidating. She was grateful that Grayson kept his arm around her as he led her into the crowd and got them drinks. He seemed to know almost everyone, and as they began to circulate, she was introduced to so many people, she couldn't possibly remember all their names. Everyone seemed so glamorous and sophisticated, she felt a little out of her depth at first. But they were all so friendly, she started to relax as they made their way around the room, moving from circle to circle. Grayson was very popular, and it was obvious that he was held in high esteem by his colleagues and peers. She felt incredibly proud to be with him.

At dinner they shared a table with three other couples. They were interesting and entertaining, and as the evening progressed, Lisa was surprised to realise she was having fun. She had wanted to be here for Grayson, but she hadn't really expected to enjoy herself. In the past, she had only ever attended ritzy events like this when she was with Mark, and she had been too tense and anxious to take any pleasure in them. It had been a public performance and she had been entirely preoccupied with playing her role to perfection so as not to incur Mark's displeasure, fearful that she would say or do something that would get her into trouble later. Tonight she could relax and be herself. She could enjoy the company and savour the delicious food and wine. She didn't flinch when Grayson told people she was an artist, and she didn't feel the need to change the subject when someone asked her about her painting.

The award presentation got under way after dinner, and all eyes turned to the stage as a hush fell over the room. As the MC announced each of the finalists, a screen in the centre of the stage showed a short film about the building they were nominated for. Lisa's heart swelled with pride as Grayson spoke passionately about the inspiration behind his project and how he had tried to create a sense of magic and possibility in the design. His aim was for the building to inspire and uplift the local community who used it, and judging by the smiles on the faces of the children, parents and teachers who were interviewed, he had succeeded. Lisa's eyes welled up as little kids were shown enjoying the library, their faces lit up with joy as they talked about how much they loved being there.

When it came to announcing the winner, there was an agonising hush as the host opened the envelope. Lisa held her breath with anticipation, her heart hammering in her chest. She hardly dared glance at Grayson as she silently willed his name to be called, repeating it over and over in her heard like a prayer.

When the MC leaned into the microphone and said 'Grayson Fielding', she wondered for a moment if she'd imagined it. But then everyone around her was surging to their feet, and the whole room burst into riotous applause. The people at their table were shaking Grayson's hand and slapping him on the shoulder, as the clapping went on and on.

'Congratulations,' Lisa turned to him, beaming.

'Thank you.' He grabbed her hand and leaned in to give her a kiss, lingering slightly before he pulled away and bounded up to the stage to collect his award.

He made a wonderful speech, gracious to his fellow nominees, and acknowledging the contributions of his partners and co-workers. Lisa could feel how much good-will there was in the room towards him and she couldn't have been prouder or happier. She was so glad she hadn't missed this.

'Great result!' Sarah, beside her, said as Grayson finished his speech to rapturous applause. 'He really deserves it. You must be so proud of him.'

'I sure am,' Lisa said softly, wiping tears from her eyes as Grayson weaved his way slowly back to her, people stopping him every few steps along the way to shake his hand and offer their congratulations.

He was in demand for the rest of the evening, and he was friendly and affable, taking time to speak to everyone who crowded around to congratulate him. Lisa was happy just to be by his side, sharing in his triumph. Later there were press photographs and an interview, and it was after midnight by the time they left and walked to the waiting car.

She sank back against the seat with a sigh as the doors closed behind them, and she finally had Grayson to herself.

'Congratulations,' she said softly, kissing him on the mouth. 'I'm so proud of you.'

'Thanks. But you were the real prize tonight,' he said, stroking her cheek. 'Thank you for being there.'

'I wouldn't have missed it for the world,' she said before he leaned forward to capture her mouth again.

It felt strange to be in Grayson's house again. It brought back a disturbing mix of memories and associations. The last time she'd been here it was in her capacity as his paid whore – not that he'd ever treated her like one.

'Tired?' he asked as he took her coat.

She shook her head. 'No,' she said, surprised to find she wasn't. It was almost one, and it had been a very long day, but she was still wired from the excitement of the evening. 'Are you?'

'No.'

He led her into the kitchen. Her eyes were automatically drawn to the big wooden table in the centre, and a little shiver ran through her at the memory of the first time she had met Grayson and what he had done to her on that table. He followed her gaze, and something in his expression told her he was remembering it too.

'Would you like a glass of wine?' he asked, dispelling the strange atmosphere.

'Yes, please.'

He poured them both wine and they took it into the library. Grayson switched on the fire, then loosened his bow tie and undid the top buttons of his shirt, while Lisa sank into the sofa. Grayson looked at her hungrily over the rim of his glass as he took a sip of wine.

'I can't believe you're here,' he said huskily. 'I've dreamed of having you here again for so long.'

'I've dreamed of being here,' she said softly.

'Really?' He raised his eyebrows sceptically. 'It can't have very happy associations for you.'

'This room does,' she said, looking around the beautiful library. 'When I was here with you – it was the only time I was happy back then. For the first time in a very long time I felt safe and—' she broke off, about to say 'loved'. 'Cared for,' she finished.

'I'm glad,' Grayson said, sinking to his knees in front of her. 'You were cared for, Lisa. You *are* cared for … loved,' he added hesitantly, looking up at her almost warily from under his lashes, as if this declaration might be unwelcome. 'I love you, Lisa.'

Her startled gasp was stifled as he leaned forward and kissed her softly on the lips, sighing deeply as his eyes fluttered closed.

'I love you too,' she whispered as his lips travelled down her neck, and she felt his breath hot against her skin as he gasped softly.

He lifted his head, his eyes burning into hers as he gazed at her.

'I love you,' she repeated, wrapping her arms around his neck. Then they were kissing again. His lips were soft and warm, his tongue insistent as it plunged into her mouth, tangling urgently with hers. He groaned deep in his throat as she buried her hands in his hair. His eyes were dark and heavy-lidded when he pulled back.

'I've dreamt of taking this off you since I first saw you in it this evening,' he said with a crooked smile, one finger trailing along the bodice of her strapless dress, skimming lightly across the tops of her breasts. Her heart beat wildly as he pulled her forward and tugged the zip down slowly, watching as the silky material fell to her waist, revealing her naked breasts to his hungry gaze.

'You're breathtaking,' he breathed. Then he bent to take one rosy bud in his mouth, while his fingers teased and caressed the other one. Lisa held his head, watching him kiss and caress her. She found the sight of him suckling her breast wildly erotic, the gentle rasp of his tongue across her hardened nipple sending sparks of electricity through her veins. She moaned softly as he sucked harder, his fingers trailing up her legs beneath her dress. Heat built inside her and she tugged at his clothes frantically, desperate to feel his bare skin against hers. She managed to unbutton his shirt with shaking fingers and he pulled away briefly to wrench it off before returning his attention to her breasts. As he kissed her aching nipples, he slid one hand between her thighs, nudging them apart. He pushed her panties aside and her whole body thrummed as he stroked along her slick folds.

'Mmm,' he groaned thickly. 'You're so wet. I want to taste you.'

Lisa trembled with need as he lifted her slightly to pull her dress off completely. Then he pulled her down onto the rug beside him, his eyes devouring her as he slowly slid her panties down her legs and tossed them aside. Lisa whimpered, her body on fire as he buried his face between her legs, kissing and licking her to a shuddering climax.

20

———

Lisa drifted awake the next morning in a dreamy haze of happiness. She was roused slowly towards consciousness by the brush of Grayson's lips against her skin, the whisper of his warm breath on her neck. They were spooned together in his bed, her back to his front. She gave a deep sigh of contentment as she opened her eyes. She felt completely cocooned in the warmth of his body – his arms wrapped around her, their legs entwined, the gentle rise and fall of his chest at her back. She smiled sleepily as she turned to face him.

'I can't believe you're here,' he said hoarsely. He dropped a kiss on her shoulder.

'I'm so glad I came.'

'Lots of times,' he said with a crooked smile, pushing back her hair to kiss her earlobe.

She laughed softly. They had made love endlessly last night, first in the library and then here in his bed, before finally falling into an exhausted, satisfied sleep. She felt a warm glow inside as the events of the previous night seeped into her consciousness – Grayson's eyes lighting up

152

when he first saw her at Isabel's; how proud she had felt of him when he won the award; their lovemaking in the library. It had been a wonderful evening – and most wonderful of all, Grayson had told her he loved her. She replayed the scene in the library again and again in her mind – the heat in his eyes, the gentle passion of his touch, the sincerity in his voice as he'd said those three little words. It was the most magical moment of her life.

And yet there was something niggling in the back of her brain that made her uneasy, something trying to nudge to the forefront of her mind that threatened to undermine her happiness. She racked her brain, but couldn't pinpoint any reason for her sense of foreboding. Last night had been completely blissful, from the moment Grayson's face lit up when he first saw her until they'd finally collapsed exhausted in each other's arms. She couldn't remember when she'd been so happy. She shook her head slightly as if to dislodge the ominous feeling.

'I couldn't believe it when I saw you at Isabel's last night. When did the two of you concoct this plan to switch places?' Grayson asked with an amused smile.

Lisa's heart plummeted as it hit her why she was feeling so off-kilter. She had swapped places with Isabel. If she hadn't gone to the awards ceremony with Grayson last night, Isabel would have gone instead – and Isabel would probably be here in bed with him now.

She tried to shake off the treacherous thought. Grayson had said he loved her last night. But what did that mean? She knew he'd had a sexual relationship with Isabel in the past. Did he still? If she asked him, she believed he would tell her the truth. She just wasn't sure she'd want to hear it.

'I hope Isabel didn't mind me taking her place,' she said tentatively.

Grayson shook his head. 'She's not very fond of big formal functions like that. She was only coming with me to be supportive. I'm sure she was only too happy for you to replace her.'

At the awards maybe, Lisa thought, feeling suddenly cold. But what about in Grayson's bed? Then again, she probably wouldn't care. Isabel had an open, free-spirited attitude to sex. She and Grayson had never had a monogamous relationship, and they weren't possessive or jealous about each other. And after all, it was just one night. She could have Grayson to herself for the rest of the week. Lisa felt a chill come over her at the thought and she shuddered.

'Are you okay?' Grayson frowned in concern.

'Yeah, I'm fine,' she said, turning away from him and burying her head in the pillow. The closeness she'd felt with him moments earlier suddenly evaporated. She tried to push down the old feelings of insecurity that surfaced, telling herself she was being ridiculous. After all, Grayson had said he loved her. He had never been in love with Isabel. That changed things … didn't it?

'Lisa?' Grayson clasped her shoulder.

'I'm tired, that's all,' she whispered, faking a yawn. But she wasn't at all sleepy – she felt wired and edgy, her nerves jangling.

Grayson's breath was hot on her skin as he chuckled. 'Well, I guess we didn't get much sleep last night.' She felt him sink down on the pillow behind her. He wrapped an arm around her and she took his hand. Grayson gave a deep, satisfied sigh, pulling her closer. Moments later, she could tell from the even, steady rhythm of his breathing that he had fallen asleep.

She lay awake fretting, her mind spinning as she tried to rationalise her anxieties. She desperately wanted reassurance from Grayson, but she didn't know how to ask for it without appearing jealous and clingy. Maybe she'd been naive to think she could handle a long-distance relationship with him. When she was in Cornwall, it had been easier to dismiss thoughts of his life here – to just enjoy their time together, and not worry about what he did when they were apart. But tonight had brought her face to face with the reality that he had a whole life in London that didn't involve her. A life that Isabel was very much part of …

She must have fallen asleep because she dreamt that she was falling, and woke with a jolt. Grayson was still dozing as she slipped quietly out of bed. She grabbed a robe from the bathroom and padded downstairs. It was a bright, sharp autumn day, and sunlight flooded Grayson's large kitchen/diner. She was just making herself a mug of coffee when she heard the front door open and footsteps clicking down the hall.

'Oh, hi!' Isabel beamed at her as she stood in the doorway. 'I just came to drop you over your case.' She was carrying Lisa's small wheeled suitcase, and she put it down by the door.

'Oh, thanks.' Lisa smiled at her dazedly, only registering the fact that Isabel had her own key to the house.

'I didn't know if you two would still be in bed, so I let myself in. I didn't want to disturb you if you were still sleeping off last night.'

'Grayson's still asleep.' Lisa said. 'Would you like a cup of coffee?'

'No, thanks. I can't stay. I—oh, hi!' She turned as Grayson came downstairs behind her. 'I just came over to drop off Lisa's case. Good night last night?'

'Yes, very good.'

'Congratulations!' She gave him a quick peck on the cheek. He had texted her last night from the ceremony to tell her he'd won. 'Very impressive,' she said, nodding to the award that still sat on the kitchen table.

'Do you want some breakfast?' he asked her. He yawned sleepily and stretched.

'It's lunchtime for most of us mere mortals, you know,' she said. 'I had breakfast ages ago.'

'Brunch, then.' He grinned.

'Thanks, but I was just saying to Lisa, I can't stay.' She turned to go.

'Thanks for bringing my case over,' Lisa said as they saw her to the door. 'And for … everything.'

'My pleasure,' Isabel said, pulling her into a hug. 'It was fun. I hope we'll see you back in London again soon.' She turned to Grayson. 'And I'll see you next Thursday,' she said, giving him a quick peck on the cheek.

'Yeah, see you then.'

As they watched her drive off, Lisa felt unsettled again and found herself wishing she didn't like Isabel so much. It would be a lot easier if she was a bitch, and Lisa could just hate her, and demand that Grayson cut her out of his life. She was disconcerted by the reminder of just how close they were. The way she'd said 'I hope *we'll* see you in London again soon', as if she and Grayson were a couple, a unit, drove home what an integral part of his life she was. She didn't imagine for a moment that Isabel was marking her territory or had meant to unnerve her, but it played on her insecurities.

When she was back in Cornwall, Grayson and Isabel would still be here in London, carrying on with their lives as usual. Isabel was going to an orgy next week. Would Grayson go with her, she wondered, her stomach turning over sickeningly. They were seeing each other on Thursday. Maybe that was the day of Isabel's party …

'So, brunch?' Grayson said as they went back to the kitchen, oblivious to the turmoil going on in Lisa's head.

She nodded. As they cooked, Lisa turned everything over in her mind, trying to sort out her feelings. She'd been so happy when she woke up this morning, still glowing from Grayson telling her he loved her. She didn't doubt his sincerity, but was it enough? The problem was she didn't know what that meant to him – whether it implied being faithful or not. She knew he wasn't in love with Isabel, and she had nothing to worry about on that score. But that hadn't stopped him sleeping with her in the past. Did he still play Isabel's games with her when he was here in London? Would he go to her orgy with her if she asked him to?

'What's next Thursday?' she asked, trying to make it sound like a casual question, while inside she was burning to know. She was glad Grayson had his back to her, watching over bacon on the stove while she set the table. She didn't think she could look as blasé as she was pretending to be. If they were facing each other, he'd see the jealousy and insecurity written on her face – all the gauche, uncool things she was feeling.

'Hmmm?' Grayson asked distractedly.

'You're seeing Isabel next Thursday?'

'Oh, yeah.' He half turned to her as he turned bacon in a pan. 'It's an opening at her gallery – an artist I'm interested in buying.'

'Oh.' At least it wasn't an orgy. But would they sleep together afterwards, she wondered. Part of her longed to ask, to push for more information. He'd always been honest with her, and she believed he would tell her the truth if she asked. But what if the truth was the last thing she wanted to hear?

She was quiet as they sat at the counter and ate, her mind in a whirl. She knew sex wasn't a big deal to him, and sleeping with Isabel wouldn't change anything. But no matter how much she tried to rationalise it, Lisa knew she could never feel that way about it. There were people who could compartmentalise sex and love, but she wasn't one of those people and never would be. Mark had always mocked her naiveté, but she couldn't help it. For her, it was all or nothing, and even though the thought of losing Grayson filled her with dread, she knew that sharing him would be worse torture in the long run. The jealousy would eat her up until there was nothing left. She couldn't let herself get consumed by him as she had by Mark, albeit in a different way. If she couldn't have him completely, she would have to end this and save herself. The thought made her so miserable, she could hardly eat.

'Lisa?'

She looked up to find Grayson frowning at her, concerned.

'What's wrong?' he asked.

'Nothing.' She smiled. 'I'm just not as hungry as I thought I was.'

'You're crying.'

She gasped and touched a hand to her face, surprised to find it wet with tears. She hadn't even realised.

'What is it?'

'I'm just—' She shook her head, putting down her fork in defeat. 'I'm just not sure this is going to work,' she said, swiping away tears with the back of her hand. 'Us,' she added as Grayson looked at her with a puzzled frown.

'What?' He reared back in shock, his eyes wide.

She bit her lip, bracing herself for a confrontation.

'But last night—you said—' he stuttered.

He looked so hurt and bewildered, her heart wrenched. 'I know, and I meant it,' she said, taking his hand. 'I love you, Grayson. I'm so happy when I'm with you. But next week, I'll be in Cornwall and you'll be here.'

'Is this about the long-distance thing? But it's only been a few weeks. We've hardly even given it a chance.' He squeezed her hand, looking into her eyes earnestly. 'We love each other. We want to be together. We can make it work.'

She sighed. 'It's not about that. It's just—' She cast around in her mind for a way to explain. 'I'm not like Isabel,' she blurted.

Grayson frowned uncomprehendingly. 'This is about Isabel?'

She took a deep, shaky breath. 'I know she didn't mind me taking her place last night. But I'm not like that. If it was the other way around, I couldn't bear it. I'd go crazy with jealousy thinking of her being with you instead of me. I know that's not very evolved, but … it's how I feel. I can't be like this with you and not mind.'

Grayson looked at her aghast as if he hardly understood what she was saying. 'Lisa,' he said slowly, 'are you saying … you think you took Isabel's place last night in my *bed*? You think if she'd gone to the dinner with me, she'd be here now instead of you?'

Lisa said nothing, but she didn't need to – her silence spoke volumes.

'Isabel and I are just friends. I thought—'

'I know,' she said quickly. 'I know you're not in love, and sex doesn't have to mean anything, but—'

She broke off, cringing inwardly as Grayson's face changed. His jaw slackened and he released her hand, leaning back in his chair. She braced herself for an angry denial. But when he finally spoke, his voice was barely above a whisper.

'You think I'm still sleeping with Isabel?'

'I don't know,' she said with a helpless shrug. 'I don't know, and it's driving me crazy.'

He looked stricken. 'Christ!' he said, raking a hand through his hair. 'I thought you understood how I feel about you. Didn't you hear what I said last night? I love you, Lisa.'

'I love you too, Grayson,' she said softly, reaching across to cup his face. 'So much.' She looked deeply into his eyes, wanting to erase all the hurt and confusion there. 'But I don't know if that changes anything.'

'It changes everything,' he said huskily. 'I've never felt this way about anyone before. I'm in love with you.'

'I know – and I get that what you have with Isabel is different,' she said. 'But——'

'No! It's not like that,' he said, putting his hand over hers where it rested on his face. 'I'm not sleeping with Isabel.'

'You're not?'

'No,' he said forcefully, holding her gaze. 'Not with her or anyone else.' He lifted her hand, playing with her fingers. 'I'm sorry. I thought you understood.' He gave a crooked smile. 'I guess I should have made myself clearer. I don't want anyone else, Lisa. Only you.'

Her breath caught at the love pouring out of his eyes, and she knew he meant every word he said. 'But ... we only see each other at weekends. All those nights you're on your own here——'

'Are torture,' he smiled ruefully.

'It's the same for me,' she whispered. The relief was overwhelming. She didn't have to hold back to protect herself anymore. She could let herself love Grayson unreservedly and wholeheartedly. It gave her such a sense of freedom, she felt like whooping for joy.

He leaned in and gave her a soft, lingering kiss, pulling her bottom lip into his mouth. 'I must admit, I do spend a lot of time thinking about you,' he said, pulling back. 'Imagining you here with me, fantasising about what we'd do.'

'Really?' She grinned at him. 'Tell me more. Maybe we could make some of these fantasies come true.'

'Well, we spend a lot of time in bed,' he said, smiling. 'When we're not there, we're mostly in the shower together, or the hot tub …'

'Oh!' Lisa gasped, flushing as an image suddenly flashed across her mind – Isabel straddling Mark in Grayson's hot tub, while he pounded into her.

'Hey,' Grayson touched the space between her eyebrows, and Lisa realised she was frowning.

She shook off her gloomy thoughts. 'I never did try your hot tub,' she said, smiling up at him.

'Well, we could remedy that later, if you like,' he said, looking at her uncertainly. 'But right now, I could really do with a shower.' He raised an eyebrow suggestively at her as he stood and took her hand.

Lisa grinned and slid off her stool.

21

THAT EVENING, Grayson sat in the hot tub, steam rising into the cool night air as the water bubbled and swirled around him. He had opened a bottle of champagne and it was sitting with two glasses on the edge of the tub.

He'd felt like such a dick this morning for mentioning his hot tub fantasy. He'd regretted it as soon as the words were out of his mouth. Lisa's smile had faded, and she'd zoned out, a troubled expression in her eyes. No doubt she was remembering the first time she'd come here and had witnessed her boyfriend fucking Isabel in this very tub. It couldn't be a pleasant memory for her, no matter how she felt about Mark.

He'd tried to distract her, quickly changing the subject, and he hadn't brought it up again. He'd been surprised when she mentioned it herself, and suggested they use it after dinner.

He looked up as she stepped out through the double doors onto the patio, wearing a short white cotton bathrobe. She smiled shyly at him as she came to the side of the tub.

She untied her robe and shrugged it off, letting it drop to the tiled floor. Grayson's breath caught in his throat as the light from the lanterns shone on her naked body, illuminating her pale skin. She was literally breathtaking. His eyes roamed hungrily over her full, high breasts, the curves of her hips, the slight swell of her stomach and her long, shapely legs. He stood as she stepped towards him and held out a hand to help her into the tub, still never taking his eyes off her. He was hard already, his body stirring in response to the sight of her.

He sank back into the seat and pulled her into his lap, his hands running over her bare, slippery skin, while his lips nuzzled her face and neck.

'I want you so much,' he whispered against her skin, loving the feel of her naked body against his. God, he'd never get enough of her.

He took her breasts in his hands, caressing and fondling them as he gazed into her eyes. She moaned softly and bit down on her lip as he teased her nipples into hardened points. She wrapped her arms around him and kissed him, gasping into his mouth as he reached between her legs and began massaging her clit. He was glad to find she was already wet and ready for him because he didn't want to wait another minute to be inside her again.

With his hands at her waist, he lifted her slightly, then brought her down onto his cock. She gave him a warm, satisfied smile as he filled her, and rocked against him as he began thrusting slowly, pushing deeper and deeper inside her. He kept up the relentless massaging of her clit, and soon she was gasping and whimpering, arching backwards in his arms as she came around his cock.

'Grayson!' She screamed his name and he buried his face in her neck as he felt her pulse and throb around him, her hands clutching at his shoulders feverishly.

With a few vigorous thrusts, he joined her, gazing into her eyes as his body jerked violently and he came with a loud groan. Lisa went limp in his arms and he pulled her close, holding her tightly as their breathing calmed.

When they had both recovered, he stood and poured them champagne.

'Sorry,' he said ruefully as he handed Lisa a glass. 'You make me forget my manners. I should have offered you a drink first, but I got … distracted.'

She smiled as he sank back into the warm water beside her and they clinked glasses. 'I'm not objecting,' she said. 'It was a very nice distraction.'

Grayson sighed and relaxed back against the bench, putting an arm around her. He kissed her forehead and she lay her head on his shoulder. 'I wish you could be here with me all the time,' he said. He wished he could ask her to come and live with him. But he shouldn't be greedy. He was lucky she was here at all.

'We'd prune,' Lisa giggled, burrowing closer into the crook of his neck.

He laughed.

'You know, Isabel made me an offer,' she said. 'I showed her some of my paintings, and she wants to sell them. She even said she'd give me a show.'

'Did you tell her you're not interested in selling in London?'

'Yes, but she said I could be anonymous if I wanted. We could communicate through you, so I wouldn't have to be in London at all.'

He looked at her carefully. 'And what do you think?'

She shrugged. 'I don't know. I thought I'd jump at the chance. I mean, it seems like the perfect solution for me. But the more I think about it …'She fell silent, and he couldn't tell what she was thinking. She appeared to be wrestling with some inner conflict. He was surprised because it seemed like the perfect opportunity for her to have the artistic career she'd always wanted without threatening her peaceful, secluded life in Cornwall.

'It sounds like a great idea to me,' he said carefully, not wanting to push her. 'Best of both worlds.'

'It is,' she said, but she didn't sound convinced.

Did she still have doubts about his relationship with Isabel? Was that what was putting her off? 'So what's the problem, then?'

'It's the anonymous part,' she said finally, lifting her head to look at him. ' I want to put my name to my work. I want people to know who I am. And … I've been thinking about moving back here.'

'Moving back to London?'

To Lisa's surprise, Grayson seemed shocked and not especially pleased.

'Yes,' she said, hesitant now. She'd thought he'd be delighted. Had she read the signals wrong? Had he just been saying what he thought she wanted to hear, and now she'd called his bluff?

He looked at her in silence for a moment as though weighing something up. 'You know you can trust me, don't you, Lisa?'

'Yes,' she frowned. 'Of course.'

'You do believe me when I say I'm not sleeping with Isabel – or anyone else?'

She smiled. 'Yes, I do. Don't worry, I'm not thinking about moving back here so I can keep an eye on you.'

'Good.' He pulled her into his lap, and she relaxed back against his chest.

'It's not that. But wouldn't you like if I was living here and we could be together more?'

'Of course I would,' he said. 'But I don't want you to move back here for my sake.' He dropped a kiss on her shoulder. 'We'll work it out.'

Lisa smiled. 'You're not the only attraction London has to offer, you know,' she said teasingly. 'What makes you so sure I'd just be moving here for you?'

He laughed ruefully. 'Sorry. Blame my over-inflated ego, thanks to last night's ceremony. But don't worry – it won't last.'

Lisa sighed as his arms tightened around her, feeling perfectly at peace – sated, secure, happy. She couldn't remember when she'd felt so complete. There was just one thing missing, one thing that had been niggling her since she'd stepped off the train at Euston.

She turned in his arms so they were facing each other. 'London's my home,' she said earnestly. 'It always was, and being back here has made me realise how much I've missed it. I mean, I love my life in Porth Heron and all the friends I've made. I'll always want to have a connection to that place. But this is where I belong.'

She had always seen herself returning to London at some point, although she hadn't thought about when that might be. It was just a vague date in the future when enough time had passed for her to feel safe again, and strong enough to face Mark if she had to.

'But it's not just that,' she continued. 'Being with you last night … it made me realise some things about myself.'

'Like what?'

'I want to get my career back on track. I want to really go all in to try to make it as an artist.'

Being with Grayson last night had sparked something

inside her. Because even as her heart had burst with pride, she had been surprised to find herself experiencing a twinge of envy and dissatisfaction. Seeing the recognition and acclaim he got for his work, the respect and admiration he had earned from his peers, she had realised that it wasn't enough for her to stand on the sidelines and applaud his achievements. She wanted a bit of that for herself. She wanted her work to be praised and celebrated. She wanted to be at the centre of her world as he was at the centre of his. She felt a sharp pang of loss for the career she could have had, the career she was on her way to before Mark had sabotaged it. But it was accompanied by a flicker of determination inside her that she hadn't felt in a long time.

Maybe she would never make it in the London art world anyway. But she knew she had to try. She would go as far as her talents could take her, however far that was. Even as she thought about it now, she felt a tingling of excitement course through her, and felt a little shock of recognition as she realised what it was: ambition. She was ambitious. It was a part of herself she'd almost forgotten.

'What do you think?' she asked.

'I think it's great. But are you sure it's not too soon? Only last week you didn't even want to come to London for a single night.'

She shrugged. 'I guess I won't know until I try. But now that I'm here, I've got some perspective and it doesn't seem so scary. I think I'd built it up in my head and blew it all out of proportion. You were right – London's a big place. I don't have to worry about bumping into Mark around every corner. Even if I did, he's with someone else now. We've both moved on.' She huffed out a laugh. 'He probably doesn't give me a second thought anymore.'

Grayson frowned, concerned. 'Just don't rush into anything,' he said.

'I won't. I haven't even decided for sure yet. I'll see how I feel this week.'

He nodded. 'There's no hurry. London will be here for you whenever you're ready. And so will I.'

<h1 style="text-align:center">22</h1>

<hr>

'I wish I'd known you were going to be here for the week,' Grayson said the next morning at breakfast. 'I could have moved things around so I could spend more time with you.'

She had got up to share toast and coffee with him before he left for work. She was still in her robe, but he was dressed in a dark suit and crisp white shirt, and had a day of planning meetings ahead.

'It's fine,' Lisa smiled. Much as she'd love to spend more time with Grayson, part of her was glad that he was going to work, and this week would be more like everyday life than a holiday. It would give her a better idea of how she felt about being back in London, just living day to day without Grayson constantly by her side.

'I was thinking of looking up some old college friends while I'm here.' She looked at him cautiously, instinctively anticipating a fight.

'That sounds like a good idea.' He smiled at her.

Lisa smiled back. When was she going to stop doing that? She should have known Grayson wouldn't have a

169

problem with her looking up her friends. 'I may not even be able to find them. We lost touch when …' She broke off. When Mark drove them away. When she let him. She felt bad that she hadn't stood up for herself more; that she hadn't stuck up for her friends. 'We sort of drifted apart and I haven't seen them in ages,' she finished sadly.

'Well, I'm sure they'd love to hear from you,' Grayson said. 'They must miss you.'

'Do you think so?'

'Of course. Anyone would miss you, Lisa.'

She sighed. 'I'm not even sure where to start. I mean, I know where they used to live, but chances are they've moved by now.' They might not even be in the country anymore.

'If they were college friends, they're artists, right?' Grayson drained his coffee and got up to leave. 'You could ask Isabel if she knows anything.'

'Good idea,' she smiled, brightening. 'I'll start there.'

Later that morning, Lisa felt a mixture of excitement and trepidation as she made her way to the Tube. Isabel had immediately recognised Susie's name and told Lisa that her friend was working in ceramics and shared a studio in Hoxton with several other artists.

It was a beautiful sunny day, and Lisa's mood veered between optimism and nervousness. She didn't know how pleased Susie would be to see her. They'd been so close at art college, but when she was with Mark, she'd let her friendships drop off. In the end, she had cut her friends out of her life altogether because she couldn't handle the conflict they caused with him. She had dumped people she loved to keep Mark happy, and she wouldn't blame them if they hated her for it.

She found the studio easily. It was a wide square building, the ground floor entirely glass. Lisa pushed open the door and stepped into a brightly lit shop space, where the artworks were for sale. There were a handful of customers browsing the shelves of ceramics and peering into glass-topped counters displaying jewellery. A young red-headed woman with a nose piercing and a full sleeve of tattoos on one arm stood behind a cash desk near the door.

'Hello,' Lisa said, approaching her, encouraged by the girl's welcoming smile. 'I'm looking for Susie Smith. I was told she works here.'

'Yes. Sure. Just wait here and I'll get her for you.'

'Thanks.' The girl disappeared behind a door at the far end of the room, and Lisa waited, wringing her hands nervously, her throat dry.

Moments later two people came back through the door – the redhead and Susie. Lisa's heart leapt at the sight of her familiar friendly face. The redhead waved in her direction as she said something to Susie, and then Susie was walking towards her. There was no emotion in her face as she narrowed her eyes at Lisa, frowning slightly questioningly. But as she came closer, her face suddenly lit up with recognition.

'Lisa!' She broke into a wide grin, quickening her steps. 'Oh my God, is it really you?' She stared at her wide-eyed.

Lisa smiled bashfully, and then Susie threw her arms around her and pulled her into a tight hug.

'I can't believe it's you!' she said, still grinning at Lisa as she pulled back. 'God, it's so good to see you.'

Lisa was weak with relief and happiness. She needn't have worried about her welcome. Susie hadn't changed towards her at all. She was just as friendly as if they'd seen each other only last week.

'I know,' she said sheepishly. 'It's been way too long. It's so good to see you too, Susie.'

'So, what are you up to? We have so much to catch up on. You look amazing, by the way.'

'Thanks. There's not a lot to tell.' That wasn't true, but she didn't really know where to start. 'I haven't been doing much.'

A shadow passed over Susie's face. 'Are you—are you still with Mark?' There was a tension in her voice, and Lisa could tell she was trying to sound neutral.

'No,' Lisa shook her head. 'We … broke up a while back. I'm living in Cornwall now.'

The relief in Susie's face was obvious and Lisa felt a pang of guilt. 'I'm sorry we lost touch,' she said.

'No, *I'm* sorry,' Susie said, to Lisa's surprise. 'God, we all felt so guilty about the way we stopped seeing you.'

'It wasn't your fault,' Lisa said, tears stinging her eyes. It had never occurred to her that her friends would blame themselves for letting the friendship slide.

Susie sighed. 'We should have made more of an effort – been more supportive. We were so worried about you, Lisa.' Her brow furrowed and her expression was troubled as she remembered. 'We just didn't know what to do.'

'It really wasn't your fault.'

Susie sighed. 'Well, we obviously have a lot of catching up to do.' She glanced at her watch. 'Can you do lunch?'

'Yes! Lunch would be great.' Lisa couldn't believe it had been that easy. She was bubbling with happiness as Susie went to get her coat and tell her co-workers where she was going.

They went to a little cafe near the studio and ordered BLTs, but they were so busy talking, they barely ate, their sentences overlapping as they tried to catch up on a couple of years in the space of an hour. Lisa was hardly aware of time passing as they chattered, falling easily back into an old familiarity. It felt like only yesterday since they'd last seen each other, and the time flew by as they talked and talked, flitting giddily from one subject to the next – Susie's move into ceramics, Lisa's recent painting, the current London art scene. Susie filled her in on what their mutual friends were doing.

'So when did you and Mark split up?' she asked eventually.

'Around March. We didn't exactly split up,' Lisa admitted, fidgeting nervously under the table. 'I left him. I just walked out one day. I sent him a text and didn't tell him where I was going. I suppose I ran away, really. He was—' Her voice caught, and she felt a lump in her throat as she tried to explain what had happened with Mark.

'He was an asshole,' Susie said, leaning forward and taking Lisa's hand, smiling gently.

'Yeah,' Lisa gave a relieved laugh. 'It just took me a while to figure that out. Way too long.'

'Don't beat yourself up about it. You got there in the end. And you went to Cornwall?'

'Yeah, I've been living there most of this year. But I'm thinking of moving back to London soon. I love it there, but—'

'You were always a London girl at heart.'

'Yeah,' Lisa smiled. 'And I've started painting again – seriously. Isabel Salas has offered me a show.'

Susie gave a low whistle, her eyes widening. 'So you're back to take the London art scene by storm!'

Lisa laughed. It was something they had all talked about endlessly in the old days – half joking, half serious. 'I'm going to give it a try,' she shrugged.

'Have you seen Daniel?'

'No. You were the only one I knew where to find. You still see each other?'

'All the time! Right, we have to arrange a big night out – the three musketeers reunited!'

Lisa giggled. 'That sounds really good.' She felt like her old self again – young, carefree and light-hearted. 'I did see Rose not that long ago,' she said. 'Just before I left London.'

Susie made a face. They had never got along. 'She was doing well earlier this year,' she said. 'I saw her show at Gallery Six. It was really good. But I haven't heard anything of her since then, now that I think about it.'

Lisa felt a twinge of disquiet. 'Apparently she's with Mark now,' she said.

They exchanged a meaningful look.

Susie frowned. 'Well, you know I was never Rose's biggest fan, but she doesn't deserve that. I wouldn't wish Mark on my worst enemy.' She gave Lisa a wary look as if afraid she had over-stepped the mark.

But Lisa smiled in response and agreed. 'No. Me neither. But maybe he'll be different with her,' she said, trying to shake off her uneasiness. 'And it might do her career a lot of good.'

'It didn't do anything for yours,' Susie said, her lip curling in disgust.

'No,' Lisa said softly.

'Anyway, let's not waste another second talking about Mark. When will we get together? How long are you in London for?'

'Just for the week at the moment.'

'How about drinks Friday? Ooh, I can't wait to tell Daniel that I've seen you,' Susie said, suddenly grasping Lisa's arm excitedly.

Lisa grinned. 'Drinks Friday sounds good.'

They had lost track of time as they chatted, and Susie suddenly realised with a shock that it was after three. 'Oh my God, I have to get back!' she said with a startled look at the clock.

Lisa walked back to the studio with her, and after they had exchanged numbers and arranged to meet on Friday, they parted. Susie pulled her into a fierce hug again in the doorway, and Lisa noticed her eyes were shining with tears as she pulled away.

'See you on Friday,' she said, her voice a little croaky.

'Can't wait,' Lisa said. She realised her own eyes were welling with tears as she turned to go.

As she walked to the tube, she let tears flow down her cheeks unchecked, too overcome with emotion to control them. She couldn't believe she was getting her friends back. After years of desolation, her life was panning out the way she'd always dreamed it would – she had work, friends, a beautiful man who loved her. She couldn't quite believe that she could have it all. As she reached the station the sun suddenly burst out from behind a cloud and she looked up, grinning at the sky as she wiped away her tears. She felt like the luckiest girl in the world.

Instead of feeling nervous and dreading telling Grayson about her day, she couldn't wait for him to come home so she could share it with him. As soon as she heard his key in the lock, she bounded out to the hallway and threw herself into his arms, smiling at him happily.

'Well, no need to ask how today went, I guess,' he said, grinning back at her as he wrapped his arms around her. They kissed as he kicked the door closed behind him, dropping a portfolio case on the floor with a thud.

Finally they pulled apart.

'I take it you found your friend, then?' he asked, smiling at her as he slid his arm around her waist and they went into the library.

'Susie, yes,' Lisa said, flopping onto the sofa.

'And?' he asked softly as he sat beside her. 'It went well?'

Lisa nodded. 'She was so happy to see me,' she said, almost wonderingly.

'Of course she was,' Grayson said. 'I told you she would be.'

'We're going out for drinks on Friday – with Daniel too.'

'That's great!'

Lisa smiled. She knew she could ask him to come along if she wanted to, and he'd be happy to join them. But she also knew that he was happy for her to have a night out with her old friends and didn't expect to be invited. It was so … normal, she thought delightedly. Her life was wonderfully, beautifully ordinary, and she loved it.

23

THE MORE LISA thought about moving back to London, the more she knew that deep down it was what she wanted. The idea of starting to build a career as an artist was exciting. If it took off, she may even be able to make a living doing what she loved. It was what she'd always wanted. She'd be close to Grayson and able to share his life fully, with no more long separations. She could see Susie and Daniel again. She'd have friends, a relationship and a shot at achieving the professional success she aspired to. It was the life she'd been on the brink of years ago before she met Mark and got steered off course, and she felt the same heady thrill when she contemplated it now as she had then. Life seemed full of promise and possibility.

Of course, Mark was the one major stumbling block in all this. She couldn't hide from him forever if she wanted to be part of the London art scene. She would come to his attention sooner or later. Did she have the strength to face him? Was she crazy to even contemplate it? Only a few days ago, the idea of coming to London had terrified her, even though there was almost no chance of bumping into him. She'd ruled it out without a second thought.

But now that she was here, she felt different. She wasn't the same cowering, insecure girl who'd run away six months ago. She had changed. In Cornwall she'd healed and rediscovered her sense of self. She'd reclaimed her self-respect and learned to stand on her own two feet.

In the following days, when Grayson was at work, she would walk the streets alone, testing how she felt about being there. She walked around Hampstead, past the house she used to share with Mark, and tried to imagine coming face to face with him. Would she be able to hold her nerve with him now, or would she regress to the pathetic, timid creature she'd been before? Even though the memories that house threw up made her ache with sadness for the lost, lonely girl she'd been then and the miserable life she'd lived there, she found she didn't quail at the thought of seeing Mark now. The idea of him no longer terrified her. She felt confident she could face him when the time came.

Everything she loved and wanted most in the world was here in London. It was where Grayson lived; it was the centre of the art world; it was where her grandparents were buried. The streets echoed with her childhood memories. London was where she belonged, and she was ready to come home.

Grayson was pleased when she told him, though he tried not to appear too eager. 'If you're sure it's what you want,' he said, but she could tell he was making an effort to sound offhand. He didn't want to influence her decision.

'I am,' she said. 'I'm not letting Mark rule my life anymore.'

'You really wouldn't be doing it for me?' he asked, a slow smile spreading across his face.

'No.' She shook her head slowly, holding his gaze so he would know she was telling him the truth. 'You're just a bonus.' She leaned in and kissed him, and their lips clung together lingeringly.

'So, what do you think?' she asked, pulling back.

'I can't wait,' he grinned. 'When do you plan to move?'

She thought. 'As soon as possible. I'll have to wait until Martha finds someone to replace me in the cafe. I don't want to leave her in the lurch. I'll have to give notice for my flat too. So I suppose in about a month. Then I'll have to find a job here, and somewhere to live—'

Grayson took her hand. 'Move in with me,' he said. 'Please.'

Lisa was torn. She would like nothing better than to live with Grayson. But she didn't want to be financially dependent on him. He was looking at her anxiously.

'I'd love to live with you,' she said, and his face lit up with a smile. He was leaning in to kiss her, but she held up a finger, halting him. 'On condition that I pay my way,' she said.

Grayson sighed. 'Well, I don't have a mortgage.'

'I'll pay my share of the bills, then, and contribute to the groceries and so forth. We'll split everything down the middle – fifty/fifty.'

Grayson hesitated. 'You don't earn as much as me. That doesn't seem fair.'

'I'll still be saving on rent,' Lisa said.

'How about eighty/twenty?'

'Fine,' Lisa shrugged, 'as long as I'm paying the eighty.'

'No way.'

'Fifty is as low as I'm prepared to go. Take it or leave it.'

Grayson gave an exasperated sigh. 'You drive a hard bargain. Okay.' He nodded. 'If that's what it takes for you to move in, you've got yourself a deal.'

Lisa grinned, holding out her hand to shake on it, but Grayson pulled her into a kiss instead.

'I'll have to find a studio too,' she said when they pulled apart. 'I can ask Susie about that. She might know of somewhere.' Now that the decision was made, she was excited and couldn't wait to start making plans for this new phase of her life.

'If you're going to be paying rent on studio space, maybe I should let you off the bills,' Grayson said.

'No, we made a deal,' Lisa grinned. 'You kissed on it. You can't back out now.'

Lisa couldn't wait to see Daniel and Susie again and tell them that she was moving back to London. On Friday she met them in a bar near Susie's studio. It was jam packed with the after-work crowd kicking off the weekend, and the atmosphere was lively and high-spirited. Daniel was as overjoyed to see her as Susie had been, and pulled her into a fierce bear hug, squeezing her so tightly she could hardly breathe. After jostling for drinks at the crowded bar, they sat together at a long, scrubbed wooden table.

'Cheers!' Daniel said as they clinked glasses. 'This is like old times.'

'It is,' Lisa said, grinning at him over the rim of her glass. The three of them had spent so many Friday nights like this when they were in college. It seemed such a long time ago, but as they talked and talked, catching up on each other's lives and filling in the missing years, it started to feel like they'd never been apart.

'We should do this more often,' Lisa said.

'Well, whenever you're in town, it's a date,' Daniel smiled.

'Yeah,' Susie said. 'Now that we've got you back, we're not going to let you get away again.'

'Absolutely not,' Daniel said. 'I still can't believe you're really here.'

'Well, now that we're all together,' Lisa said, 'there's something I want to ask you. Do either of you know of a studio that's available for rent?'

Daniel looked puzzled, but Susie got it immediately. Her face broke into an ear-splitting grin. 'Oh my God, you're moving back!' she squealed.

Daniel's eyes widened in delight and he beamed at her. 'Really?'

Lisa nodded slowly, grinning back at them. 'Yep.'

'Oh my God, this is fantastic!' Daniel said excitedly. 'There's a space available in my building.'

'Really? Where is it?' Since she had last seen him, Daniel had forged a modestly successful career for himself as a painter, supplementing his income by doing freelance book cover design.

'In Limehouse. Hang on.' He got out his phone and started thumbing through it. 'This is it,' he said, holding it out to Lisa and showing her a listing on a property website for the vacant studio.

Lisa took the phone from him and studied the details. The rent was two hundred and fifty pounds a month, and the studio looked ideal.

'It's a great place,' Daniel said. 'The landlord's a decent guy, and the rent's pretty reasonable for the loca-tion. It's not easy to get somewhere so central.'

'It looks perfect,' Lisa said, handing the phone back to him.

'We could be neighbours,' Daniel said, grinning

excitedly.

'Well, I think this calls for another round of drinks,' Susie said, crashing her empty glass onto the table. 'My shout,' she said, getting up.

The next day Daniel took Lisa to view the studio.

'I know you're not moving back to London immediately,' he told her on the way there, 'but if you want it, you should probably take it straight away and pay a deposit. Places like this are hard to find and they don't come up that often.'

The studio was perfect, and she already felt excited about working there as she looked around. It was on the top floor of the building, a large, bright room flooded with light.

'If you need help making up your mind,' Daniel said, 'the pizza at the place across the road is to die for.'

'Well, that would definitely swing it,' Lisa said. 'But I've already made up my mind. I'll take it,' she told the estate agent.

<h1 style="text-align:center">24</h1>

LISA GAVE Martha her notice as soon as she got back to Porth Heron, and Martha found a replacement for her before the month was up. It was a bittersweet time as she wound up her life in the little village that would always have a special place in her heart. She was looking forward to moving in with Grayson and starting her new life in London, but she was sad to be saying goodbye to the friends who had been such an important part of her life. She would always be grateful to them and to this place for the second chance they had given her. Together they had helped her to heal and start over.

Katya and Martha were sorry she was leaving, but not surprised. It seemed that after meeting Grayson, they had both decided it was only a matter of time before she would move back to London to be with him.

'Just don't forget about us,' Katya sniffed as they said goodbye. Grayson had driven down the day before, and this time, Lisa was getting the flight back to London with him. Most of her belongings had already been sent to

London. Martha and Katya had come to help her pack up the last of her things and wave them off.

'Don't worry, I'll keep in touch. Anyway, Grayson's parents are near here and we'll be visiting them often. I'll come and see you guys whenever we're down here.' It made it easier to leave knowing that she'd be back regularly.

'And you're both welcome to come and stay with us anytime,' Grayson said.

She was glad that her first few weeks in London were too busy to allow her time to brood, as she was immediately thrown into preparations for her show at the end of the month. Luckily, she didn't have to find a job right away. She had been working most of her time in Porth Heron and she had been careful with her money, so she still had some savings to live on while she concentrated on painting. She spent long days in her studio, putting finishing touches to the pieces for her show, and she worked closely with Isabel, doing what she could to help raise her profile ahead of the opening.

Isabel had been thrilled when Lisa told her she wanted to take her up on her offer. She had immediately swung into action, organising catalogues and invitations, and helping Lisa make the final selection of paintings. She was a powerhouse of energy, and her excitement about launching Lisa as a new artist was inspiring. Despite working harder and longer than she'd ever worked in her life, Lisa felt energised and invigorated by it rather than exhausted.

She'd never been happier. Living with Grayson was bliss. She loved her new studio, and it was wonderful having time to concentrate on her art. She was looking forward to putting it out in the world, though a little nervous about how it would be received. But whenever she had a wobble and doubted herself, Isabel's faith in her boosted her confidence. She just hoped she could do it justice.

The only cloud on the horizon as the big day approached was the thought of seeing Mark again. So far she had managed to avoid bumping into him since coming back to London, even though she had visited Isabel's Mayfair gallery many times. She had even hung around the area longer than necessary, half hoping that she would run into him and get it over with. Now it seemed likely that the first time she'd see him would be at her show. She wondered how he'd felt when he got the invitation.

'I don't have to invite Mark if you don't want me to,' Isabel had said when they were discussing the guest list.

'Wouldn't that be weird?'

'Well, he would usually come to openings at my gallery,' Isabel shrugged. 'But if you don't want him there ....'

'No, I want you to invite him,' she'd said. 'The London art world is pretty small, so I'll have to face him sometime. It might as well be now.' She didn't want to be a coward. Besides, it would put her mind at rest if she saw him with Rose and could reassure herself that they were a couple now and he had moved on.

'Well, Grayson and I will be there with you,' Isabel said kindly.

'I know,' Lisa said, smiling at her. 'That means a lot.'

The weeks flew by in a blur of activity, and before she knew it, the big night arrived. Despite all the planning and preparation, Lisa still didn't feel ready as she sipped a glass of champagne, watching the guests start to stream into the gallery.

'Nervous?' Grayson asked, putting an arm around her and pulling her into his side. He gave her a soft kiss on her temple.

'Yes,' she breathed.

'You don't have to be,' he said. 'The show is amazing. They're going to love it.'

Lisa smiled at him shakily. But the truth was, she was less nervous about the show going well than she was about seeing Mark again. Her heart was thudding in her chest and her palms were clammy as she watched the door. She tried to turn away, to focus on something else, but her eyes were always drawn back to the entrance. The anticipation was agony. She wished he would just come and get it over with.

And then suddenly he was there. Her skin prickled and her heart leapt into her throat as he walked in, his arm around Rose's waist. Her eyes flew to Rose. Was she imagining it, or was her smile a little forced and tense? They looked every inch the glamorous, successful couple and probably no one in the room but her would question if they were really as relaxed and happy together as they appeared. But all she could see was the slightly pinched look to Rose's features, the tightness of Mark's grip around her narrow waist. Rose was wearing a very revealing dress, the plunging neckline slashed almost to her waist, showing off her waifishly thin body. It was a marked departure from her usual arty, bohemian style. Her quirky individuality was gone, and she looked chic and sophisticated, but older than her years. Mark appeared suave and genial as he surveyed the room, but his eyes became flinty as they came to rest on Lisa, and she felt paralysed by the intensity in his gaze.

She was relieved when Isabel moved forward to greet them, diverting his attention away from her. Mark smiled easily as Isabel welcomed them and handed them drinks. Then they were coming towards her. Lisa steeled herself as they approached, grateful when Grayson slid an arm lightly around her waist.

'I don't need to introduce you to our wonderful artist,' Isabel said to them.

'Lisa,' Mark nodded at her in greeting, a sardonic twist to his lips.

'Hello, Mark.' His eyes burned into hers with such intensity, she had to look away. 'Hi, Rose,' she turned to the girl with a smile. 'Thank you both for coming.'

'I wouldn't have missed it for the world,' Mark said, his eyes scanning the room briefly. 'Congratulations!' He raised his glass of champagne to her.

'Thanks.'

'Yes, well done,' Rose said, a glint of triumph in her smile as she nestled closer to Mark. 'We've heard great things from Isabel.' There was something smug in the 'we' and the way she curled herself into Mark's body that Lisa knew was meant to unsettle her and make her jealous. But Lisa had once been exactly where Rose was now, and all she could feel was pity.

'Grayson,' Mark greeted him with a cursory nod, then proceeded to introduce him to Rose.

'Nice to meet you, Rose,' Grayson shook her hand. 'I hear you're a very talented artist yourself.'

'Yes, what are you working on these days?' Lisa asked her. 'Last time I saw you you were about to have your first solo show.'

Lisa recognised the nervous glance Rose threw Mark with a sinking heart.

'Oh, I'm taking a bit of a break at the moment,' she said airily. 'I need some time out to … develop.'

Lisa recognised that line all too well. It was Rose's voice, but they were Mark's words. 'Well, don't leave it too long,' she said. 'Sometimes you just need to dive in and put it out there.'

Rose gave her a sour smirk. 'Really, Lisa? One show and you consider yourself an expert, qualified to dole out career advice to the rest of us?'

'Oh, no – I didn't mean it like—'

But with a toss of her head, Rose stalked off before she could finish.

'Rose didn't do herself any favours by putting her work out prematurely,' Mark said coldly. 'It's not helpful to rub her nose in it.'

Lisa gasped. 'I wasn't—' she protested hotly. 'I didn't mean—'

Mark smiled. 'No, I'm sure you didn't mean it like that, Lisa. I know you don't have a spiteful bone in your body. But it's a bit of a sore point with Rose. She's very sensitive about it. So you'd be doing her a kindness if you didn't needle her about her career, especially when you're doing so well.'

Lisa nodded dumbly as Mark moved off to look at the paintings and Isabel brought more guests over to meet her. She hardly knew what she was saying, her mind still spinning from her encounter with Mark, going over all the things she should have said. She couldn't believe how easy it was for him to wrong-foot her still, leaving her speechless and gasping, hardly knowing what she'd said or what she'd meant by it. Had she come off as bitchy to Rose? It was unintentional, but maybe she *had* sounded like she was lording it over her now that she was having some success, while Rose's star seemed to be in the descendent.

'You didn't say anything wrong,' Grayson murmured in her ear. 'Don't pay any attention to him.'

She turned to him, dazed. He was right. She mustn't let Mark get into her head and manipulate her as he always had. She was distracted by Daniel and Susie arriving, squealing with excitement as they hugged and congratulated her.

'Ugh, what's he doing here?' Daniel said, throwing daggers looks at Mark.

Lisa shrugged. 'I was going to have to see him some time. Might as well get the kudos of having him come to my show.'

'Well, just don't let him kill your buzz,' Susie said.

'Don't worry,' she smiled. 'I won't.'

'Come on, Dan,' Susie said, grabbing his hand. 'Let's go and say hi. He must have missed us dreadfully. I'm sure he'll be dying for a catch-up.'

Lisa giggled as she dragged Daniel off.

The gallery quickly filled up, and Lisa was kept busy talking to guests and answering questions about her work. But she was always aware of where Mark was in the room, without even seeking him out. She knew she was being cowardly, but she made sure she was always on the opposite side of the gallery to him or surrounded by other people. She didn't want to be on her own with him. She did want to speak to Rose in private, though, and she watched for an opportunity to get her alone. It wouldn't be easy because she always stayed close to Mark. But just as she finished talking to a potential buyer, she spotted Rose standing alone at the other side of the room. Now was her chance.

25

'IT's good to see you again, Lisa.'

She gasped, and turned around. She'd been so preoccupied with watching Rose, she hadn't heard Mark come up behind her.

'You look well,' he said, his eyes raking over her body, lingering on the soft swell of her breasts and the curve of her hips. 'The work is very good.' He nodded to the painting on the wall behind her. 'I'm impressed.'

'Thanks,' she breathed.

'You're very talented. But of course, that's no surprise to me. I always knew you had it in you.'

Lisa frowned. 'You told me I wasn't good enough.'

He cocked his head to the side and gave her a pitying smile. 'Come on, Lisa. We both know that's not true. I told you you needed to develop – and I gave you the time and space to do that.'

She stared at him aghast. She couldn't believe he was still trying to gaslight her. For a moment he almost made her doubt herself and question the truth of what had happened between them.

190

'And I was right,' he said, looking around at the paintings. 'You've put in the time, and it's paid off.'

She shook her head. 'You didn't support me. You sabotaged my career. You took my paintings and pretended you were trying to sell them, and instead you buried them—'

He sighed. 'Because you weren't ready. You were always too impatient. I didn't want a little early success to go to your head and ruin the career you could have. Those paintings weren't—'

'Don't tell me they weren't good enough,' she said vehemently. 'Because they were. *I* was good enough.'

He shrugged. 'Yes, they probably would have sold. But would you really have been happy with just being "good enough"? I couldn't let you settle for that when I knew you were capable of so much more. I just wanted you to achieve all your potential, Lisa. Maybe your work was "good enough" then. But this – this is magnificent.'

Once more she was rendered speechless, and she was relieved when Isabel found her and pulled her away to meet someone. She'd forgotten just how insidious Mark could be, what a gift he had for twisting things until you hardly knew which way was up. She was more determined than ever to find an opportunity to speak to Rose. She had to try and warn her. It would probably fall on deaf ears, but at least she wouldn't have it on her conscience that she didn't try.

She kept a watch on Rose out of the corner of her eye, and when she saw her going towards the bathroom, she excused herself as soon as she could and followed her.

When she entered, Rose was standing in front of the washbasins, touching up her lipstick in the mirror. Lisa glanced around quickly, relieved to find they were alone.

'Hi, Rose,' she said, with a sidelong glance in the

mirror. She took the pins out of her hair and began to rearrange it as an excuse to linger.

'Hi.' Rose gave her a wary glance.

'I'm sorry if I said anything to upset you earlier. I didn't mean to sound patronising—'

'Good. Because I have Mark guiding my career now. I really don't need advice from the likes of you.'

Lisa decided to ignore her rudeness. She had more important things to say to her. 'So, you and Mark are … together now?' she asked. 'How long have you been seeing each other?'

'A couple of months,' Rose said with a little frown. She appeared surprised by Lisa's interest.

'Is it serious?'

Rose raised her eyebrows and shot Lisa a cold glance. 'Not that it's any of your business, but yes, it is. We're living together, if you must know,' she added with a haughty look.

That was quick. 'Still, it's early days, isn't it?' Lisa said. She was aware of how intrusive she was being, but she forced herself to continue. 'I know how Mark can sweep you off your feet, but … don't let him rush you into things.'

'What are you trying to say?' Rose narrowed her eyes.

'I just mean Mark can be pretty … intense. Don't let him bully you.'

'Bully me?' She put her hands on her hips. 'What's your problem, Lisa? Are you jealous?'

'*Jealous*? No, of course not!'

'Good, because you threw Mark over, and if you regret it now, that's tough. But trying to cause trouble between us or split us up is just pathetic, especially after what you did to him—'

Lisa frowned. 'What do you mean? What is it you think I did to him?'

'Oh, I know what you did, Lisa. He told me how you cheated on him with Grayson, and then disappeared without even a word – just a couple of lines of text.' Her lip curled contemptuously.

'I didn't cheat on him with Grayson or anyone else,' Lisa protested. She didn't want to go into the details of what had happened with Grayson, but she couldn't let that pass.

'Whatever,' Rose said with a dismissive shrug. 'You dumped him and he's moved on. He's over you and he's with me now. We're very happy together, so just leave us alone, please.'

Lisa nodded silently. But she felt compelled to say something more. 'How are Anna and Nikki these days?' she asked, trying a different tack.

Some emotion Lisa couldn't place flickered across Rose's face. 'I haven't seen much of them lately,' she said, but there was an air of bravado about her casual shrug.

Lisa felt a chill creep up her spine. Mark was alienating Rose's friends like he had hers, isolating her so she had no one to turn to. He'd already persuaded her to put her career on hold, exactly as he'd done with her. She shivered. 'Is that Mark's doing?' she asked tentatively.

'No!' Rose almost screamed the word in exasperation. 'God, Lisa!' She turned to her, her face a mask of fury. 'Mark warned me you might do this, you know.'

'Do what?'

'Try to turn me against him. What's your problem, exactly? Is it that you can't stand seeing him happy with someone else? Or do you regret leaving him for Grayson and want him back?' She heaved an exasperated sigh. 'He told me you were spiteful and jealous, but I never expected you to be this vindictive.'

Lisa sighed. It was hopeless. Mark had already poisoned Rose's mind against her. There was nothing she could say that would convince her.

'I don't have any problem,' she said quietly. 'I'm very happy with Grayson, and I don't regret leaving Mark for one second. I just wanted to warn you to be careful. He's a controlling, abusive man. Believe me, I know – and I hope you never have to find out for yourself.' She took a deep, shaky breath. 'Just … take care of yourself, Rose. And if you ever need a friend or just someone to talk to, feel free to call me.' She took a card out of her bag and held it out to her.

Rose stared at it. 'What's this about – all this pretence of being concerned for me? We're not friends, Lisa. We've never been friends.'

'You're right,' Lisa said. 'We haven't been friends. But if you ever need help and you have no one else to turn to, I will honestly do my best to be a friend to you.'

Before Rose could say anything else, she put the card down on the sink surround, turned on her heel and left the bathroom.

'You were right,' she said to Grayson later as they watched the last guests trail out of the gallery. 'She didn't want to hear it.'

'You did all you could,' he said, rubbing her arm comfortingly.

'I just wish I could have convinced her.'

'I know. But don't let it spoil your night.' The show had been a great success, and one by one red dots had appeared on painting after painting throughout the evening. She looked around, and there didn't seem to be a single one unsold.

Grayson slid an arm around her waist, pulling her closer to his side. 'It's been quite a night,' he murmured softly in her ear. 'You're a star. I'm so proud of you.'

Lisa relaxed, curling into him, comforted by the solid warmth of his body. Desire spiked deep inside her as she breathed in the smell of his aftershave at his neck. She closed her eyes, laying her head on his shoulder.

'Tired?' he asked.

She shook her head. 'Not at all. Just ready for bed.' She looked meaningfully into his eyes, and his pupils darkened.

She tried to put her worries about Rose out of her head as Grayson bent to kiss her. He was right – she'd tried and there was nothing more she could do. She wouldn't let Mark ruin this wonderful night.

'Come on,' Grayson said. 'Let's go home.'

She gave Isabel a hug on the way out. 'Thank you so much for everything.'

'Thank *you*,' Isabel said. 'You're the star. Everyone's crazy about your work, Lisa. I can't tell you how many people asked me where you've been hiding all this time.'

At least the worst was over, she thought, as she got into the back of the car beside Grayson. She was satisfied that Mark was with Rose now. He'd accepted they were over and moved on. He was still trying to twist things, still lying about what had happened between them to anyone who would listen. But she didn't have to deal with that anymore, and she wasn't going to waste another second worrying about it. He was out of her life and she could put him well and truly behind her.

26

LISA WENT to work in her studio the following day full of enthusiasm, still buzzing from the success of her show. It had completely sold out, and Isabel had had several queries already about when further work would be available from her.

'Get painting!' she'd told Lisa on the phone that morning. 'You're in demand. I like to give my customers what they want, and what they want is you.'

She was only too happy to oblige. If this kept up, she would be able to paint full-time. It would be a dream come true to earn a living doing what she loved.

She was happily engrossed in her work, making preliminary sketches for a new painting, when she was interrupted by a tap on her door. She glanced at the clock, surprised to find it was almost lunchtime already. Daniel had promised to buy her lunch at the pizza place across the road to celebrate last night's triumph.

She hopped off her stool and wiped her hands on a rag.

'Delivery for you!' When she threw open the door,

Daniel was hidden behind an enormous bunch of red roses, only his legs visible.

He thrust them at Lisa and she took them from his outstretched hand.

'Thanks!' she gasped in surprise. They were beautiful – there must have been at least two dozen perfect blooms on long graceful stems.

'Someone loves you,' Daniel grinned as he followed her inside. 'No need to guess who they're from.'

'No,' Lisa smiled, touched by the gesture. It gave her a warm glow knowing that Grayson was thinking about her when they were apart.

'You ready for lunch?'

She nodded. 'I'll just stick these in water and I'll meet you downstairs in five.'

'See you then.' Daniel turned on his heel and left.

Lisa hugged the bouquet to her in both arms, breathing in the scent of the flowers. It was such a lovely surprise, so thoughtful of Grayson. She laid them carefully on the workbench, then went to find something to put them in. She filled a clean bucket with water – it would have to do for now. She took the card and headed for the door, smiling in anticipation as she pulled it out of its little envelope. But she stopped dead in her tracks and her face fell as she read the message:

Congratulations on last night, Lisa! You were stunning.
All my love, Mark x

She felt suddenly queasy, her stomach turning over. She glanced at the flowers and they appeared malevolent now, threatening – like poisoned roses from a fairytale. There were too many of them, and they were too big and overbearing, sucking all the air out of the room. Her first instinct was to grab them and throw them in the bin on the way out. But what if Daniel saw her? He thought they were from Grayson, and she didn't want to tell him the truth – it would only worry him. She'd think about it later. She sighed as she pulled the door behind her and went downstairs to meet Daniel.

She felt more relaxed after a glass of wine and a gossipy lunch with Daniel, and Mark's flowers didn't seem quite so menacing when she returned to her studio in the afternoon. She told herself she had over-reacted and there was nothing sinister in it. It wasn't as if he'd sent her flowers out of the blue. He was just congratulating her on her show in his professional capacity as an important dealer. He would do the same for any artist whose show he'd attended. She knew he would. She'd ordered the flowers herself sometimes when she'd worked at his gallery. It didn't mean anything, she told herself, studying the card again and again, going over the words repeatedly, as if she could decipher some hidden meaning in them.

But no matter how hard she tried, she couldn't convince herself. Why did he say '*you* were stunning' – not the work, not the paintings – if he was congratulating her on her show? It wasn't about the opening, it was about her. *You, love*, the little 'x' by her name– the words leapt out at her, and they looked all wrong.

Finally, frustrated with herself for wasting so much time fretting over it, she tore the card up into little pieces and tossed it in the bin. She had resolved that she'd never let Mark control or manipulate her again, and here she was doing just that – letting him preoccupy her thoughts and take her from her work. If that was what he hoped to achieve by sending her the flowers, he wasn't going to win. She wouldn't let him unsettle her.

Maybe he wanted her to get in touch to thank him. She wouldn't. She'd take the flowers with her when she was leaving and give them to someone on the way home – one of the girls in the coffee shop downstairs would appreciate them – and that would be that.

'These were delivered for you earlier.' Grayson came to join her in the hall as she took off her coat.

Her heart started pounding as she looked up and saw him holding a large cellophane-wrapped bouquet.

'Oh.' She hung up her coat, looking at him warily as he held them out to her.

'They're not going to bite,' he said, laughing at her expression.

She blinked. 'No. Thanks,' she said, taking them from him. Her heart was in her mouth as she opened the envelope and dug out the little card.

'Oh, they're from Isabel,' she smiled, melting with relief as she read:

> *Congratulations on a wonderful show, Lisa! A star is born.*
> *It's a real honour to work with you, and thank you for*
> *gracing my gallery with your art.*
> *All my love, Isabel.*

'Oh, that's so sweet of her,' she said, blinking back tears. 'They're beautiful.'

'Are you okay?' Grayson frowned. 'You seem a bit tense.'

'Just tired,' she said, giving him a reassuring smile. 'I

think all the nerves and excitement are just catching up with me now.'

'How was your day?' he asked as she followed him into the kitchen.

'It was good,' she said. She wasn't going to tell Grayson about Mark's flowers. It would only make him angry and worried. 'I started a new painting.'

As the talk turned to work, she started to relax and forget about Mark. She would simply ignore him. He would get the message when he didn't hear from her, and that would be the end of it.

But the next day, there were more red roses. She was glad that she accepted the delivery herself, so Daniel didn't see them. She didn't have any illusions this time about who they were from. Reluctantly, she forced herself to read the card. Her blood ran cold when she saw what he'd written:

I have to see you, Lisa. I love you as much as ever. I'd say I love you more, but that's not possible. Call me. Mark x

She could barely breathe as she stared at the words. She felt hunted, panicked. The walls seemed to close in on her, and the room spun giddily. So much for trying to convince herself she was over-reacting. She flopped down onto a chair, gasping for breath. She'd been an idiot to think Mark would let her go so easily. Fleetingly, she longed for the peaceful seclusion of Porth Heron. Had she made a mistake coming back to London?

But no, she mustn't think like that. Everything else in her life was going so well – she wouldn't let Mark ruin it for her. She would just keep ignoring him and eventually he'd give up.

. . .

She didn't visit the studio over the weekend, and for two days she just relaxed with Grayson and almost managed to put Mark out of her mind.

But the following week, it started again. Monday brought yet more red roses, this time accompanied by a handwritten letter. Her heart pounded as she opened the envelope and unfolded a page of thick paper covered in Mark's bold handwriting.

Lisa, I've been in agony since you left me. My life is meaningless. I can't work, can't eat, can't sleep. All I can think of is you and what we had – what I lost. Please come back to me. I know I made mistakes with you in the past, but I can change. I'll do anything to get you back, but I can't live without you. I sleepwalk through the days, going through the motions. But it's not living, because I don't have you. We belong together, Lisa. You promised, remember – you said you were only mine. And I am and will always be
Yours, Mark x

Very poetic, she thought disgustedly, tossing the letter onto the bench. She felt dirty just touching it. There was a time when words like those from Mark would have meant the world to her. Now they made her feel sick and claustrophobic, like she couldn't breathe. She picked it up and tore it into little pieces, then threw the pieces in the bin.

27

Day after day more flowers and letters came until Lisa started to almost dread going to her studio. She tried to dump them without anyone noticing, but they came faster than she could get rid of them, until her little space looked more like a florist's shop than an artist's studio. It became harder and harder to ignore them and focus on her work. Their presence was overwhelming and oppressive, a constant reminder of Mark.

Should she tell someone about this, she wondered, biting her lip as she looked around at the flower-filled studio? Did it constitute harassment? It seemed ridiculous to think of going to the police because someone sent you flowers. They would probably laugh at her and tell her she should be more appreciative. She knew Grayson would want to do something about it if she told him, but she would prefer to keep him out of it and handle it herself if she could. She didn't want Mark anywhere near her relationship with Grayson.

But she had to tell someone. It was eating her up. So

she was relieved when Susie turned up unannounced at the studio on Friday afternoon.

'Oh wow!' she gasped, looking around in awe. 'Grayson's got it bad. Either that or he's cheating on you.'

'Hey, I'm joking,' she added when she caught Lisa's worried expression.

Lisa shook her head. 'It's not that.' She took a deep breath. 'They're not from Grayson.'

Susie's eyebrows shot up. 'They're not?' Her eyes widened. 'You've got someone else? Or a mysterious secret admirer maybe?' she asked teasingly.

Lisa shook her head, swallowing hard. 'No. I know who they're from.'

'Who?' Susie frowned, intrigued.

'Mark.'

Susie let her mouth drop open, stunned into silence for a moment. 'Mark?' she said finally, all the mischief going out of her eyes.

Lisa nodded. 'He's been sending them every day. Letters too.'

'Christ!' Susie flopped down onto a chair. 'He wants you back.' It wasn't a question.

'Yes,' Lisa nodded.

Susie glanced at her uncertainly, then looked around at the flowers again. 'Lisa,' she said hesitantly, 'you don't—I mean, you don't want to get back with him, do you?'

'No!' She shook her head vehemently. 'God, no.'

Susie gave a relieved sigh. 'I didn't think so, but …'

Lisa knew what she was thinking. She'd been in love with him once. She'd been a total idiot where Mark was concerned, completely taken in by him. She'd dropped her friends and given up her career, sacrificing everything to be with him. She couldn't blame Susie for doubting her.

'I don't know what to do,' she said. It was such a relief just to talk about it to someone, it already didn't seem like such a big deal.

'Have you told Grayson?'

'No.' She shook her head. 'I don't want to involve him if I can help it.'

'But this is … it's not normal behaviour, Lisa. It's harassment – stalking maybe. You have to do something to stop it.'

'I know. It's starting to really get to me. I can't concentrate on my work.'

'You won't even have any room to do it, if this keeps up much longer,' Susie laughed, lightening the atmosphere. 'I thought he was with Rose now anyway? They were together at your show.'

'Yeah, he is,' Lisa sighed. 'Which makes this even creepier.'

'God, poor Rose.'

'I know. I talked to her the other night. I tried to warn her off, but—'

'You did?' Susie's eyebrows shot up, and Lisa felt a pang of shame. Susie wasn't used to her standing up for herself or anyone else.

'Yeah, I've changed,' she said with a shaky smile.

Susie grinned. 'I like it.' She nodded approvingly. 'I mean, I loved the old Lisa, but I'm really digging this new you.'

Lisa shrugged. 'It didn't do much good anyway. She basically told me to fuck off. She accused me of being jealous.'

'Yeah, right,' Susie huffed. 'Have you kept the letters Mark sent?'

'Not the first one – I tore it up and threw it away. It didn't occur to me to keep it; that it might be—'

'Evidence,' Susie finished for her, her face hard.

'Yeah. It seems ridiculous even thinking like that, but—'

'It's not ridiculous,' Susie frowned. 'It's realistic – sensible. This sort of thing can escalate and get out of control.'

Lisa knew she was right. In a way, it did seem silly to be frightened of someone you used to live with; someone you used to love. She had felt foolish thinking of letters from an ex-boyfriend as evidence. And yet some instinct had made her see them that way, and after impulsively tearing up the first one, she had kept all the rest, along with the cards from all the flowers that had been delivered. She had even kept a record of the dates and times so that they could be easily verified by the florists. She shuddered. It was frightening to realise what she subconsciously feared.

'Are the letters threatening at all?' Susie asked.

'Not really. They're very intense, but he just keeps saying that he loves me and wants me back.' She took a deep breath. 'He says that he can't live without me, we're not meant to live without each other – stuff like that.'

'So he hasn't made any direct threats,' Susie clarified.

'No, but—'

'But there are implied threats in all this can't live without you stuff.' Susie frowned, and Lisa felt oddly comforted that she was taking this so seriously.

'Yes, that's how it feels,' she said, feeling vindicated. Those words had scared her most of all. 'And the last couple ...' She bit her lip. The last two letters had been different. The tone was more aggressive, the content sexual and explicit, verging on pornographic.

I miss your beautiful body, and the way you fucked me.
Nobody fucks like you, Lisa. Believe me, I know. I've fucked
countless other women trying to get over you, but none of

them even come close to how you make me feel. You have a unique combination of innocence and whorishness that's completely beguiling. I spend every day surrounded by beautiful things, but I've never seen anything to match the sight of you kneeling naked on the floor, your mouth filled with my cock, my cum dripping from your swollen lips. The way you'd look up at me then from beneath your eyelashes, so eager to please – you can't tell me that's not love. It makes me hard just thinking of the look in your eyes. It was love, Lisa – pure, worshipful love.

They got more graphic by the day.

You're mine, Lisa. I can't bear to think of you giving someone else what's mine. What we had was special. Just come back to me, baby and we can have it again. I miss you so much. I miss fucking your tight little ass. You were so sweetly submissive, always willing to give me whatever I wanted, ready to bear your own pain for the sake of my pleasure. You wouldn't have done that if you didn't love me. Do you do that for him? Do you let him flip you over and bury himself so deep inside you it hurts? Do you kneel on cold tile for him and let him fuck your mouth so hard it brings tears to your eyes? Does he bite your beautiful soft skin? Has he left his mark on you?

She shuddered. She couldn't bear for anyone else to see those letters and read those things about her. She hated the thought of having to show them to the police, but more than that she couldn't stand the thought of Grayson reading them. She knew that was partly why she hadn't told anyone. She had kept it to herself, hoping Mark would get the message and lose interest when she didn't respond. But instead it had got worse. Maybe that was what he wanted – to humiliate and intimidate her into keeping it to herself, so it would be like a guilty secret between them and she was colluding in her own persecution.

'Has he ever turned up here – called, tried to see you?'

'No. Not so far.' But she felt like it was only a matter of time. She had started to look behind her when she was out on the street, and her stomach dropped with dread now whenever the phone rang.

Susie sighed. 'What are you going to do?' she asked.

Lisa had been mulling over that very question before Susie turned up. Ignoring him hadn't worked. She was going to have to try a different approach.

'I have to tell him that I want this to stop. Then if he keeps it up—'

'It definitely constitutes harassment,' Susie finished for her.

Lisa nodded. 'I'm going to go and see him – confront him about it. I'm going to tell him straight out that I want it to stop.'

Susie's eyes widened in shock. 'Do you think that's wise? Couldn't you just call him?'

'I think it'll work better face to face. And what's he going to do? I'll go to the gallery, so we'll be in a public place. He won't try anything there. He'll have to maintain his perfect professional facade.'

'Are you going to tell Grayson?'

'No, not if I can help it. I really don't want anyone to see those letters, Susie. The things he wrote ...'

'Well, I think someone should go with you at least. Do you want me to come?'

'No,' Lisa shook her head. 'Thanks, but honestly, it'll be fine. I'll just talk to him, try to make him see reason.'

Susie still looked worried. 'I don't know. I don't think Mark and reason are really on speaking terms.'

Lisa gave a little laugh. 'I know what you mean. But

don't worry. We'll be at his place of work. There'll be people around. What can he do?'

28

SHE WASN'T FEELING SO brave the next day as she made her way to Mark's gallery. Her heart was in her mouth and her legs felt like lead. She was sorely tempted to back out. But she had to put a stop to his harassment, so she forced herself to carry on.

She hadn't expected Greta to be at the reception desk. That was awkward.

'Lisa!' She greeted her with a warm smile. Lisa wondered how much she knew about her and Mark's break-up. 'How nice to see you. How are you doing?'

'Great, thanks. I was wondering could I see Mark. It won't take long. I just want to talk to him to … tie up some loose ends.'

Greta picked up the phone and spoke to Mark. 'He said you can go up,' she said as she put down the receiver. 'You know where his office is?'

'Yes. Thank you.' Lisa felt shaky as she crossed the floor to the stairs. But Greta knew she was here. It wasn't as if Mark could kidnap her, she thought, trying to laugh away her nerves. Still her heart was pounding as she walked up to the first floor.

She knocked softly on the door.

'Come in,' Mark's voice boomed.

She opened the door and stepped inside, deliberately not closing it behind her.

'Lisa!' Mark sprang up from his desk and crossed the room to her. In one move he closed the door and pinned her back against it.

'Finally,' he said, reaching out to lightly caress her cheek as he looked down at her. 'I thought you'd never come.' He smiled, and Lisa's stomach turned over as she realised he'd completely misread the situation. She knew at once she'd made a huge mistake coming here alone. What had she been thinking? But it hadn't occurred to her that he could actually believe his attentions were welcome.

'You really know how to draw out the agony,' he said with a crooked smile. His face was flushed with passion. 'I've been dying here, Lisa, without a word from you.'

'Mark, stop!' She shook off his hand, and wriggled out from where she was trapped between him and the door. She took a step away from him, putting distance between them. 'I didn't come here for this.'

He frowned, his expression like thunder. 'What are you here for, then? You got my flowers? My letters?'

'Yes, I got them,' she said tightly. 'But I don't want them. I came here to tell you that you have to stop. Stop sending me flowers, stop writing to me.'

'Lisa,' he looked at her forlornly. 'Is that really all you have to say to me after all this time?' He moved closer and took her arm, his fingers digging into her flesh. 'What do you want? Just tell me and it's yours.'

'I don't want anything from you, Mark. I just want you to leave me alone.'

'You can't mean that,' he said. 'What we had – it doesn't just disappear. I've missed you so much, Lisa,' he said, his eyes glittering dangerously. 'Haven't you missed me?'

'No,' she said, appalled by how shaky her voice sounded. 'I told you we're over, Mark. I've … moved on. We both have,' she added desperately.

'Ah yes, Grayson.' He smiled nastily. 'I suppose I only have myself to blame for that. I should never have shared you.' He released his grip on her arm, but instead his hand slid down her body, brushing against the side of her breast, curling around the curve of her hip. His eyes darkened as they followed its trail. 'I should have known you couldn't handle it, that you wouldn't take it for what it was. It was just a bit of fun. You were only meant to fuck him, not run off into the sunset with him.'

'Mark,' she choked, pushing him away. 'Please stop!'

To her relief, he let her go. 'Shall I tell you something funny?' he said, striding to his desk. 'This will give you a laugh. Remember I told you I had another surprise for you when I got back from China?'

Lisa nodded wordlessly, her throat dry.

'Aren't you curious what it was?' He pulled something out of one of the drawers and slammed it shut.

She shook her head. 'It—it doesn't matter. Mark, I have to—'

But as she turned to go, he strode up to her and grabbed her arm roughly. 'It was this.' To her horror, he pulled out her hand and placed a small velvet ring box on the flat of her palm.

'Open it,' he snapped.

'No,' she shook her head, the box balanced on her outstretched hand.

He grabbed it and flipped it open, revealing a large

sapphire and diamond ring couched on a bed of white satin.

'I was going to ask you to marry me, Lisa,' he said accusingly. 'I wanted to spend the rest of my life with you. I was coming home to propose, and instead I find you've run off without a word – with him!' His lip curled in a sneer and he flung the ring box to the ground with such force that it bounced and hit off the far wall.

She flinched, and her heart pounded, feeling an old familiar terror as he raged on.

'You couldn't even be bothered to tell me in person,' he said, panting in anger. 'You just sent me a text. Do you really think that was all I deserved after all the time we'd been together?'

Lisa sagged defeatedly. 'But you wouldn't listen. I tried to tell you. So many times I tried to—'

'Really?' His voice was dripping with sarcasm as he cocked his head to the side and raised an eyebrow. 'When did you try to me tell me? When you said you loved me? Was I supposed to deduce it from that? Or maybe you tried to show me, since you're so inept with words? Hmm? When you got on your knees and sucked my cock, was that your way of telling me it was over? Really, I'm interested. When you let me fuck your ass until you couldn't stand, was that it? Did I misread the signals?'

'Stop it!' She put her hands over her ears. 'Mark, please!'

He sighed heavily, hands on his hips, his head hanging contritely. 'Sorry, baby,' he said, lifting his head, his eyes full of remorse. 'But if you weren't happy, couldn't you have just talked to me about it, instead of running off like that as if you were afraid of me? I never did anything to hurt you, did I?'

She looked at him aghast.

'Well, never more than you could stand,' he amended with a sardonic smile that made her feel sick. He took a step towards her, backing her up against the door. 'I'm sorry I shouted. I just love you so much, Lisa, it drives me crazy. You're all I want – all I've ever wanted.'

'That's not true, Mark. I was never enough for you. You wanted me to have surgery. You wanted to have sex with other people.'

' I know I made mistakes with you,' he said, curving a hand around her hip. 'But just come back to me, baby, and I promise things will be different. Please. I like the way you look now – you're sexier than ever.' His eyes roamed over her breasts. 'We can do it your way. I promise I'll never share you again. I'll never even look at another woman, if that's what you need.'

She shook her head. 'I can't listen to this,' she said, steadying her voice with an effort. 'I don't love you anymore, Mark. There's nothing else to say.' She pushed away from the door, and this time he released her. 'Stop sending me flowers, stop writing to me. It won't change anything.'

Before he could say anything else, she quickly opened the door and left, her heart pounding as she raced down the stairs to the gallery. She didn't look back, but she heard Mark's door open, and she could feel his eyes on her as she crossed the floor and made her way outside.

29

'So, when are you off to Cornwall?' Daniel asked her a week later. It was the second Friday in December, and Lisa had met up with Susie and Daniel for a pre-Christmas drink before they all went their separate ways for the holiday. They were crammed around a little table in the muggy warmth of a crowded pub festooned with tinsel and twinkling fairy lights.

'We're flying down on the twenty-third.' They were spending Christmas with Grayson's family. She was looking forward to it, though she was a little nervous about meeting his sisters for the first time. They planned to celebrate the New Year in Porth Heron, and she was excited about seeing all her old friends again. They kept in touch regularly by email and phone, but it wasn't the same as being together in person.

'It'll be good to get away,' she said, poking her straw in her drink broodingly.

'Is Mark still pestering you?' Susie asked.

She nodded. 'He's still sending letters almost every day.'

Daniel threw her a sympathetic look. He'd noticed how tense and edgy she was lately whenever they met up at the studio, and when he'd expressed concern, she'd confided in him about Mark's harassment.

Mark had stopped sending flowers since the day she went to his office, but the letters kept on coming. She still hadn't told Grayson about them. Right now she didn't want to have to think about it. She felt worn down by it, and she just wanted to get out of London and put it all out of her mind for a while. Maybe Mark would lose interest over the break …

'I still can't believe you went over there on your own to confront him,' Daniel said. 'Please don't ever do that again without bringing at least one of us for back-up.'

Lisa smiled at him gratefully. 'Don't worry, I've learned my lesson.'

'Have you seen him since?' Susie asked.

'No. But he'll be at Isabel's party tomorrow.' Isabel was throwing a lavish end-of-year bash at the gallery.

Susie pulled a face. 'Do you have to go?'

'No. Grayson's happy to skip it if I want, and I know Isabel would understand. But I feel I owe it to her to be there. Besides,' she shrugged, 'there'll be lots of people there who I *do* want to see. Hopefully I'll be able to avoid Mark for the night.'

'Good luck with that,' Daniel said.

'So, have we all finished our Christmas shopping?' Susie asked, and Lisa was grateful to her for changing the subject.

'I just have a few last-minute things to get for Grayson's family. I'll finish it tomorrow.'

'Ugh, I don't envy you,' Daniel grimaced. 'I did all my shopping online. I couldn't face those crowds.'

'You're such a Grinch!' Susie said, giving him a playful slap.

'Face it, London's a nightmare at this time of year. I can't wait to get out.'

'I love it,' Lisa said. She drained her glass.

'Weirdo! Another one?' Daniel stood and headed for the bar.

Lisa was looking forward to getting away to Cornwall this year, but she loved London in the run-up to Christmas. Everything about it was cheering and brought back happy memories – the smell of roasting chestnuts rising in wafts of steam from street vendors' stalls; the glittery shop window displays; even the crowded pavements as shoppers jostled together laden down with bags and brightly wrapped gifts.

It was most magical at night, when garlands of lights sparkled above the streets, brightly decorated pubs and restaurants glowed welcomingly in the darkness, and glamorous partygoers tumbled from black cabs and spilled out of bars like colourful birds, shivering in their finery.

'This city,' she sighed, looking out the window of the cab as she and Grayson made their way to Isabel's gallery the following evening.

'It's something else, isn't it?'

He looked devastatingly handsome in a black dinner jacket and snowy white shirt, his copper-coloured hair artfully unruly.

He took her hand. 'You okay?'

'Yeah, I'm fine.' She gave him a shaky smile. She wished she could just throw herself into the festive cheer and enjoy having a glamorous party to go to with a beautiful man by her side. But Mark's presence cast a shadow over it all.

'We don't have to stay long,' Grayson said, giving her hand a squeeze. 'Whenever you want to leave, just say the word.'

The gallery was thronged, buzzing with the hum of voices and the tinkle of champagne glasses, but Lisa's eyes were drawn to Mark as soon as they entered. She felt a frisson of nerves as he looked over and nodded hello. Rose gave her a sidelong glance, but quickly turned away and said something to Mark, drawing his attention back to her.

Isabel had worked her usual magic, and the party was as dazzling and stylish as everything she put her hand do. As the evening went on, Lisa began to relax and have fun. The champagne helped loosen her up and she enjoyed mingling with the broad mix of people that Isabel had brought together from all corners of the art world. She felt a glow of pride that she had been invited in her own right as one of Isabel's artists, and she wasn't just tagging along as Grayson's date. She was glad she hadn't let Mark put her off coming.

She found it easy to stay out of his way, and she quickly realised that she had Rose to thank for that. She seemed as determined as Lisa to keep them apart, and whenever their paths were about to cross, she would steer him off in the opposite direction or pull him away to meet someone else. It suited Lisa just fine.

But Rose must have let her guard down, because as Lisa made her way back from the bathroom, down a long, snaking corridor at the back of the gallery, suddenly Mark was standing in front of her blocking her path.

'Hello, Lisa.'

'Mark.' She nodded brusquely and tried to step past

him, but he grabbed her hand and pulled her into an alcove, pressing her up against the wall.

'You haven't spoken to me all evening. I get the feeling you've been avoiding me,' he said, his eyes glinting dangerously. 'Did you get my letters?'

'Yes, but I didn't read them. I told you I don't want them. We're over, Mark. Let me go.'

He shook his head. 'We'll never be over, Lisa. We belong to each other. You know that. You said you were mine – only mine. You promised.'

'People change. I'm not yours anymore. I never was really. People don't own each other.'

'But we belong together. We were made for each other. I can't live without you. And you're not supposed to live without me. Surely you see that.'

She swallowed hard. 'I can't listen to this anymore,' she said, trying to keep her voice steady, while inside she was struggling not to panic. 'I need to get back to the party. Grayson will be wondering where I am.'

She tried to push past him, but he shoved her back against the wall.

'*Grayson*,' he snarled, his lips twisting in contempt. 'Let him wonder. Anyway, I'm sure he wouldn't mind letting me have a turn with you. He's not selfish like that, is he? In fact, why don't the two of you come for dinner with me and Rose some time? Then we could take our time.' He reached out and cupped her face with one hand, his thumb stroking over her lips. 'We're all grown-ups, after all. This doesn't have to be furtive.'

Lisa's eyes widened as she grabbed his hand and pushed it away, her heart beating wildly in her chest. 'Grayson would never—'

'Oh, come on, Lisa,' Mark drawled with a sneer, 'grow up. You know Grayson is good at sharing. He never minded bringing Isabel around for me to fuck, did he? Are you forgetting how you two love-birds met?'

Lisa hated that he had that to taunt her with. But everything was different now. Grayson loved her. He didn't want anyone else.

Mark laughed, watching her face. 'What do you think Grayson did here in London all the time you were shut away in Cornwall?' he mocked. 'You think he hasn't had Rose?'

'I know he hasn't. But I don't want to discuss this with you, Mark,' she said stiffly. 'My relationship with Grayson is none of your business.'

'Still so uptight,' he sighed. 'I thought I'd cured you of that. Look, why don't I invite you and Grayson over? And then we'll see.'

'We won't come,' she said tightly.

'Oh, you'll come,' he said with a laugh. 'I could always make you come, couldn't I?'

To her horror, his hand was on her leg now, sliding up under her skirt. She tried to push it away, barely able to breathe. She twisted her head, looking to the door at the end of the corridor, desperately hoping someone would come and interrupt them. But the corridor was deserted. Besides, if anyone did come, they would just look like two people who had slipped away from the party for a quick fumble in private.

'You're not going to tell me it's the same with him, are you? Maybe you need a reminder of how it is between us.' He leaned closer, his breath hot on her face, while his hand slid up her thigh.

'Stop.' She slapped his hand, but he was too strong for her. Her eyes darted to the door and she tried to wriggle away from him, but he grabbed her hands, pinning them over her head against the wall, while he pressed his body against hers. Lisa writhed helplessly, struggling not to panic. But he overpowered her easily and she was trapped, her hands immobile, his big body holding her in place.

'Don't tell me this doesn't excite you,' he said softly, his eyes dropping to her breasts. Her chest was heaving, her heart pounding as she struggled to break free. Dear God, what was he going to do?

'What—what about Rose?' she choked, her throat so dry it was difficult to get the words out.

'I don't give a fuck about Rose,' he said. 'Is that what this is about? Is that why you haven't answered my letters? Are you trying to punish me for being with someone else?'

'Of course not. I don't care—'

'Because I know how you feel. It's torture seeing you with *him*. But don't worry about Rose. She's just a diversion, nothing more.' He transferred her hands to one of his, the other cupping her cheek, his thumb trailing over her lips. 'She's good for a fuck, but she's not you, Lisa. You know I've never loved anyone but you.'

She was aghast, realising she was supposed to be flattered. He actually thought talking about Rose like that would win her over.

'I've never wanted anyone as much as I want you,' he continued, his eyes burning into hers. His intensity scared her. 'And you want me too,' he said, running one finger slowly down over the curve of her breast.

'No. I don't.'

His finger stroked her nipple through the thin fabric of her dress, pinching and massaging until it was hard and taut. He smiled in satisfaction as his eyes dropped to her breasts. 'You say one thing,' he said softly, raising his eyes to hers, 'but your body says another.'

Lisa cursed her involuntary response to the stimulation

of his fingers. She writhed desperately beneath him, struggling to get away as his hand moved slowly down her body.

'Please, stop.' Her heart hammered in her ears, but she fought to stem the trembling of her body. She must try to appear calm and in control. 'Stop,' she whimpered. 'I don't want this.'

But he just pressed closer, pinning her to the wall. His physical size was overwhelming, his big body solid and immovable. His mouth crashed down on hers, their teeth clashing as he forced her mouth open, his tongue plunging inside as he ground his hips into hers. She could feel how turned on he was by this. Her heart pounded and she gasped for air as he held her trapped against the wall, powerless to escape the relentless onslaught of his tongue. She whimpered helplessly, writhing against him, but he only took it as encouragement.

'Feels good, doesn't it?' he murmured throatily, lifting his head a fraction. His eyes glittered dangerously as his free hand trailed down her body, lingering on the fullness of her breasts. He looked down at her hardened nipple poking through the thin material of her dress and smiled.

'You like that, don't you, baby?' he said, massaging her breast. Then he bent his head and sucked the hardened peak, nipping it with his teeth until she squealed.

'Good girl,' he said, lifting his head and stroking his hand over her breast in a soothing gesture. 'Are you wet for me?' he said. She squirmed desperately, struggling to get away as his hand moved slowly down her body. He grabbed the hem of her dress and lifted it, hiking it up her thighs.

'Stop, Mark!' she choked, bile rising in her throat as his hand slid up her leg to the edge of her underwear. 'Let me go.'

He shook his head slowly. 'Not without taking back what's mine.'

Oh God, he was going to rape her, right here. Tears stung her eyes as she struggled ineffectually against him. Why didn't someone come?

'This is mine,' he said, his hand cupping her between her legs. She thought she might pass out with fright as he tugged her panties aside and slid one finger inside her.

'No!' she shouted, finally finding her voice, despite her terror. She opened her mouth to scream, but his mouth clamped down on hers in a bruising kiss. She twisted her head trying to escape his grinding lips, her heart beating wildly as she felt his erection pressed against her. She tried to raise a leg to kick him, flailing around for any means of escape, but he was too strong for her, his body as big and solid as a wall.

'Mark, no—' she gasped when he lifted his head.

'You want this as much as I do, Lisa,' he said. His eyes were predatory, glittering with lust, and she thought she might throw up as he pumped his finger inside her.

Suddenly there was a crash at the far end of the corridor, the hum of the distant party drifting momentarily through an open door. Thank God!

Mark turned in the direction of the noise and withdrew his finger, breathing heavily.

'We should get back to the party,' Lisa said shakily, trying to regain control.

To her relief, Mark released his grip on her hands.

'You're probably right,' he said regretfully. To Lisa's horror, he helped her adjust her clothing, and she shivered because it made her feel complicit, as if they had been in this together, sharing a clandestine kiss and grope behind their partners' backs. She just wanted him to stop touching her. She couldn't bear to have his hands on her a moment longer.

He was tugging down her skirt, his hands lingering unnecessarily on her legs, when suddenly she heard the rapid click of heels along the corridor, followed by a loud gasp. She twisted her head towards the sound and froze. Rose was standing there, watching them, her mouth open in a strangled scream.

30

MARK STILLED as he turned and saw Rose, but he didn't seem perturbed about being caught. He pulled away from Lisa slowly, giving her a lazy smile as she finished tugging her dress down. Her hands shook as she quickly smoothed her hair. Rose was glaring at her, her eyes hard.

Lisa didn't waste another second now that she was free. Without a backward glance, she raced down the corridor past Rose and pushed through the door to the main gallery, dimly aware of Mark's slower footsteps behind her.

Once she was back in the crowded gallery, she took a moment to collect herself. She breathed hard, struggling not to collapse to the floor in a sobbing heap. She quickly glanced around the room to locate Grayson. He was in a group of people by the far wall, and he hadn't seen her yet. She had to compose herself before he did. She didn't want to tell him what had happened with Mark. It would only make him worry.

She took a glass of wine from a passing waiter and took several deep gulps, her breathing slowly returning to normal as she calmed herself. She could feel her face crumple, and it was an effort not to break down and cry. She forced herself not to turn around as she heard Mark came back into the room behind her. Instead she fixed a smile onto her face and started to weave through the throng towards Grayson.

He slid an arm around her waist as she joined him. She tried to appear calm and unruffled, as if nothing had happened. But she knew her smile was faltering, and she couldn't concentrate on what was being said. She was afraid to speak because she knew she wouldn't be able to stop her voice from shaking. She just listened and smiled, sipping her wine to steady her nerves, and taking comfort from the warmth of Grayson's body next to hers.

Out of the corner of her eye she saw Rose crash through the door behind Mark, and she was alarmed to see she was making a beeline straight for her, racing across the crowded floor like she was on a mission. Lisa tried to ignore her, joining in the laughter as someone finished speaking, even though she had no idea what the joke had been.

But Rose broke through the circle around her and marched straight up to her. Before Lisa realised her intent, she drew back her arm and slapped her so hard across the face, her head snapped to the side painfully. There was a second's hush followed by a chorus of startled gasps and exclamations. Lisa's glass slipped from her fingers and crashed to the ground, smashing into pieces, wine splashing over her dress as it fell. She gasped for breath as her hand flew to her cheek, tears smarting her eyes. She was dimly aware of Grayson's arm tightening around her briefly before he pushed her behind him.

'What the hell?' He glowered at Rose, shielding Lisa from her with his body.

Rose was seething, rigid with fury, her eyes flashing as she faced Grayson.

'What the fuck do you think you're doing?' he shouted, fuming.

'Why don't you ask your girlfriend?' Rose sneered, baring her teeth as she glared at Lisa, her eyes sparking fury.

'Are you okay?' Grayson turned to Lisa, frowning in concern.

She nodded, holding a hand to her cheek, her eyes still smarting from the blow.

'You little slut!' Rose yelled at her. There were horrified gasps all around. 'Why don't you ask her what she was doing in the corridor with Mark just now?' she said to Grayson. 'They were all over each other. You think I don't know you still have the hots for him?' she said to Lisa. 'You act the innocent – pure, sweet little Lisa, pretending you want to be my friend,' she mocked. 'Butter wouldn't melt. Well, you may have fooled him,' she jerked her head at Grayson. 'But you don't fool me.'

Grayson turned to Lisa, his hand closing almost painfully around her wrist. 'Is this true?' he asked her, his eyes blazing, his mouth tight. 'Did he touch you?' He was fuming, and Lisa cringed.

Before she could answer, Mark came storming across the floor to them.

'That's enough, Rose,' he snapped at her, grabbing her wrist tightly and pulling her back.

'Did you touch her?' Grayson asked Mark, his voice tight. 'Did you put your hands on her?' He was so consumed with rage, he was almost shaking.

Mark gave a little laugh, his lip curling contemptuously. 'I didn't put my hands anywhere she didn't want them. Did I, Lisa?' His eyes glittered cruelly.

Lisa was speechless. All she could do was shake her head mutely in protest.

'You know what she's like,' he said mockingly to Grayson. 'Always so desperate for it.'

Grayson made a lunge for Mark, but Lisa pulled him back. 'Please,' she whispered. 'Can we just go?'

He turned to her, his eyes blank, hardly seeing her he was so incensed.

'Please?' She was desperate to get away, not sure how much longer she could hold it together. 'I want to leave now,' she said, reminding him of his promise that they would go any time she wanted.

He blinked several times, then let out a heavy breath. He nodded.

'Just keep your hands off my boyfriend in future,' Rose spat as Grayson slid an arm around Lisa's waist and they turned to go.

'You shut the fuck up,' Lisa heard Mark hiss as they walked away, and despite everything, she felt sorry for Rose.

Grayson found her shrug and helped her into it, then put an arm around her, pulling her close into his side, and led her to the door. Lisa found the solid warmth of his body immensely comforting. She could tell he was still seething, his jaw clenched, his movements sharp and jerky.

'You don't usually get fisticuffs thrown in at these shindigs,' she heard an amused voice drawl as they made their way to the exit. 'Hats off to Isabel. Never a dull moment at one of her parties.'

She was glad that Isabel was nowhere to be seen as they made their way out, wanting as little fuss as possible.

.   .   .

It was only when they were sitting side by side in the back of the car that Lisa realised she was shaking. She was still in shock, she supposed, first from Mark's attack and then Rose's. Her teeth were chattering, and she couldn't stop trembling.

'Come here,' Grayson said, pulling her into his side. He put on her seat belt for her, then did his own as the driver slid into the front seat. 'Are you cold?' he asked, shrugging out of his jacket without waiting for an answer. He draped it around her shoulders and pulled her closer.

'No.' Lisa shook her head.

'You're shaking.' He rubbed her arm comfortingly, warming and soothing her. He leaned forward and asked the driver to turn the heat up.

Lisa put a hand tentatively to her cheek.

'Does it hurt?' Grayson asked.

She shook her head. 'It just stings a bit.'

Grayson kissed the top of her head. He was silent for a few minutes, and Lisa could feel him relax, the adrenalin slowly leaving his body.

'Why didn't you tell me?' he asked as they pulled into the traffic.

'I didn't get a chance,' she said. 'There were too many people around. I didn't want to make a scene.'

'Would you have told me? If Rose hadn't hit you, would you have said anything?'

She hung her head. 'I didn't want to worry you.'

He sighed deeply, leaning his head wearily against the back of the seat.

'He assaulted you?'

Lisa was overwhelmed with relief that he didn't question even for a moment whether she had wanted it. She nodded, tears streaming down her face. She drew a ragged breath. 'I—I thought he was going to rape me. If Rose hadn't come—'

'Has he tried anything like this before?' he asked, his voice loaded with concern.

'It's the first time he's been so … aggressive.'

His jaw hardened at the word. 'What else has he done?' he asked tightly.

She told him about the letters and flowers, and what had happened when she'd gone to confront him about them. 'I thought it would be okay because he's with Rose now,' she said, feeling foolish. 'I thought he'd moved on. But he won't leave me alone.'

'Jesus, Lisa! That's stalking and harassment. We should report it,' Grayson said.

Lisa lifted her head. 'You mean, the police?'

'Yes. He's obsessed with you, Lisa.'

'He used to say …'

'What?'

She hesitated to say it out loud and make it real. 'He used to say that he couldn't live without me – that he didn't want to live without me. Sometimes I'm afraid …'

'You're afraid of what he'll do?'

She nodded.

'You can't let him control you like that. Besides, it's not just stalking and threats now. He attacked you tonight. We should get the police involved.'

'There's no point.' She sighed defeatedly. 'He'll just say I wanted him. It's his word against mine. And Rose would probably back him up.'

'I still think we should report it,' Grayson said. 'At least there'd be a record if he tries anything else. And you could definitely have Rose up for assault. There were plenty of witnesses to that.'

'I don't want to make trouble for Rose,' she said. Rose

was going home with Mark – that was punishment enough. He had been furious with her for making such a public scene, and Lisa dreaded to think what lay in store for her tonight when they got back to his house. She shivered at the thought. Besides, she was grateful to Rose for rescuing her. However unwittingly it was done, she had saved her from being raped by Mark. She'd take any amount of slaps from Rose if she could be spared that.

'I didn't want it, you know,' she said, looking at Grayson earnestly. 'I don't want him.'

He frowned. 'I know that, Lisa.'

She smiled. It felt so good to be believed; to be trusted so completely and unquestioningly.

'You have proof of the harassment,' Grayson said. 'You could get a restraining order at least.'

She nodded. 'If it continues, I will. I promise. Right now I just want to enjoy Christmas and forget about it all for a while.'

Grayson sighed, nodding reluctantly. 'But if you hear another word from him, we're going to the police. He's dangerous, Lisa. If Rose hadn't found you tonight—' He broke off, his fist clenching until the knuckles turned white.

She shuddered. If Rose hadn't found them, Mark would have raped her. She was sure of that now.

Grayson was quiet for a while, staring out the window, seemingly lost in thought. When he turned back to her, he looked troubled. 'If I hadn't come back into your life, this wouldn't be happening,' he said broodingly. 'You were living peacefully in Cornwall, and you'd still be there if I hadn't come along. You wouldn't be in any danger from Mark.'

'I also wouldn't be represented by one of the most prestigious galleries in London,' she said softly, smiling at him as she took his hand. 'I wouldn't have the career I've always dreamed of. I wouldn't have Susie and Daniel back in my life.' She drew a shaky breath. 'I wouldn't have you,' she said, her voice wobbling. 'I wouldn't know what it felt like to be loved by you. I don't regret any of it, Grayson. Not for one second.'

He blinked at her, speechless, his eyes glittering wetly.

'What did I do to deserve you?' he said finally. He put an arm around her and she laid her head on his shoulder. The car had heated up as they drove, and she felt cosy and warm as she snuggled into him, her eyes drooping closed.

'Almost home,' he murmured in her ear, his fingers lightly playing with her hair.

She sighed happily, nuzzling his neck. 'I'm already there.'

31

Lisa struggled with her umbrella as she made a dash from the cab to the door, the wind driving icy sleet into her face and soaking her hair. She wrestled with it as it was buffeted by the wind, pulling it closed as she reached the shelter of the porch and fumbled for her key.

It was a relief to step into the warmth of the hall. She shoved her umbrella into a stand and swept her wet hair off her face, shivering as she unbuttoned her coat.

'It's wild out there,' she said to Grayson as he appeared in the doorway of the library.

He smiled and came forward to give her a soft kiss. She sighed, sinking into the warmth and comfort of his body as he wrapped his arms around her.

'I thought we'd have supper in the library,' he said, jerking his head in the direction of the door. 'Why don't you go take a bath and relax, and come down when you're ready.'

'Mmm, that sounds good,' Lisa said pulling away. 'I could do with a bath,' she laughed, holding up her paint-spattered hands, daubed with smudges of cobalt blue and vermilion. She had spent a long day at her studio, finishing things up before the Christmas break. 'I probably stink of turps and oil paint.'

Grayson gave her a crooked grin. 'The smell of turps gives me a hard-on at this stage,' he said.

Lisa laughed, raising her eyebrows. 'Really?'

'Call it a Pavlovian response.'

'That's perverse.'

Grayson shrugged. 'What can I say?'

She felt all the stress and tension of the day melt away as she enjoyed a long soak in a hot bubble bath. The water soothed her aching muscles, stiff and sore after long hours of standing at her easel and bending over drawing boards. It had been a busy, tiring week, but as she lingered in the fragrant foam, she started to unwind and ease into holiday mode. Tomorrow was Christmas Eve and they were flying to Cornwall in the morning. She felt in need of some rest and relaxation, and she was looking forward to a quiet, lazy week of sea air and sleeping late.

She hadn't heard from Mark since Isabel's party. There had been no letters from him this week, but she didn't allow herself to feel complacent about it just yet. It could just be that he was out of town for Christmas. Anyway, she was glad of the respite for now, and she wasn't going to worry about it over the holiday.

When she had finished her bath, she pulled on a pair of yoga pants and a soft creamy sweater, then padded downstairs to join Grayson in the library. He met her in the doorway and took her hand, drawing her inside. Her breath caught as she looked around the room. A fire was blazing in the grate, a blanket spread out on the floor in front of it. The room was lit by dozens of flickering candles and strings of fairy lights, and in the bay window, the Christmas tree sparkled, light dancing off the coloured baubles. A picnic basket was placed on the blanket, with a bottle of champagne sitting in an ice bucket alongside two long-stemmed crystal flutes.

Lisa flushed with pleasure at the romantic gesture. 'Wow, you've been busy,' she said. She hadn't expected this. They had an early flight in the morning, and she'd thought they'd have a quick supper in the kitchen before an early night. Grayson obviously had other ideas. He'd really gone all out.

She suddenly had a flashback to the first time they'd had a picnic together in this room, when she'd been having sex with him for money and had baulked at the romance.

'I thought we could start the holiday tonight, just the two of us,' he said.

'It looks great!'

'But first …' With an almost shy smile he led her over to the fireplace. He stood facing her, taking both her hands in his. 'I have something I want to give you before Christmas day.' He licked his lips, and if she didn't know better, she'd have said he was nervous. 'Something I want to ask you.'

Lisa raised her eyebrows questioningly, baffled.

By way of an answer, Grayson simply sank to one knee in front of her. Lisa gasped as he pulled a small box from his pocket and flipped it open, holding it up to her.

'Will you marry me, Lisa?'

She was suddenly filled with inexplicable dread. She felt cornered, suffocated. She stood horrified but speechless as she watched Grayson's hopeful expression fade. She couldn't bear the hurt and disappointment in his face. She knew what she could say to instantly make it better. But still she couldn't bring herself to say that one little word.

'Grayson, I—' she looked away, struggling to make sense of her feelings. 'Sorry. This is just so unexpected. I—' she tucked a lock of hair behind her ear nervously. 'I don't know what to say.'

'Yes would be good,' he said, trying to smile, but his face seemed frozen.

She sank to the floor beside him, dazed. She had been so happy a moment ago. How had everything changed so fast? She didn't know what happened now. Had she ruined everything? Would Grayson even want her to join his family for Christmas now?

'Lisa?' he said, pulling her back to the present. She realised she had zoned out. 'It's fine,' he said, getting up and pulling her to her feet. 'Not the answer I was hoping for, but—'

She hated how wounded he looked, and she couldn't bear for him to think it was because she didn't love him enough. 'I wish I could say yes,' she told him, clutching his hands and looking pleadingly into his eyes.

'But you can't.'

'No,' she whispered. 'I'm sorry.' She wished she could explain, but she didn't even understand it herself. She'd have thought she'd jump at the chance to marry Grayson, but the moment he'd said it, she'd felt trapped and she'd recoiled instinctively. It wasn't that she thought she'd ever want to leave Grayson. But it still felt like a threat, something she had to avoid to protect herself.

She bit her lip. 'Grayson,' she said earnestly 'it's not you. It's—'

'Please don't say it's not you, it's me,' he joked, his wry smile not reaching his eyes.

'No, it's not me, it's … marriage. I love you so much,

Grayson,' she said. 'I want to be with you. But—I just can't. I'm so sorry.'

Grayson swallowed hard and nodded. 'You don't want to marry me.'

She shook her head. 'If I wanted to marry anyone, it'd be you. But I don't.' She hadn't actually thought about it before, but now that she was confronted with it, she knew it was true. She couldn't say why, but every fibre of her being rejected the idea.

'Is it really just the idea of marriage?' he asked her.

'Yes. It just—it scares me, I guess,' she admitted, feeling foolish.

He sighed. 'Will you take this ring anyway?' he asked, lifting it out of the box.

'I—it doesn't seem right.'

'Please, Lisa. I want you to have it. You can wear it on your other hand. It doesn't have to mean anything.' He shrugged. 'Just take it as a Christmas gift.'

She took it from him tentatively.

'There's no one else I want to give it to,' he said softly. 'There never will be.'

She slipped it on to the ring finger of her right hand. It was stunning – a delicate art nouveau design, with pearls and diamonds in an antique gold setting.

'It's so beautiful, Grayson,' she said, her eyes shining with tears as she looked up at him. 'Thank you.'

'Well, let's not let this spoil our night,' he said, pulling her down onto the blanket.

But Lisa felt she'd already spoiled it, and as Grayson poured champagne into two glasses, she knew they were both aware that this was meant to be a celebration of their engagement.

'Happy Christmas,' he said softly, clinking glasses.

'Happy Christmas,' she whispered, desperately trying

not to cry as she took a sip. But it was no use. A sob escaped her chest and she was helpless to stop the tears that rolled down her cheeks.

'Lisa!' Grayson's eyes widened in alarm. 'Please forget I said anything. I didn't mean to upset you. Can't we just pretend that didn't happen and start over?' He looked pained.

'I just—' her voice broke. 'I love you so much,' she said, wiping away tears. 'I can't bear the thought of losing you.'

Grayson frowned in concern, taking her glass from her and putting it on the floor. Then he pulled her into his arms. 'You're not losing me, Lisa.'

'But I will.'

'Why? Because I asked you to marry me and you turned me down?'

She hated the way it sounded, like she'd rejected him. But then, she supposed she had, in a way. She nodded.

'It wasn't meant to be an ultimatum. Nothing's changed, Lisa. I love you. You're still the person I want to be with.'

'But you want to get married,' she protested. What kind of future could their relationship have when they both wanted such fundamentally different things?

'No,' he said. 'I don't.'

'But—'

He shook his head. 'It's not like it's something I want to tick off a list, like some kind of life goal. I'd like to be married to *you*. But if you don't want that, then I want to live with you for the rest of my life and have children with you, and—' he broke off suddenly. 'God, I don't know if that's something you even want.' He smiled ruefully. 'I should shut up before I scare you off completely and you run for the hills.'

'Children?' She looked at him. 'Yes, it is. Not so much

as a life goal,' she said, echoing his words. 'But I want to have children with *you*.' She had thought about having a baby with Mark in the early days, but he had always found some reason to put it off. Deep down she knew it was just that he was too possessive and selfish. He didn't want her body to change. He didn't want her to get fat. He wasn't willing to share her with a baby. For once she was grateful for his control over her life. It would have been so much harder to leave if there had been a child involved.

'Lisa?' Grayson was frowning at her in concern.

She shook off the dark thoughts and gave him a reassuring smile. 'Sorry. I was miles away.

'Come on, let's eat,' he said, flipping open the picnic basket. 'We've got an early start in the morning.'

They sat cross-legged on the blanket, and even though they weren't engaged, it felt like a celebration as they ate lobster and drank champagne in front of the flickering fire, talking about their trip to Cornwall.

'I can't wait for you to meet the rest of my family,' Grayson said.

Lisa sighed. 'I just wish you could have met mine,' she said sadly.

'You must miss your grandparents a lot, especially at this time of year.'

She nodded. 'I do.' She would have loved them to meet Grayson.

'I wish I could have known them.'

'They'd have loved you,' she said. 'They'd have loved you for making me so happy. And for your mad chess skills, of course,' she added, laughing. 'Any tips for getting your sisters to like me?'

'Nah.' He grinned. 'Just act like you think I walk on water and you'll be golden.'

'Okay, now you're making me nervous.'
'Don't be.' He leaned in and kissed the tip of her nose.
'Just be yourself. They'll adore you.'

32

Snow was falling in light flurries when they pulled up outside Grayson's parents' house on Christmas Eve. The short driveway was lit with little shrubs strung with fairy lights, throwing a lambent glow into the surrounding darkness. Lisa felt a flutter of nerves as Grayson unloaded their bags from the boot, a little daunted at meeting the rest of his large family. He handed her the bags of presents, and he carried their luggage in both hands. The door swung open as they approached, and they were greeted by a smiling Janet ushering them inside.

When they had dropped their bags, she threw her arms around Grayson and gave him a kiss on the cheek, then pulled Lisa into a hug.

'I'm so glad to see you both. We were worried the snow would pick up and you wouldn't make it.'

'It's not bad at the moment, but it looks set to get worse later,' Grayson said.

'Well, you got here, that's all that matters,' Janet said.

Lisa could hear voices elsewhere in the house, and she

was glad that everyone hadn't come out to meet her at once.

'Well, you two get settled, and then you can come straight down. Supper's almost ready. We're having it early so the children can eat with us before they go to bed.'

They went upstairs and dumped their bags in Grayson's room. 'Hungry?' he asked her.

Lisa nodded. 'Starving.' The sound of voices and laughter drifted up from below, and she felt nervous about going down and joining Grayson's family.

'Come on,' Grayson said, taking her hand. 'They won't bite, I promise.'

In the dining room, everyone was seated around the long table in front of the window, while Janet and Don set out dishes and poured wine. They all looked up expectantly as Lisa and Grayson entered, and there was a chorus of hellos. The three young women who were obviously Grayson's sisters looked at her with open curiosity, and Lisa felt she was being thoroughly scrutinised.

'Everyone, this is Lisa,' Grayson said, putting his hands on her shoulders. They all nodded in acknowledgement, smiling as Grayson introduced her to them in turn and they shook hands. His sisters Alison, Emma and Sarah were stunning, with the same slanting green eyes and copper-coloured hair as Grayson. Their husbands were Ben, Patrick and James, but Lisa quickly forgot who belonged to who. Sarah's daughters Daisy and Poppy were seated together at one end of the table, while Alison wrestled a squirming toddler in her lap, and a baby sat in a high chair between Janet and Don.

'You can sit here, Lisa.' Janet guided her to an empty space between Emma and Sarah, and Grayson sat opposite her.

Lisa soon forgot her shyness as Janet and Don took

their seats, and everyone started talking at once as they passed dishes around the table. Dinner was a delicious fish pie with side dishes of buttered leeks and carrots.

Grayson's sisters were full of questions for Lisa, tripping over each other in their eagerness to quiz her about herself. She got the feeling she was a bit of a novelty for them.

'Mum tells us you're an artist,' Alison said.

'So how did you two meet?' Sarah asked simultaneously.

Lisa laughed. 'Um …'Her eyes met Grayson's across the table and she blushed. 'Yes, I'm an artist. We met through Isabel.'

'Oh, you know Isabel?' Emma's eyes widened significantly.

'Isabel represents Lisa,' Grayson said smoothly, as if implying that was how they'd met.

'She gave me my first solo show,' Lisa said, keeping up the semi-fiction.

One of the husbands – Patrick? – rolled his eyes sympathetically at Lisa. 'You'll have to forgive them. We all had to go through this grilling the first time, didn't we?' He looked around at the other men, who nodded.

'Sorry,' Emma said, without a hint of contrition. 'It's just that Grayson's never brought a girlfriend home before.'

'Shut up, Emma,' Grayson said good-naturedly.

'We don't know how to behave because we haven't had any practice,' she continued undaunted, throwing her brother a teasing glance.

'Mum said you used to live in Porth Heron,' Sarah said.

'That's right. But I'm from London originally.'

'Are your family in London?' Alison asked.

'Lisa doesn't have any family,' Janet told her quietly.

'I was raised by my grandparents,' she said, 'but they're dead now.'

'Oh, I'm so sorry,' Alison said.

'Thanks.' Everyone looked at her sympathetically. Lisa was touched by their compassion, but she hated being an object of pity.

'Well, you've got us now!' Emma said gaily. 'Marry Grayson and you'll have more family than you know what to do with.'

Lisa blushed, throwing a cautious glance at Grayson.

'Who said anything about marriage?' he said tetchily to his sister.

'Are you going to marry Uncle Grayson?' Poppy asked Lisa in her high, childish voice.

Lisa shifted uncomfortably, not knowing how to answer as she suddenly felt all eyes on her.

'Poppy,' Sarah chided. 'You shouldn't ask questions like that.'

'Why not?' Poppy said. 'I think it would be nice. Lisa could be my auntie.'

'Would you like that?' Sarah said indulgently to her daughter.

Poppy nodded, beaming at Lisa.

'I agree,' Sarah said. 'I think it would be very nice. So, how about it, Grayson?' She turned to him. 'When are we going to hear wedding bells?' she asked with a playful wink.

'Not everyone is as obsessed with weddings as you three,' Grayson snapped. Everyone looked startled by his reaction, and Lisa flinched. Out of the corner of her eye, she noticed Janet's eyes fly to the ring on her finger.

'Sorry,' Grayson sighed, giving his sister an apologetic smile. 'But it serves you right for being nosy.'

'Sore subject, obviously,' Sarah said with a roll of her eyes.

There was an awkward silence, the atmosphere around the table suddenly strained. Janet threw a shrewd look at Grayson.

'Don't mind him,' Emma said to Sarah with a little laugh. 'He's just touchy about it because we always made him be the groom when we played at weddings. We've probably put him off for life.'

'Well, I think they should get married,' Poppy piped up, relieving the tension. 'Lisa looks nice. She's got lovely hair.' She turned to her little sister for support.

Daisy nodded solemnly. 'I like her,' she said quietly.

Grayson smiled fondly at his niece, then at Lisa. 'I like her too.'

'It'd be nice being married to Uncle Grayson,' Daisy said, turning to Lisa. 'He's good at telling stories. And he buys you lots of sweets when you go to the cinema.'

'Well, that's quite a recommendation,' Lisa said seriously as everyone laughed. 'I'll definitely have to think about it.'

After dinner, Don went to the local pub for a traditional Christmas Eve drink with some friends, while Grayson and his sisters put the children to bed and read them stories. Their husbands were sorting presents in the garage, preparing to sneak back into the house and play Santa Claus once the children were asleep. Lisa helped Janet clear up, and when they had finished, Janet made them hot port and they sat at the kitchen table enjoying a moment of calm.

Lisa felt Janet's eyes going to her hands, cupped around the steaming glass.

'Can I ask you something, Lisa?' she asked gently.

There was something ominous in her tentative tone, but Lisa nodded.

'Of course you don't have to answer,' Janet said with a light laugh. 'You can tell me to mind my own business.'

Lisa smiled at her in response.

Janet took a deep breath. 'Did Grayson ask you to marry him?'

Lisa clenched her fist on the table. 'Yes,' she said faintly, dropping her gaze, not able to look Janet in the eye.

'And you said no.'

It wasn't a question. Lisa looked up at her. 'Yes, I did.' She frowned. 'How did you know?'

'That ring,' Janet nodded to Lisa's finger. 'It was my mother's engagement ring. But you're wearing it on your right hand.'

'Oh,' Lisa whispered, appalled. She felt awful. What must Janet think of her? She started to twist the ring off her finger. She should never have accepted it.

'No,' Janet frowned, putting a hand over hers to stop her. 'It's yours. Grayson obviously wanted you to have it.'

'But—it's an engagement ring, and I'm not going to marry him.'

'No,' Janet sighed. 'But it's not as if he's going to marry anyone else, is it? I've seen the way he is with you, Lisa. He clearly adores you. Keep the ring. It was his to give to whomever he chose.' Her hand closed over Lisa's. 'But—can I ask you something else?'

Lisa nodded, biting her lip.

'Why don't you want to marry him? I'm not sure I've ever seen two people so much in love – unless I'm very much mistaken.'

Lisa shook her head. 'It's not that I don't want to marry Grayson,' she said, looking earnestly at Janet, pleading with her to understand. 'I don't want to marry anyone.'

'You don't believe in marriage?'

'It's not that I don't believe in it. It's just … not for me. It scares me, to be honest,' she said with a little self-deprecating laugh. She felt like such an idiot admitting that. 'I know it's silly, and I don't even know why exactly—'

'Well, it is a big step …'

'I love Grayson – so much. And I know he loves me. I want us to be together always. It's not that I'm afraid of the commitment. But the idea of marriage. … when I think about it, I panic and I feel like I can't breathe.'

Janet just nodded understandingly.

'I wish I could say yes. I'd do anything to make him happy—'

'You make him very happy, Lisa.' Janet squeezed her hand. 'You love each other. You're happy together. That's all that matters.'

Lisa smiled, relieved. She was grateful to Janet for being so kind and understanding. Her calm, accepting presence was so comforting. Lisa could see how just talking to her could be healing. She must have been a wonderful therapist.

'I'm sorry Sarah embarrassed you, but she didn't mean any harm. Forget her talk of weddings, but I'll stand by the rest of what she said. Married or not, I hope we can be your family now,' she said.

'I'd like that,' Lisa said, her eyes welling with tears. 'More than anything.'

33

THE NEXT MORNING she and Grayson were woken by
Poppy bursting into their room announcing that it was
Christmas and demanding that they get up. They quickly
pulled on dressing gowns and joined everyone else in the
race downstairs, led by the excited children, to see what
Santa had brought. Lisa had helped lay out all the presents
in the living room last night, and she loved being part of
the excitement. She'd never had a family Christmas like
this before. It had always just been her and her grandparents. Their Christmases were always wonderful, but they'd
been quiet. Grayson's large, boisterous family was very
different, and she loved joining in the fun, watching the
children's wide-eyed wonder as they discovered the
presents that had magically appeared under the tree. They
squealed and shouted over each other in delight as they
tore at wrapping paper, while the adults looked on fondly,
snapping photos.

Lisa had been reticent at first about blending in with
Grayson's family, but her shyness soon evaporated as she
found herself swept up in helping with dinner prepara-

tions. She was glad they let her help instead of treating her like a guest, and she felt like one of the family as she joined Grayson's mother and sisters in the kitchen. They chatted easily as they worked, Grayson's sisters telling her funny stories about their childhood and the tortures they'd inflicted on each other. Soon it was as if they'd known each other all their lives, and any awkwardness from last night's dinner was forgotten.

Once dinner preparations were under control, everyone assembled in the living room to exchange presents. Lisa had never had so many parcels to open on Christmas Day. Grayson's sisters gave her jewellery, luxurious bath oils and scented candles, and his parents gave her a stunning piece of abstract glass sculpture made by a local artist. She had bought most of their gifts from her friends – ceramic pieces by Susie for Grayson's sisters, and one of Daniel's paintings for Don and Janet. She was pleased the children seemed delighted with the books she had given to all of them. She had chosen them with care after quizzing Grayson about their preferences.

She gave Grayson his present last. He raised his eyebrows quizzically as she handed him the heavy parcel. She held her breath as he opened it, uncovering the intricately carved wooden box. His face lit up delightedly as he lifted the lid and saw the vintage Italian wooden chess set, each piece exquisitely hand carved and painted. She had spent a long time searching for the perfect gift for Grayson, and she had been so pleased to find the chess set in a little antique shop in Mayfair – even more so that after her show, she had been able to afford it. She thought it would look right at home in Grayson's library.

'It's perfect,' he breathed reverently, picking up a knight to examine it. 'Thank you.' He leaned forward and gave her a peck on the lips. 'Winning will be sweeter than ever.'

'It doesn't have magical properties, you know,' she said with a wry smile.

'Okay, that's fighting talk. You and me, after dinner.'

'You're on.'

Still laughing, Grayson took a long cylindrical parcel from under the tree and handed it to her. 'This is for you,' he said. 'Happy Christmas.'

Intrigued, Lisa unwrapped it. Inside was a plastic tube. She glanced at Grayson quizzically as she opened it, puzzled as to what it could be. She pulled out three large sheets of drafting paper and unrolled them, flattening them out on the floor. They were architectural drawings, she realised, but she still wasn't sure what exactly she was looking at as her eyes scanned the plans and sketches – until she saw the legend in the top right-hand corner: Lisa's studio. She gasped, her eyes flying up to Grayson's.

'Really?' she breathed, eyes wide.

He smiled and came to sit beside her on the floor as she bent her head over the plans again and he interpreted them for her. He planned to build the studio to the side of his house, connected but with its own separate entrance. He became boyishly excited as he pointed out the different features of the structure and how he'd designed the space to optimise natural light. As he spoke, Lisa stopped looking at the plans and watched his face, loving his enthusiasm.

'You can see what you think,' he said. 'Nothing is set in stone. Anything you see here can be changed if you have other ideas.'

'I can't believe it,' Lisa said. 'Thank you so much.' She threw her arms around him, squeezing him tight. 'This is the best thing anyone's ever given me.' She couldn't wait to see it taking shape, already excited at the thought of working there.

'I can't wait to get started on it,' Grayson said, echoing her thoughts as he hugged her back. 'But I got you something else, since you can't use this right away,' he said, nodding to the plans still in Lisa's lap as his sisters crowded around to peer at them over her shoulder. He got up and went behind the tree, pulling out a surf board with a big red ribbon tied around the middle.

'You'll never guess what it is,' he joked, grinning as he presented it to Lisa.

'Hmm, I think I may have an idea,' she said, standing up to take it from him. She gave a puzzled frown as she untied the ribbon. 'A surf board!' she squealed in surprise, clapping her hands playfully.

Grayson laughed.

Lisa ran her hand over the surface of the board. It was beautiful – sleek and polished, with a colourful tie-dye design in pinks and blues. 'It's gorgeous! I can't wait to try it out,' she grinned.

Grayson smiled at her and not for the first time, she wondered what she'd done to deserve this beautiful man. When she was with him, she felt so … cherished. It was the only word for it. Had she been wrong to turn him down when he proposed? She loved him with all her being, and she knew he loved her. She trusted him absolutely. She wanted to have a life with him – a life like this, filled with love and family – and it was hers for the taking. Why couldn't she just reach out and grab it?

Later as she watched Grayson playing with his nieces and nephews, helping Poppy build a Lego fire station, or putting together a train set with Daisy, she couldn't help thinking what a wonderful father he would make. She had never been broody before, but he was so good with his sisters' children, and watching him with them, she felt a sudden pang of longing for a baby *–his* baby. As if he felt her gaze, he looked up. His eyes dropped to Daisy, cradled in her lap, admiring a sketch of a horse Lisa had done for her, and she got the distinct feeling he was feeling the same thing as her.

'Do another one!' Daisy said, pulling her attention back. She was delighted with Lisa's drawing skills, demanding one sketch after another from her.

'Okay, what shall I draw next?'

'Do a monkey!'

'Hmm, okay. Why don't we both do one,' she said, handing a box of crayons to Daisy, 'and then Uncle Grayson can decide which one is best.'

Christmas dinner was a joyous affair. They ate at the long table in the dining room, children squeezed in between adults. As chatter and laughter flowed around her, Lisa felt incredibly lucky to be welcomed into this happy, loving family. There was so much warmth and affection here, and as she cast her eyes around the table at their friendly, smiling faces, she couldn't prevent her mind from drifting back to last Christmas with Mark. The contrast couldn't have been more stark.

They had eaten dinner alone, just the two of them. Mark's father was dead, and he was estranged from his mother, who had remarried and moved to France. Lisa had felt tense and on edge all day, miserable that Christmas, which had been such a happy time when her grandparents were alive, had become so lonely and empty. The whole thing had become just another exercise in creating the picture-perfect magazine life.

They had an artfully decorated tree, carefully colour-themed in white and blue. It looked bleak and chilly to Lisa, but Mark refused to let her use any of the gaudy multi-coloured decorations she had saved from her childhood. They hosted a champagne reception in the morning, and Lisa had spent days beforehand making elegant canapés to serve to Mark's important friends instead of the fruit-laden puddings, booze-soaked cakes and buttery mince pies she'd have made with her grandmother in the lead-up to the holiday.

Lisa found the whole thing exhausting and depressing, and there was no reward at the end of it for all her hard work – no thanks or appreciation, none of the enjoyment or fun of sharing it all with someone who really cared for her. Mark had chosen her clothes, of course, and she had been uncomfortable all day in a figure-hugging jersey dress and spiky heels.

Instead of the traditional roast turkey dinner, they had shared a seafood platter filled with the crab, oysters and lobster that Mark loved, and which moreover wouldn't make Lisa fat. He had given her expensive jewellery she didn't care about and sexy lingerie that was just for him, and she had forced a smile onto her lips and pretended to be pleased because she knew how angry he'd be if she didn't play her part right. She'd almost let her facade slip when she'd opened her final present and Mark explained to her what it was – a butt plug. Even now she flinched at the thought of it. She had been in danger of bursting into tears, and it had taken all her strength not to show how despondent and miserable she'd felt.

Mark had talked before about wanting anal sex, but she had always resisted and put him off.

'We're going to start training that ass of yours,' he'd said then, as if it was a fun activity for them both. 'No more excuses,' he said, grinning at her mischievously. 'You're going to love it, Lisa. You'll see.'

She didn't love it. But at least he couldn't see her face as she wept into her pillow a few nights later as he pushed inside her. He had quickly lost patience with her 'training' and decided she was ready for the real thing. It hurt, and she had gritted her teeth and clutched the pillow, but still a sharp cry had escaped her lips when he rammed himself balls-deep inside her.

'Ssh,' he had said roughly, his voice thick with excitement. 'Don't make such a fuss. Just let go, and you'll get used to it. It'll be better for you if you relax. God, you feel amazing, Lisa.' And she was forgotten as he lost himself in his own pleasure.

She had never grown to enjoy it, but she did get used to it. She'd had no choice. Mark loved it, and it became a regular part of their sex life. Deep down, she suspected that he knew she didn't like it − and that that only made it more exciting for him.

'Lisa,' Grayson murmured in her ear, his hand lightly touching hers, jolting her back to the present. She blinked, looking around the table, grounding herself in the moment. She was still in this bright, cheery room with Grayson's family, surrounded by love and laughter. She turned to Grayson with a grateful smile before she resumed eating. He always seemed to know when her mind strayed and she got lost in that dark place, but one touch of his hand could bring her out of the shadows and back to the light.

But that night her thoughts turned gloomy again as she sat on Grayson's bed, waiting for him. She had come up early, claiming she was tired, leaving him downstairs having a nightcap with his parents. She'd had a wonderful day. Everyone had been so friendly and welcoming, and she loved being part of their family Christmas. And yet she'd had a sudden, overwhelming need to get away and be on her own.

She felt so out of place at times, like an imposter in the midst of Grayson's family. It was as if she was here under false pretences, tricking these kind, decent people into liking and accepting her, when all along she knew there was this poison deep inside her and she didn't deserve their trust and friendship. If they knew the things she'd done, would they still be happy to welcome her into the family? Would they let her play with their children? Would they think she was good enough for Grayson? She wished there had been no Mark and she could have come to Grayson whole and unscarred. Instead she felt tainted and damaged, unworthy of him.

'Well, my family adore you,' Grayson said, coming into the room.

'I pass the test with your sisters?'

'Definitely.' He closed the door quietly behind him and crossed to the bed. 'And Poppy and Daisy are huge fans.'

'They're adorable. I love your family.' She plucked at the bedspread broodingly, unable to shake off the dark thoughts troubling her.

'What?' The bed dipped as Grayson sat beside her.

She heaved a sigh. 'I wish—I wish I could be … normal.'

Grayson frowned. 'You are normal.'

'Better, then. Not—not broken … corrupted.' He deserved someone who would love him wholeheartedly and unreservedly. Someone who would say yes when he asked her to marry him. She hated that she was always holding back with him, even now.

'Everyone has their demons, Lisa. Tell me.'

She shook her head. 'I don't think I can.' She felt so ashamed of the things she'd done with Mark, the things she'd let him do to her.

'I may not be able to slay all the dragons, like in a fairy-tale,' he said. 'But sometimes just talking about them makes them less scary. I was reading Rumpelstiltskin to Poppy tonight.' He smiled. 'You know how it ends?'

She nodded. 'When the miller's daughter guesses his name, the goblin vanishes.'

'Right, she says it out loud. So maybe when you name your fears, they don't have power over you anymore.'

'Is that the moral of the story?'

He smiled. 'That's what Mum always told me it meant.'

'I like that interpretation.' She looked at him carefully. He couldn't want to hear what she'd have to say. And yet, she knew she could tell him anything and it wouldn't change how he felt about her. He wanted to know her completely, and she didn't have to hide any part of herself from him.

So she started to talk, slowly and quietly, and she told him the whole sordid story of last Christmas with Mark – how she had cried when he pushed inside her, how she had hated it, but still let him do it over and over, because she was too weak to say no. How he kept on going even when she begged him to stop. And when she finished, Grayson was still looking at her the same way, like she was the most precious thing on earth.

He touched the space between her eyebrows. 'I wish I could erase those memories – whatever you're thinking of when you look like that.'

She heaved a shaky breath. 'I don't think you can.' But

he was right – it felt less threatening now that she'd said it out loud.

He sighed. 'Maybe not. But we can make new memories.'

She nodded, giving him a wobbly smile. He leaned in and kissed her, his lips soft and firm on hers. He slowly peeled off her pyjama top, his hands gentle on her breasts as he stroked and massaged them. He stood to undress, then he removed the rest of her clothes and lay down beside her, kissing and caressing every inch of her skin until all the nerve endings in her body were on fire and she was shaking with need. The low hum of voices still drifted up from other parts of the house, and when Grayson thrust powerfully inside her, she clamped her mouth shut, swallowing the screams of pleasure that threatened to escape so that his family wouldn't hear.

'Let go, baby,' he said as her head thrashed on the pillow and she stifled a whimper as she writhed beneath him. 'No one can hear you.'

'Are you sure?' she breathed.

He gave a crooked smile as his fingers worked her clit, pushing her over the edge. 'I built this house, remember? I can vouch for the soundproofing.'

Relieved, Lisa let go and screamed her release. Grayson followed quickly after, his body jerking violently as he came inside her.

'Well, that's one way to drive away the demons,' Lisa grinned as he collapsed heavily on top of her.

Grayson chuckled as he rolled away. 'Happy Christmas,' he said softly, pulling her into his arms.

'Happy Christmas, Grayson.'

34

RETURNING TO LONDON IN JANUARY, Lisa felt stronger than she had in a long time. They'd stayed with Grayson's parents for a few days after Christmas, then saw in the New Year with Lisa's friends in Porth Heron. The break had done her good, and she felt refreshed and energised, ready to take on anything – even Mark. So far there hadn't been any more letters, and she hoped he had finally got the message that there was nothing he could do to make her change her mind.

She threw herself into her work with renewed enthusiasm, able to enjoy her studio again now that she wasn't constantly being bombarded with messages from Mark. She had made some decisions too. She had felt so much better after talking to Grayson, and it made her think. Since that first night, she had opened up to him more and more, telling him about her life with Mark. But it wasn't fair to burden him with it all, and while it was good to share and be open with each other, ultimately she didn't think it was the best thing for their relationship to turn him into her therapist. Nevertheless, she felt talking was the key

257

to healing. The way she'd felt when Janet had listened to her so patiently and non-judgmentally had stuck with her, and she wanted more of that.

'I've decided I'm going to talk to someone,' she told him over dinner one night.

He raised his eyebrows.

'A therapist,' she clarified.

'That sounds like a good idea,' he said. He didn't seem surprised, and she was relieved. She'd been a little nervous that he'd tell her she didn't need it and try to talk her out of it.

It had never occurred to her that she could have PTSD, but Grayson had mentioned it tentatively to her one night when she was talking about Mark, and she'd started researching domestic abuse and its after-effects on the internet as soon as she got home.

She'd cried when she'd read the stories women shared on blogs and websites – partly because she felt sorry for them, but also because it could have been her writing those things. It was her story as much as theirs, and she felt a strange sense of relief that she wasn't alone.

'I've been reading up on domestic abuse and PTSD,' she told Grayson, 'and … well, I relate to so much of it.'

'Do you know anyone?' he asked. 'I could get mum to recommend someone, if you like.'

She shook her head. 'Thanks, but Daniel's already given me the name of a therapist. He says she's really good.'

To her relief, when she broached the subject with her friends, it turned out that most of them had been in therapy themselves at some stage, and they were reassuringly matter-of-fact about it.

'Anything from Mark today?' he asked.

She shook her head. 'No, nothing. I think he's finally given up on me.'

'Let's hope so.'

But she could tell neither of them really believed it.

The next day she met Isabel for a catch-up over lunch at a trendy Bond Street restaurant. They had just parted ways and she was on her way back to the studio when she saw two young women coming towards her who seemed vaguely familiar. It took her a moment to realise it was Anna and Nikki from her class at art college. They spotted her just at the same moment she recognised them.

'Hi!' She smiled, stopping.

'Hi, Lisa,' Nikki said. 'How are you?'

'I'm fine thanks.'

'Congratulations on your show, by the way,' Anna said.

'Yeah, you're doing really well. Congratulations! I wasn't able to make it, but I heard great things.'

'Thanks. So what are you two up to?

'I'm teaching,' Nikki said with a roll of her eyes.

'I'm doing an MA,' Anna told her.

'Oh, good for you! Well, I'd better get on.' They had never been close, and they didn't have much to say to each other beyond idle small talk. They'd been Rose's friends at college. But as she turned to go, Lisa wheeled back towards them. 'How's Rose?' she asked as an afterthought.

'Rose?' Anna frowned. 'I don't know. I haven't seen her in ages.'

'Me either,' Nikki said with a shrug. Then a sly smile spread across her face. 'Why do you ask?'

Lisa shrugged. 'Just wondering. She was at my opening, and I saw her at a party just before Christmas. But I haven't heard anything of her since.'

'Well, I suppose you know she's with Mark now?' Nikki said with a smirk.

'Yes, I know that.' Lisa said, keeping her expression neutral. If Nikki thought she was imparting bad news, she was very much mistaken. 'They were together at my show.'

Lisa could tell Nikki was disappointed that she hadn't managed to upset her. She'd always had a malicious streak.

'Is she working on something, I wonder,' Lisa prompted. 'Her solo show did well, didn't it? She must be doing something to follow it up.'

'Wouldn't have a clue,' Anna said. 'She doesn't really keep in touch.'

'Well, if you see her, say hello for me,' she said.

'I doubt we'll be seeing her anytime soon,' Nikki said bitterly, her lip curling. 'She seems to have forgotten who her friends are. Now that she's hooked up with Mark Reader, she thinks she's too important to hang out with the likes of us.'

Lisa couldn't put the meeting out of her mind as she made her way home later that evening. It sounded like Mark was isolating Rose the way he had her, alienating all her friends. She wished there was a way she could reach out to Rose somehow. She knew it probably wouldn't be welcome, but she felt she had to try. But how? She couldn't rely on bumping into her by chance. She remembered when she had met her earlier in the year, she said she was working at a recruitment agency, but she didn't know which one, and anyway, it was unlikely she was still working there – not if Mark had anything to do with it. So how could she get in touch with her? Unless she was just upfront about it …

'Grayson,' she said tentatively that night as they ate

dinner.

'Hmm?'

'How would you feel about inviting Mark and Rose over?'

His eyes shot to hers, widening. 'You're kidding, right?'

She quailed a little, knowing she would have a fight on her hands. But she stood her ground. 'No.' She shook her head slowly. 'I'd like to.'

'Lisa … no. Why are you even saying this?'

'I'm worried about Rose,' she said. 'I'm afraid he's cutting her off from everyone like he did with me, and I want to talk to her, to—'

'You tried, remember?' he said. 'She cut you dead.'

'But it might be different now. I know what Mark's like. In the beginning he can be so charming, and everything seems great, but—'

'I don't want to hear it,' Grayson said flatly, cutting her off. 'I don't want that man in my house, and I don't want him anywhere near you. I can't believe you do.'

'I don't,' she said pleadingly. 'Believe me, I have no more desire to see Mark than you do.'

'Christ, Lisa! This is the man who attacked you the last time you saw him. And now you're suggesting we just casually have him over for dinner? No.' He shook his head emphatically. 'No way.'

'I just want Rose to know there are people she can turn to if she needs help – if she decides she wants help,' she amended.

Grayson sighed. 'You did your best, and she didn't want to know. You can't save people from themselves, Lisa.'

'You saved me,' she said in a small voice.

'No, I didn't. You saved yourself. I just provided the means.'

Lisa sighed. She could tell she wasn't going to win this

one – and part of her was relieved to give it up. Grayson was right – it really wasn't a good idea to invite Mark back into her life when she'd worked so hard to get rid of him. Besides, what if he were to start harassing her again? It wouldn't look very convincing on a police report if she was having him over for dinner.

'You're right,' she said to Grayson. 'Sorry. I shouldn't have brought it up. It was a crazy idea.'

'You're not responsible for Mark,' he said, his tone softer now.

She nodded. 'I know. But that doesn't stop me feeling it sometimes. I guess that's one more thing I'll have to work through with my therapist,' she said with a wry smile.

The following evening, they were playing chess in the library after dinner when the doorbell rang. As Grayson got up to answer it, it rang again several times in rapid succession.

Lisa leapt up and followed him into the hall, alarmed by the urgency of the persistent ringing. It sounded like someone was in trouble. She hung back in the doorway of the library as Grayson threw the front door open. She stifled a gasp as she saw Rose standing in the porch, pale and shivering, her arms wrapped around herself defensively.

Grayson didn't step aside, but stayed blocking the door, frowning forbiddingly at her.

'Can I see Lisa?' Rose asked, her voice shaky. 'Please?'

'I don't think that's a good idea—'

'I'm sorry about what happened,' she said quickly, glancing over his shoulder at Lisa. 'I don't want to make trouble.'

'Let her in,' Lisa said, coming forward to stand behind

Grayson. He turned and frowned at her in concern.

Rose looked to her pleadingly. 'I just want to talk.'

'Grayson,' Lisa touched his back. 'It's fine. Come in, Rose.'

Grayson reluctantly stepped aside, and Lisa ushered Rose inside and into the library. In the light of the room she saw that there was a livid red bruise on Rose's jaw, and her stomach turned over in revulsion.

'I'm sorry I hit you at Isabel's party,' Rose was babbling as Lisa urged her onto the sofa. 'I know we've never been friends, but I didn't know where else to go. I had nowhere to go,' she wailed desperately. 'And you said—'

Lisa nodded. 'It's fine. She sat beside Rose and put an arm around her narrow shoulders. 'I said if you were in trouble I'd try to help you,' she said as much to reassure Grayson as anything else. He was hovering over them anxiously.

'I'm really sorry – about everything,' Rose said, starting to cry quietly. 'You were right,' she sniffed, wiping away tears with the back of her hand. 'About Mark.'

'Did he hit you?' Lisa asked quietly.

Rose nodded. 'Yesterday.' Her face crumpled and she swallowed a sob.

Grayson's eyes sparked fury, and his jaw clenched. 'Asshole!' he muttered under his breath. He went to the drinks cabinet and poured a large glass of brandy.

'Drink this,' he said, handing it to Rose.

'Thank you,' she whispered, looking up at him shyly as she took it from him. She took a small sip and put it down on the table in front of her.

'He accused me of sleeping with someone else,' she said, wringing her hands, while Lisa rubbed her back soothingly.

Grayson sat down on her other side. His expression

had softened, his eyes full of sympathy now as he listened to Rose.

'I didn't sleep with anyone,' she said. She took a deep gulp of brandy. 'Christ! How could I? I never see anyone anymore. No one but him. I don't think he even believed I had, really – he just wanted to pick a fight. I think—' she gulped. 'I think he just wanted an excuse to hit me.'

'Does he know you're here?' Lisa asked.

Rose shook her head. 'He's out of town tonight. He's gone to Paris. It was my only chance to get away. He watches me all the time. I didn't know where else to go, I just ran—'

'You can stay here for now,' Lisa said. 'Can't she?' She looked across at Grayson.

'Of course,' he nodded. 'Do you want to go to the police?' he asked Rose.

'Police? I hadn't thought—'

'He assaulted you,' Grayson said through gritted teeth, his rage barely suppressed. 'It's a crime. It should be reported.'

Rose took a big swig of brandy, and Lisa saw her expression hardening.

'Yes,' she said firmly, turning to Grayson, a new steel in her voice. 'Yes, I want to report him.' She took another gulp of brandy, and it seemed to be giving her strength. 'You're right,' she said, a determined set to her jaw, 'he shouldn't get away with this!'

Grayson nodded, the ghost of a smile hovering around his mouth. 'Good.'

Lisa felt a shock of admiration for Rose, along with a small stab of envy. She wished *she'd* had a bit of that courage and determination. If she'd stood up for herself, maybe Rose wouldn't even be in this situation now. If only she hadn't been so pathetic.

'We should probably go to the police station now,' Grayson said to Rose. 'The sooner, the better.'

She nodded and drained the last of her drink. She looked stronger already than she had when she'd arrived. There was some colour in her cheeks, and a spark of fire in her eyes.

'I'll get the spare room ready,' Lisa said. She looked shrewdly at Rose as she stood to go. 'And I'll make you something to eat for when you get back,' she added. 'You're probably hungry.'

Rose nodded and gave Lisa the ghost of a smile. 'I'm always hungry these days,' she said wearily.

While Grayson took Rose to the police station, Lisa made up a bed for her in the spare room. When they returned, she made Rose a bowl of pasta carbonara, watching her wolf it down with a kind of hunger that Lisa recognised with a stab of pain. Grayson put an arm around her and pulled her into his side, as if instinctively knowing she needed comfort.

'Don't beat yourself up about it,' he said later in bed, when Rose was tucked up in the spare room. 'None of this is your fault. You can't blame yourself. You tried to warn her, but she's a grown woman. She made her own decisions.'

'I know,' Lisa chewed her lip. 'But I can't help thinking if I'd been braver ... if I'd been more like her and stood up for myself back then ...'

'You didn't have someone like you to turn to,' Grayson said, pulling her into his arms.

'But I had you,' she said, curling into him. 'Thank God I found you.'

35

GRAYSON BREATHED a sigh of relief as he pulled up in front of his house on Friday evening, after driving Rose to Hastings to stay with her parents. It had been a long week, and he was looking forward to a quiet night in with just him and Lisa. The day after Rose made her report, Mark had gone to the police station and accepted a caution, with the condition that he didn't contact Rose again. From what the police said, he had obviously implied that he was just accepting the caution as a formality to spare everyone the stress and expense of going to court – still playing the good guy, as if he was admitting guilt for everyone else's sake and not because he was actually culpable. Lisa and Rose knew just how charming he would have been with the police, how reasonable he could make himself appear, and they seethed over the way he could take people in. But frustrating as it was, at least it seemed to have the desired effect, and he hadn't attempted to contact Rose since.

He was disappointed to see the house was in darkness, meaning Lisa wasn't home yet, but he wasn't exactly surprised. It was the first day she had gone back to her studio since Rose had appeared on their doorstep, and no doubt she had a lot to catch up on. While Rose was with them, Lisa had stayed at home with her, fussing over her like a mother hen, feeding her up, encouraging her to talk about Mark, and persuading her to contact family and friends. It was touching to see how Lisa took care of her, he thought with a smile. Rose seemed to bring out her maternal instincts, even though they were the same age. Rose had been aloof at first, but she had gradually thawed and relaxed. Lisa's patience and kindness had slowly broken through her defences, and they had seen another side to her – a lively, funny girl with a kind and loyal heart under her caustic exterior. They had all become genuinely fond of each other, and he and Lisa were almost sorry to see her go. But it would be nice to have the house to themselves again.

His phone rang just as he got out of the car. He pulled it from his pocket, as he locked the car with his other hand. He smiled to himself when he saw it was Lisa.

'Hi, sweetheart.'

'Hi, are you back yet?'

'I'm just home this minute.'

'Is Rose okay?'

'Yes. I left her with her parents. They seem really nice. She'll be fine.'

'Okay. I got delayed, but I'm just leaving now, so I'll be home in about half an hour.'

'Great.' Grayson pushed open the gate. 'I can't wait to—'

Suddenly there was a movement in the shadows, a rustling in the bushes that bordered the garden. He was startled by a shape looming in the darkness out of the corner of his eye. He turned towards it, and then it was rushing towards him, and he saw a man's face illuminated by the light from the street lamp. 'Mark—'

He was cut off as something heavy hit his shoulder, then his chest. His phone fell to the ground with a clatter. He thought Mark was punching him, and he fought to hit back, but his limbs felt weak and powerless, his head spinning dizzily. As he dropped to the ground, he felt a wet warmth spreading across his chest, and realised he was bleeding. He saw the flash of something silver in Mark's hand, and as his head hit the tarmac of the drive, it fell to the ground beside him with a metallic clink. He was dimly aware of footsteps receding into the distance and Lisa's voice calling his name as if from very far away before he lost consciousness.

'Grayson!' Lisa shouted his name repeatedly into the phone as she ran down the stairs and out to the street, her heart pounding. She looked around desperately for a taxi. Oh God, what was happening? Her head was spinning as she hailed a cab and scrambled inside.

Once they were speeding towards Grayson's house, she dialled 999 with shaking fingers, and asked for an ambulance. She had no idea what had happened, but there was no time to hesitate. All she knew was that Grayson had suddenly gone silent mid-sentence, and 'Mark' was the last thing he'd said before the phone went dead. She told the dispatcher that she thought he'd been attacked and needed help. She felt sick with fear, barely able to breathe. Why was the traffic so slow? Her mind raced, cycling through every nightmare scenario she could think of. Had Mark hurt Grayson? Was he lying injured outside? Why wasn't he able to speak to her? She dialled his phone again and again, but it was out of service now.

Her stomach lurched when they turned into Grayson's road and she saw the flashing blue lights illuminating the darkness. She felt a mixture of relief and panic at the sight of the ambulance, glad that it had arrived so quickly, but still hoping that she had over-reacted and it wouldn't be needed. That hope was quickly dashed as she saw that there was a police car too, and a couple of officers were milling around in front of the house alongside the ambulance crew.

She paid the driver and stumbled out of the cab just as a team of paramedics were carrying a stretcher through the gate. She rushed up to them, and her worst fears were confirmed as she saw Grayson lying on it. He was unconscious and frighteningly pale. She was dimly aware of a policewoman standing by the ambulance saying something about stab wounds into her walkie-talkie.

'What happened?' she asked breathlessly. 'I'm his girl-friend. I'm the one who called you.' She could hardly speak, her heart hammering in her throat.

'He was stabbed,' one of the paramedics said, giving her a sympathetic look.

Lisa looked around wildly. Grayson's phone was lying on the driveway, a blood-stained knife beside it. She shuddered. 'Will he—is he going to be okay?'

'We're doing all we can, miss. We have to get him to hospital as fast as possible.'

Lisa just latched onto the fact that he was still alive. They were loading him into the ambulance now, setting up drips, hooking him up to machines.

'Can I come with you?' she asked.

The paramedic looked to the policewoman.

'You're the person who called this in?' the police-woman asked her.

'Yes,' she said agitatedly. She just wanted to be with

Grayson. A policeman had got into the ambulance with him now and the doors were closing.

'I'm sorry, you'll have to stay here for now. We'll need to talk to you,' the policewoman said, nodding over Lisa's shoulder to an unmarked car that had just pulled up outside the house. Two men got out and were coming towards them, pulling phones and notebooks from their pockets.

She nodded, trying to swallow down her impatience as the ambulance sped off, sirens blaring. Of course, this was a crime. They would need to question her. It all seemed so surreal, as if it was happening to someone else. She felt dizzy and disoriented as she tried to take it all in.

'Any witnesses?' one of the detectives asked as he approached the house. He was the older of the two, tall and wiry. 'Who called the ambulance?'

'I did,' Lisa said. 'But I wasn't a witness. I'm his girlfriend.'

'Okay, I'll need to take a statement from you.' He quickly issued instructions to his partner, who started barking orders at the uniformed officers about securing the scene and making house-to-house enquiries, while he drew Lisa away a little to interview her.

He introduced himself as DCI Watson.

'You called the ambulance?' he asked her, flipping open his notebook.

'Yes.'

'But you didn't see what happened?'

'No. I wasn't here at the time.'

'How did you know the victim was injured?

'I was on the phone to him. I'd called him to say I'd be late home. Then suddenly he stopped talking, as if he'd been startled by something.' Tears stung her eyes as she relived those awful moments. 'He said "Mark" – and then he went silent.'

'Mark?' DCI Watson raised his eyebrows, his expression blank. 'Does that name mean something to you?'

Lisa nodded. 'He's my ex-boyfriend.'

'And you believe this Mark attacked Mr Fielding?'

'Yes.' Lisa's voice came out as a croak. 'I do. He'd been … stalking me.'

'Had he made threats?'

'No, not threats exactly.'

'Any history of violent behaviour?' ' He wrote quickly in his notebook as they spoke.

'Yes. He tried to … assault me recently. And he's been violent in the past – with me, and with his latest girlfriend, Rose. There's a report,' she said, with a rush of gratitude to Rose for her bravery. Thanks to her there was evidence, a record. 'He was cautioned.'

DCI Watson nodded. 'Good. Well, if you could give me the details of where I can find Mark …' He broke off, his pen hovering over his notepad.

'Mark Reader.' Lisa gave him Mark's details.

He called the younger detective over and relayed the information to him, then got Lisa to go over the timeline of events again. 'I'm sorry,' he said, 'but we need to get all the information we can as quickly as possible.'

'I understand,' she said, and went through it all again. Finally he took Rose's name and contact details, and asked her about any places Mark might go apart from his house.

'Thank you, Miss Matthews,' he said finally, flipping his notebook closed. 'We'll probably need to talk to you again, but that's all for now.'

36

A POLICE CAR took her to the hospital. Only when they were on their way did she succumb to tears, not bothering to stop them as they streamed down her face. She whispered Grayson's name over and over in her head, silently begging him to be all right. He was still being treated in the emergency room when she arrived.

'He's fairly stable now,' a young doctor told her, her tone sympathetic. 'The blade missed the heart, so he should be fine.'

Lisa nodded gratefully, too choked up to speak. She paced the corridors, unable to sit still, while doctors and nurses came and went. She lost all sense of time, and she didn't know how many hours had passed when she was told that Grayson was being taken into surgery. The staff were kind, keeping her updated on what was happening and trying to reassure her, but it was torture having nothing to do but wait and worry.

It was almost a relief when the police arrived to interview her again. It was a welcome distraction from what might be happening to Grayson right now. DCI Watson and his partner, who he introduced as DS Patel, took her into a small private room with a desk.

There was something strange in DCI Watson's demeanour this time that sent chills up her spine, and she immediately got the sense that something had happened. They went over some of the details in her statement again, and after a few cursory questions, DS Patel slid a photo of Mark across the desk and they asked her to identify him. And then, very slowly and solemnly, DCI Watson told her that they had gone to take Mark in for questioning on the basis of her evidence. Police officers had called to his house – and found him hanging from a ceiling beam.

Lisa just stared at them blankly, speechless. She felt frozen and detached, unable to respond in any way. She had nothing to say. There might have been a time when she'd have cried for the man Mark once was; when she'd have grieved the loss of the handsome lover who'd swept her off her feet; when she'd have mourned the waste of a life with so much promise and potential. Maybe if he'd shown her an ounce of mercy, she could have found it in her to pity such a lonely end. But he'd been remorseless, cruel to the last, and his final act on earth was an attempt to punish her by taking away the man she loved.

He'd finally accepted that she wouldn't have him, and so he'd wanted to make sure she wouldn't have anyone. He'd left Grayson to die, like his life was nothing – just something he could destroy to make her suffer. She couldn't forgive him that. And so the only feeling seeping through the numbness was satisfaction that he'd done his worst and hadn't succeeded – and relief that he was finally out of her life forever.

'Thank you,' she said finally when the interview was over. Her legs were shaking as she stood, but somehow she managed to make it out to the corridor and into a toilet cubicle before she was violently sick.

As she went back to her vigil, she felt increasingly helpless and scared. Ridiculously, she found herself wishing Grayson were here to put his arms around her and tell her everything would be okay. She didn't know what to do without him. She couldn't handle this on her own, and suddenly she felt more alone than she'd been in a long time.

Then slowly it dawned on her that she didn't have to be – not anymore. There were other people who cared about her besides Grayson, friends who she could count on to be there for her. She pulled out her phone and dialled Susie's number.

'Well, that's that, I guess,' Susie said when Lisa finished telling her about Mark. She cast a worried glance at Lisa. 'Sorry, does that sound heartless?' She shrugged. 'I don't know what to say.' She was clearly just as flummoxed for an appropriate response as Lisa had been.

Lisa shook her head. 'No. That's exactly how I feel.'

Susie had come straight to the hospital when Lisa told her what had happened, and hadn't left her side since, sitting with her as they waited for news of Grayson, holding her hand as she fretted, and listening as she talked about the dramatic events of the night. She was still there at four in the morning when Grayson was finally out of surgery and the doctor came to talk to her.

'Your boyfriend was lucky,' he told her. 'He was stabbed in the chest, but the knife missed the heart. He did suffer a punctured lung.'

Lisa's eyes widened at this, fear gripping her.

'Don't worry,' the doctor said, 'it's not as alarming as it

sounds. It's quite a simple injury. We've reinflated the lung, and he'll be fine. We'll be keeping him in for a few days. He'll be a bit stiff and sore for a while, but he should be back to normal within a few weeks.'

'Thank you,' Lisa smiled, blinking away tears. Relief coursed through her body, and all the feelings she'd been holding in for the past few hours flooded to the surface.

'Can I see him?'

'He's not conscious yet, but you can look in on him briefly. Then I suggest you go home and get some sleep, and come back later on.'

Lisa bit her lip. She wasn't sure she'd get any sleep if she went home, even though she was bone weary.

'I think it's a good idea,' Susie said, as if reading her thoughts. 'You can come back to my place, though. You shouldn't be on your own.'

'Thanks,' Lisa nodded, gratefully. It was a relief to let someone else take over. She didn't think she could manage even the simplest decision right now.

So after she looked in on Grayson, she let Susie drive her back to her flat. They went to Grayson's house first so Lisa could collect some things. She was alarmed when they pulled up outside to find the police still standing guard and the entrance cordoned off by bright yellow tape. Of course, she thought dazedly – this was a crime scene now. It hardly seemed real. Her stomach turned over at the sight, bringing to mind all too vividly what had happened here earlier tonight. She kept seeing that knife going into Grayson's chest, him lying bleeding on the drive, helpless and alone.

She had to ask one of the police officers if she could go into the house, and one of them escorted her inside, hovering while she collected pyjamas and threw some things into a cosmetics bag. She didn't linger, getting out again as quickly as she could, and averting her eyes as they passed the dark patch on the driveway that she knew was Grayson's blood.

Back at her flat, Susie gave her wine and cooked a pizza from the freezer. Lisa wouldn't have thought she was hungry, but once she started eating, she realised she was ravenous. She wolfed the food down mindlessly, hardly tasting it. Despite how keyed up she was, she felt drowsiness overtake her, and she fell asleep almost as soon as her head hit the pillow.

She woke with a start the next morning, the events of the previous night flooding her brain as soon as she was conscious. She glanced at the bedside clock, shocked to discover it was almost ten. She was amazed she'd slept so well, and felt guilty as her thoughts immediately went to Grayson lying alone right now in a hospital bed – and all because of her.

She had a quick shower and got dressed. Susie had taken the morning off, and insisted on making breakfast for them both before Lisa went back to the hospital.

'Have you spoken to any of Grayson's family?' she asked as she slid an omelette onto Lisa's plate.

'Oh God!' Lisa gasped. In all the panic and stress of last night, it hadn't even occurred to her to call Grayson's parents. 'I never even thought—'

'It's probably just as well,' Susie said soothingly. 'Now you can tell them that he's going to be okay. You'd just have worried them needlessly last night.'

'I suppose you're right,' Lisa said. She still felt guilty, though, and she dreaded having to tell Grayson's family what had happened. They'd all been so kind to her. And now thanks to her, he was lying in hospital. He could have been killed. She didn't know how she'd ever face them again.

Despite all the doctor's assurances that Grayson would be okay, she still felt anxious as she made her way down the hospital corridor later that morning, dreading what she might find. So she was weak with relief to find him awake and sitting up in bed, propped up against a mountain of pillows. He was still attached to a drip, a tube going into his arm.

'Good morning,' she said softly.

'Hey you.' He gave her a weak smile.

She took off her coat and pulled a chair up beside his bed. 'How do you feel?' She put a hand on his arm as she sat down.

'A bit sore, but they're giving me lots of painkillers.' He nodded to the stent in his hand. 'I'm going to be fine,' he told her reassuringly as she looked at him anxiously.

'Have the police been in with you?'

He nodded. 'As soon as I was conscious.'

'And you identified Mark as the person who attacked you?'

'Yes.' He looked at her warily.

It was a formality, but they had told her they wanted Grayson to positively identify him as his attacker before they closed the case, just to make sure there were no loose ends.

'They told me about Mark,' Grayson said, looking at her with concern.

She nodded. She still could think of nothing to say that would make sense of the whole sordid mess. All that mattered was that Grayson had survived. Only when she thought of what might have happened to him did her emotions surface again.

'God, if only I'd been there with you,' she said, tears stinging her eyes.

Grayson's eyes widened. 'Thank Christ you weren't!' He took her hand. 'If you'd been there, he'd probably have stabbed both of us. And then there would have been no one to call for help.'

Lisa's stomach heaved at the thought of the two of them bleeding to death on Grayson's drive. 'If I hadn't phoned you when I did …'She shuddered at the thought of how long he might have lain there bleeding, with no one knowing he'd been hurt.

'You saved me,' he said. 'Not for the first time.'

Lisa withdrew her hand. 'No.' She shook her head. 'I'm the reason you're here.'

'Don't say that.' He frowned, 'You're not responsible for his actions, Lisa.'

'But if it weren't for me—if you'd never known me …'

'Don't say that.' He frowned, looking pained. 'I don't like to think about my life without you.'

'I never thought of contacting your parents last night,' she admitted.

'That's okay. The police have been in touch with them and informed them what happened. They're on their way.'

'Oh. That's good.' Lisa glanced nervously towards the door. She didn't think she could face Grayson's family right now – not after what had happened to him. No matter what he said, this was her fault. It had only happened because she'd been gullible and stupid enough to fall in love with Mark in the first place. She'd let him into her life, and thus into Grayson's.

'Lisa, don't blame yourself for this,' Grayson said, as if he could read her mind. 'Please.'

She nodded, smiling to keep him happy. She didn't want him to be anxious. But she couldn't make the feeling go away. 'When do you think your parents will get here?'

He looked at his watch. 'They were leaving first thing this morning, so I'd say they should be here in the next hour or so. And Alison and Emma will be here shortly.'

'Well, I'll leave you to rest for a bit, then. I don't want to wear you out before they get here. I'll come back later.'

She knew she was being a coward as she scurried away, but she couldn't help it. No matter what Grayson said, she was ultimately responsible for this happening to him. If only she'd stayed in Cornwall. She'd been perfectly safe living there quietly in obscurity, out of Mark's reach. It should have been enough for her. But no, she'd had to chase her dream of making it as a professional artist – and at what cost? It was her stupid ambition that had got Grayson where he was now. How could his family ever forgive her? How could she forgive herself?

'THIS IS TORTURE,' Grayson said. 'I hate lying in this bed every night, not having you beside me, not being able to touch you.'

She smiled. She knew what he meant. It had been agony for her too, sleeping alone every night in their big bed. She spent most of her time at the hospital, but she still missed him dreadfully when she was alone in the house.

'Never mind,' she said, taking his hand. 'You're doing well. The doctor told me you'll probably be able to come home tomorrow.'

'Thank God,' he said, his thumb rubbing over her hand, even that light touch igniting fire in her belly.

'Can I get you anything?' she asked.

He shook his head. 'No. I've got everything I need right here.' His fingers tightened on hers, and Lisa swallowed a lump in her throat.

Grayson had been lucky, the doctors said. If the knife had gone in a few inches to the left … She shuddered.

'Has anyone else been to see you today?' she asked, shoving those dark thoughts to the back of her mind.

'Not yet. Mum's on her way. She should be here soon.'

'Oh.' Lisa had been avoiding Grayson's family ever since the accident. She always asked him when they were due to visit and made sure she was gone before they arrived. She felt so guilty, and she was sure they must hate her for bringing Mark into Grayson's life. She just hoped in time they'd be able to forgive her because she couldn't bear the thought of losing him. And yet, how could she be with him if his family hated her? She couldn't ask him to choose between them.

'Well, I'd better be going,' she said, standing up.

Grayson frowned. 'Really? I thought you were going to stay until after lunch.'

She shook her head, avoiding his eyes. 'I—I just remembered I'm supposed to be meeting Daniel. Sorry. But I'll be back tonight. I'll bring the chess board.' She leaned forward to give him a quick kiss, but he put his arms around her and his lips clung to hers, softly lingering.

'I miss you so much,' he whispered against her mouth, gently pushing her hair back from her face.

'Mmm,' she sighed. 'I can't wait for you to come home.' With an effort, she pulled away. 'I'll see you later.'

As she stepped out into the corridor, she saw Janet coming towards her. Damn! If only she'd left just seconds earlier. Her eyes darted around in panic, looking for somewhere to hide. But it was too late. Janet had already seen her, her face lighting up in a smile as she gave her a little wave.

'Hello, darling,' she said, bustling up to her. She was astonished as Janet pulled her into a warm hug. 'I'm surprised I haven't bumped into you here before. We seem to keep missing each other. How is he today?' She gave Lisa a sympathetic look.

'He's … doing well,' Lisa said, her eyes dropping to the

floor. 'The doctors say he can probably come home tomorrow.'

'Oh, that's great news. You must be so relieved. I know I am.'

Lisa nodded, her head still bent. She felt her eyes well up. She didn't know what to say to this lovely woman, but she had to say something. She took a deep breath and lifted her head, her vision clouded with tears. 'I'm so sorry,' she choked.

Janet frowned. 'Oh, darling,' she said, 'whatever for?'

'For … all this,' Lisa said, wiping away the tears that were escaping from her eyes.

'Don't be daft,' Janet said, putting an arm around her. 'It's been a very stressful time for all of us. You poor thing, you must be exhausted from all the worry. You cry as much as you like.'

Lisa shook her head. 'I mean I'm sorry for what happened to Grayson. I'll never forgive myself.'

Janet looked at her thoughtfully in silence for a moment, her expression grave. 'I think we should go and have a cup of tea,' she said finally.

'But—you were going to visit Grayson.'

'That can wait. Come on – just a quick cuppa.' And before Lisa had a chance to protest, she was leading her back down the corridor.

'So,' Janet said when they were seated in the cafeteria with two steaming mugs of tea, 'tell me what this is all about. Why are you apologising to me for what happened to Grayson? You're not telling me you're responsible for it?'

Lisa nodded. 'Yes,' she said. 'I am.'

'Really?' Janet raised her eyebrows sceptically. 'Well, I

find that hard to believe. You're telling me it was you who attacked him, not that man the police think did it?'

Lisa couldn't help smiling shakily. Janet knew damn well that Mark was guilty.

'No, of course not,' she said. 'But still … it's my fault. You must know it is.'

'No.' She reached forward and clasped Lisa's hand in both of hers. 'Lisa, it's not your fault. You're not responsible for that monster's actions.'

Lisa's eyes welled with tears, relief spreading through her as she realised Janet truly didn't blame her in the least for what had happened to Grayson. She was so grateful for her kindness and understanding. She just wished she could stop blaming herself.

'Still,' she said, 'the fact is if it weren't for me, Grayson wouldn't be lying in a hospital bed right now with a collapsed lung. If he'd never met me—'

'He wouldn't be half the man he is now,' Janet interrupted. 'Grayson's always been a good person. He was such a kind, affectionate boy,' she said with a fond smile, 'and he grew up into a caring and compassionate man. But there was always something missing in his life until you came along. I'd begun to think he'd never find someone he wanted to give that ring to.' She nodded at Lisa's right hand. 'And it made me sad, because I knew he was capable of so much love. You've made his life complete, Lisa. I've never seen him as happy as he is with you, and I know you love him as much he deserves to be loved. I can't tell you how glad I am that he found you.'

Lisa wiped away fresh tears, touched by Janet's words.

Janet gave her a shrewd look. 'Is this why I haven't seen you at the hospital before? Have you been avoiding us?'

Lisa nodded sheepishly. 'Sorry. I just felt so guilty. I couldn't face you.'

Janet sighed. 'Please don't let this come between you and Grayson,' she said. 'If you do, you're letting Mark win.'

Janet's words echoed in Lisa's head as she made her way home. She was bone weary, emotionally wrung out from the events of the past week. But knowing that Grayson's family didn't blame her felt like a huge weight had been lifted off her chest, and she could finally breathe again. She felt calmer than she had since the attack, and after all the turmoil and anxiety of the last few days, she was finally able to think clearly.

That night she relaxed in a long, hot bath and did a lot of thinking, mostly about Grayson – how much she loved him; how she wanted to be with him always and spend her life making him happy; how she had nearly lost him. Having him almost taken away from her like that had put things in perspective, and suddenly her fears about marrying him felt absurd. When the chance of having any future with him seemed about to be snatched away from her, she was overcome with regret that she hadn't grabbed it with both hands when she had the opportunity. It became instantly clear to her that life was too short and love too precious not to commit to it fully and give it everything you had, and she was horrified that she'd ever held back.

Miraculously, she had been given a second chance, and this time there would be no hesitation. She was going to go after what she wanted – and what she wanted was to marry Grayson. The only problem was, he was unlikely to ask her again. She'd said no, and he had respected that. She didn't think he'd try to change her mind. So if she wanted to marry him, she was just going to have to ask him.

She smiled to herself as she turned on the hot tap to top up the bath and lay back in the bubbles to plan the perfect proposal.

38

————

After giving it a lot of thought, Lisa couldn't think of anything more romantic than Grayson's proposal to her, so she had decided she would simply copy it. On the day he was to come out of hospital, she bought lobsters and champagne, and planned a picnic in the library, decorating the room with fairy lights and flowers.

When she brought Grayson home in the afternoon, she ushered him straight upstairs so as not to ruin the surprise.

'Can't wait to get me into bed, eh?' he joked.

Lisa laughed. 'No, I really want you to rest. I want you to keep all your strength for tonight,' she added to his disappointed look.

'That sounds promising,' he said with a crooked smile.

In the bedroom, he sank down onto the bed and took both her hands in his. 'You're really not going to join me?' he asked.

'No,' Lisa smiled, sweeping the hair out of his eyes. He looked tired. She knew he'd found it difficult to sleep in the hospital. 'You have a nap.' She leaned in and gave him a soft kiss, and he caught her mouth, pulling her down onto the bed. He wrapped his arms tightly around her as he deepened the kiss, his tongue sliding into her mouth. Lisa's blood pulsed in her ears as Grayson's hands roamed over her body, caressing her breasts, his thumbs stroking over her nipples until they were tight and hard.

'I've missed you so much,' he whispered, trailing butterfly kisses along her neck, his hand tugging at the collar of her shirt, pulling it out of his way as he blazed a trail to her ear, gently tugging on the lobe with his teeth.

Lisa's senses leapt in response, her whole body coming alive under his hands and mouth.

'I can't wait another minute,' he said as his fingers went to the buttons of her shirt, quickly opening it and parting the material. Then he tugged down one bra cup and bent his head to her breast, sucking the nipple into his mouth.

Lisa whimpered as he gently grazed the taut bud with his teeth, heat surging through her body. 'I've missed you too,' she said. Her hand went to the front of his jeans and a fresh stab of desire pierced through her as she felt the hardness of his erection. She didn't want to wait any longer either. She wanted him desperately, now. But she was also wary of hurting him and she didn't want him to exert himself too much.

'Lie down,' she said softly, nudging him back against the pillows.

'You really think I can nap right now?' he laughed, his eyes glittering with desire.

'Ssh,' she said, her hands going to his zipper. 'Doctor's orders. I just want you to relax. I'm going to take care of you. Just show me where it hurts.'

She quickly unzipped his jeans, and he lifted his hips as she pushed them down along with his underwear. She felt a rush of heat between her legs as his cock sprang free, erect and glorious.

'That looks painful,' she said, looking up at him coyly from beneath her lashes as she rang a finger along his thick, swollen shaft. 'Don't worry.' She bent and ran her tongue around the tip. 'I'm going to make you feel better.'

Grayson sighed deeply as she took him into her mouth. He buried his hands in her hair as she sucked him deep, groaning as she swirled her tongue around the head and stroked him with her fist. Before long, his hips were pumping upwards, thrusting deeper into her mouth as his whole body jerked and he came with a deep moan of satisfaction.

When he had finished, Lisa wiped her mouth and flopped down beside him.

'*Now* do you think you could nap?' she asked with a playful smile.

Grayson gave her a sleepy, satisfied grin. 'What about you?' he asked, his eyes fluttering closed even as he spoke.

'Later,' she whispered. But he was already asleep.

While Grayson slept, Lisa put the finishing touches to the library. The picnic basket was on the rug in front of the fire, and a bottle of champagne was chilling in an ice bucket. Candles were lighting on the mantelpiece, their flickering flames reflected in the gilt mirror above it. Everything was in place for her grand gesture. She just hoped Grayson would wake up in time for supper, she thought with a wry smile, or all this would go to waste and she would have to reschedule.

But just as she was thinking that, the library door pushed open and Grayson stood there, incredibly handsome in a soft cream cable knit sweater. He looked slightly flushed from sleep, his tousled hair still damp from the shower.

'You're just in time,' she said.

He raised his eyebrows, looking slightly bemused as he took in the room.

Lisa had been looking forward to this moment for days, but now that it was here, she suddenly felt shy and nervous. 'Before we eat,' she said, taking Grayson's hand and leading him over to the fireplace, 'there's something I want to ask you.' She licked her lips nervously.

'You can ask me anything,' he said with a little puzzled frown.

She took a deep, shaky breath, maintaining eye contact as she sank down onto one knee in front of him. 'Grayson, will you marry me?'

He gave a startled gasp, his eyes widening. 'Lisa … no,' he said softly, shaking his head.

Her heart turned over. She hadn't expected this. Now she knew how he'd felt when she'd refused him. 'No?' she repeated faintly as he pulled her up to her feet. 'You've changed your mind,' she stated flatly, trying not to feel hurt.

'No. Not at all,' he said insistently. He cupped her face, tilting it up so she had to look at him. 'I'd love to be married to you, Lisa. But I know it's not what you want.'

She opened her mouth to protest, but he interrupted. 'My mother told me she bumped into you at the hospital the other day.'

'Yes.' Lisa said, frowning. She didn't understand what that had to do with anything.

'And she told me what you talked about,' Grayson continued. 'Mark attacking me wasn't your fault,' he said, his thumb stroking her cheek gently as he looked into her eyes. 'No one blames you for it. Least of all me.'

She frowned, wondering why he was bringing that up at a time like this. 'I—I know,' she said. 'I realise that now.'

'I don't need you to marry me, Lisa. We love each other, we want to be together, and that's enough for me. I'm happy as we are.'

Then she realised: he thought she was doing this out of guilt, to atone somehow for what Mark had done.

'Is that why you think I proposed?' she asked, smiling at him gently. 'Because I feel guilty? You think I'm trying to make it up to you somehow for Mark attacking you?'

He shrugged, looking sheepish. 'Well, I know you don't want to get married, so—'

'But I do,' she insisted. 'I've changed my mind. It's a woman's prerogative, you know.'

He narrowed his eyes at her, looking at her closely as if trying to decide if she was telling the truth.

'I want to be your wife,' she said, taking his hands in hers. 'And believe me,' she said with a wry smile, 'no matter how bad I felt, I wouldn't get married as penance.'

'You really want to get married?' he asked, a smile spreading across his face, his eyes lighting up.

'I really want to marry *you*. I love you so much, Grayson. When I thought I might lose you, I couldn't bear the thought that I'd held back from you in any way. I want to go all in with you, total one hundred percent commitment.' She reached up and touched her lips to his, and he wrapped his arms around her, his mouth moving gently against hers.

'Okay then,' he said huskily as they pulled apart, his eyes dropping to the ring on her right hand. 'I'm all in too.'

'Is that a yes?' Lisa grinned.

'That's a yes.' His fingers were shaking as he slipped the ring off and slid it onto the ring finger of her left hand. 'A total one hundred percent yes.'

EPILOGUE

Lisa's phone buzzed with a message. Grayson:

Are you sure you want to do this? It's not too late to run.

She smiled, and texted back:

*You're not getting out of this now, buddy. You won't get
rid of me that easily.*

Moments later a reply came through. It was a picture of a
rose, with the caption '*I love you.*'

Love you too. See you soon. I'll be the one in white. X

She smiled to herself as she tossed the phone onto the
vanity table in front of her.

'Grayson?' Susie guessed.

'Yes,' Lisa smiled at her in the mirror. She and Katya
were standing behind her, putting the finishing touches to
her hair. It was arranged in loose, side-swept curls that

tumbled softly around her shoulders, and instead of a veil she wore a delicate floral headband of pearls and crystals.

'You look amazing,' Susie breathed.

'Stunning,' Katya agreed.

Lisa could hardly believe this day had come. She couldn't wait to be married to Grayson and to start their life together as husband and wife. She checked her watch for the umpteenth time. He would be arriving at the church around now. Her phone buzzed again, and she picked it up.

I'm just at the church. Last chance to change your mind.

She laughed softly.

Never, she texted back. *All in, remember? I can't wait.*

Half an hour later she stepped through the doors of the little chapel and onto the red carpet that led down the aisle. On either side, rows of pews were decorated with posies of white roses and babies breath tied with white ribbon. There was a rustling and murmuring as she entered and the assembled guests turned to look at her. Then a hush descended on the crowd before the organ struck up.

As Grayson turned towards her, everything else seemed to fade out, and all she could see was him. He looked impossibly gorgeous in a soft charcoal suit and crisp white shirt, his beautiful hair artfully messy. But it was the look on his face that really took her breath away – the love that shone from his eyes and the sheer happiness that seemed to radiate off him.

As he turned back to the altar, Lisa looked around her. She took a deep breath and stepped onto the carpet, Susie and Katya following slowly behind. Daniel had offered to walk down the aisle with her, but much as she loved tradition, the symbolism of one man 'giving her away' to another wasn't lost on her, and she had decided it wasn't going to be part of her wedding ceremony. She was giving herself to Grayson, and this was a walk she wanted to make alone.

There were gasps and murmurs of admiration as she passed, accompanied by the clicking of cameras. She nodded to Martha, Ellie and Connor, and Daniel gave her a little wave, grinning excitedly. Rose was even there, sitting a little stiffly beside Daniel, but she turned to Lisa as she passed and gave her a shaky smile. On the other side of the church, Isabel sat with Grayson's large family, his parents and sisters all looking so happy and proud. Tomorrow she and Grayson were going to Italy for an extended honeymoon, and she was looking forward to exploring the world with him. But today was about sharing their happiness with family and friends.

Her eyes welled with tears. She was so touched that all these people were here for her, wishing her well. A year ago, her side of the church would have been empty. She felt like the luckiest person in the world, her heart bursting with happiness. Everyone she loved was here – well almost everyone, she thought with a pang. But she could feel her grandparents looking down on her, and she knew they would approve. She had never felt so loved.

And there at the front waiting for her was the person who she knew loved her most in the world. She blinked away tears of happiness as she reached the altar and Grayson turned to her. She took his hand, and stepped into her future.